DARK WATER SERIES
SHADOWS

BOOK ONE

J.L. DRAKE

SHADOWS

DARK WATER SERIES

Copyright 2023 © J.L. Drake

All rights reserved

The unauthorized reproduction or distribution of this copyrighted work is a crime punishable by law. No part of this book may be scanned, uploaded to, or downloaded from file sharing sites or distributed in any other way via the internet or any other means, electronic or print, without the publisher's permission. Criminal copyright infringement, including infringement without monetary gain, is investigated by the FBI and is punishable by up to 5 years in federal prison and a fine of $250,000.

This is a work of fiction. Names, characters, places, and incidents either are the product of the author's imagination or are used fictitiously, and any resemblance to locales, events, business establishments, or actual persons—living or dead—is entirely coincidental.

All rights reserved. Except as permitted under the U.S. Copyright Act of 1976. No part of this publication may be reproduced, stored in, or introduced into a retrieval system or transmitted, in any form or by any means (electronic, mechanical, photocopying, recording, or otherwise), without the prior permission of J.L. Drake.

Cover Design by Deranged Doctor Design

Editing by Lori Whitwam

Formatting by RedDoor Author Services

Dedication

To all of my readers who asked for the story of how Shadows came to be, plus a little more.

Enjoy

Cast of Characters

Daniel: Cole's father, first generation Blackstone. Married to **Sue,** Cole's mother.

Edison: Cole's grandfather. Married to **Meg,** Cole's grandmother.

Abigail/Abby: Mark's adopted mother, Cole's childhood nanny, house aide. Sister to **June.**

Dr. Roberts: House psychologist. Dating Abigail.

Frank: Blackstone contact for the Army. First generation Blackstone member.

Zack: First generation Blackstone member.

Families

Cole: Owner of the Shadows safe house. Leader of the Blackstone special ops team. Married to **Savannah**. They have two kids, **Olivia** and **Easton**.

John: Blackstone member. Married to **Sloane**.

Mike: Blackstone member. Married to **Catalina**. Daughter **Gabriella**.

Keith: Member of Blackstone. Married to **Lexi**. They have two kids, **Brandon and Reagan**.

Mark: Blackstone member. Married to **Mia**. They have a set of twins, **Liam** and **Ethan**, and a daughter **Tabby**.

Paul: Blackstone member. Deceased.

Dell: North Rock member. Dusk Safehouse in North Carolina.

Davie: North Rock member. Dusk Safehouse in North Carolina.

Steve Chamness: North Rock member. Dusk Safehouse in North Carolina.

Denton Barlow: The American. Deceased.

Animals

Goats: Friendly reminders of home.

Chickens: Annoying and always in the way.

Scoot: A-hole house cat.

Butters: Mark and Mia's Husky.

Tripper: John and Sloane's German shepherd.

A note to my readers

Since Savannah and Cole's story was released years ago, I've heard from so many of you asking endless questions about Shadows and how it all started. Your request for more has been heard. After the Blackstone Series was finished, it was obvious that the story needed to be expanded because it just wasn't enough to satisfy your appetite. I'm certainly not one to argue that. After all, I could write these characters until the end of time. My imagination missed them, too, and is always eager to conjure up more adventures for my full list of Blackstone characters.

So, here I am, back with an exciting new series, and let me tell you, this is-going-to-blow-your-mind!

Let me explain a few things, before you dive into the story.

I decided to start this series a little differently. So, just how did the Shadows Safehouse come to be? Exactly who started it and why? I thought a lot about how to tell the whole story to give you all the answers you'd asked for. I considered doing a short novella with sprinkled treats and surprises throughout in a way that answered the questions. But after some thought, I wondered if it might be better to write the full story. I'd start you off in present day, then draw you back to the very beginning. Then I could move you forward to drop you back off into the present again. That way, you could hit the ground running for book two, Whiskey.

So, that's what I did.

Don't worry, this isn't a book that flips you back and forth through memories. It's a smooth transition of present, past, and present again.

I consider this to be a "bridge book" to bring you forward to the new Dark Water series. Dark Water delves into a whole new team with brand new characters I want you to meet.

In the present, I set the scene of what's to come in Whiskey. Though it will be a brand-new story, you will also be living with the Blackstone Team, old friends who have moved on to Dusk, and of course everyone else you've met along the way…and maybe, just maybe, a few other characters will pop up.

Remember to watch for the little things, I never put something on the page without a reason. I hope in writing this book I will satisfy your curiosity, but I also want you to come along with me back home again. I know I've missed everyone. I hope you enjoy the ride.

Daniel Logan

We fought for our country in an unpopular war. "Make love, not war," they said. The people back home held peace signs, drank, partied, smoked pot, and slept in fields. All the while, we fought in unfamiliar territory, dragged our heavy weapons through bug-infested swamps, suffered in hot, steamy jungles, and lost thousands of our men in unimaginable ways. "Make love," they said, but where was our love?

CHAPTER ONE

Location: Montana Shadows Safehouse
Coordinates: Classified

Present Day
Daniel

"How bad is it?" Savannah stopped me in the kitchen after our morning meeting had run several hours over. "It must be bad, because Frank's assistant has called me three times wanting to know if Cole has signed off on the paperwork yet."

"It's bad." I warmed my hands around my mug and wondered how quickly we could make things happen. "Frank said his intel should be providing an update soon. Regardless, the Cartel numbers are growing fast, and it's impossible to keep up. What's happened to Captain Brent can't be ignored. It's a wakeup call that we need to step up our game."

"Agreed." She leaned against the counter with a sigh. "I know Cole is nervous of changing the dynamics of the house, but what other moves do we have?"

I couldn't help but smile at how she looked at things. She

reminded me so much of Sue at times. It was always our problem, never just the team's problem.

"I don't think it's so much nerves as it is just a lot. Between Shadows and Dusk, there have been a lot more plates to juggle than there used to be. Cole's focus is split in too many different directions, and bringing in another team to live here and train under Blackstone, well, it's a big decision to make. The way Shadows has been run for years now works well, but a new team will be less stress on Blackstone, that's for sure."

"You're right," she nodded, "it really will."

"We're not getting any younger, Savannah," I smiled, "and the Cartels are not only increasing in number, but they're getting smarter and more sophisticated all the time. I'm all for the idea of Blackstone training another team, though. We really need the help."

"Me too." She leaned her arms on the island and bent over, taking a deep breath. "I'd always thought that once The American was removed from the picture, it would give us all breathing room, but clearly, I was wrong."

"The use of fear builds an army quicker than anything else, and most of those poor people don't have much of a choice. Once they've been approached by the Cartel, they either accept the role forced on them or they or their family could face death."

"It's sick." She rubbed her face.

"What's sick?" Olivia asked as she dropped her bookbag on the counter and looked at the two of us. "Grandpa, are you sick?" Her eyes bored into mine, and a fine line of worry, very similar to her mother's, appeared between her eyes.

"No, dear, it's just about work."

"Oh, yeah, did Daddy sign the papers yet?"

"How do you know about that?" Her mother shook her head.

"Mom, I'm a Logan. There's not much I don't know about what goes on in this house." She pulled out her binder. "If I'm going to run this place someday, I need to be in the know. So," her dark eyes took in both of us as she raised her pencil as though to take notes, "why is everyone looking stressed out?"

"No one is stressed."

"Mom," her hands went to her hips, "Uncle Mark didn't smile when I got home, and he always smiles."

"That means nothing." Savannah tried to assure her, even as we both knew it wouldn't work.

"Then why is there a full rack of cookies on the counter?"

I sipped my coffee to hide my smile. The little girl missed nothing.

"Olivia," Savannah cupped her face and stared down at her lovingly, "there are some things that are meant for adults. At this point, we don't have all the details. So, I'm asking you nicely to let it go until we have some answers. Then Daddy and I will let you know what's happening, okay?"

"Okay." She knew better than to argue with her mother, especially when she used a certain tone. Her expression went from concern to a smile. "Since Uncle Mark isn't eating those cookies, can I have some?

"Of course, you can." Savannah planted a kiss on her forehead then stepped back as Olivia jumped off the stool, grabbed two cookies, then raced off calling for the twins.

"She's quick." I chuckled.

"Daniel?" Keith popped his head around the corner. "The video chat is ready to go, and Frank should be logging on any minute now."

"Great, thanks."

"Savi?" Keith lowered his voice. "Is Lexi home?"

"I don't think so. I haven't seen her since last night." Keith nodded and looked away, then turned back, waved goodbye, and disappeared as quickly as he'd arrived. Savannah looked at me, and I closed my eyes and shook my head slowly with a deep sigh.

"One thing at a time."

"See," Olivia popped her head around the corner, "Uncle Keith didn't touch the cookies either."

"Off you go." Savannah shooed her away. "Here, Grandpa, take one for the road."

"Thanks."

I hurried downstairs and only just avoided a collision with Butters. The crazy dog was infamous for stealing socks, and his latest bright blue prize dangled from his mouth as he raced in the opposite direction to avoid being caught. Things certainly had changed around here.

My eye went to a grouping of photos on the wall, and I took a moment to study them. When I'd first put together Team Blackstone, it had consisted of only four guys—myself, Frank, Zack, and Ray. A photo of the four of us put a grin on my face. We were together, heads thrown back in laughter, while Zack hung upside down from our homemade climbing wall. He clowned around, having lost a race with Frank. I moved to another picture, one of my son Cole. It had been taken the day I'd handed the team reins over to him. Cole was so happy to take over as team leader, and it showed in the pride on his face.

Then Mark, basically our adopted son, was brought in, along with Paul and John. Mike and Keith came into play later, and then York. York was never really a full-fledged member of Blackstone. I thought of him only as a filler and the one man who would never have his picture hung on any wall at Shadows.

I studied the photos along the wall, and nostalgia filled me as I walked toward the conference room. Over the years, we'd lost a few of our men, and each one hit us hard. One hit, in particular, had been really difficult for us all. It happened just a few years back. Staff Sergeant Paul. He was a great soldier and an even better friend. He'd been killed while on a mission. We had his picture hung inside our conference room, not just to remember him, but to give us all the feeling he was still part of our meetings. I touched the frame as I entered the room. It had become a tradition for all of us.

As I sat down at the rectangular wooden table, Frank angled the camera and started in.

CHAPTER TWO

Location: Cartel House, Rosarito, Mexico
Coordinates: Unknown

Eric

Warm light peeked through the sheer curtains, and a beam of sun brushed over her bare legs. Her dark hair was tousled across the pillow, and her skin nearly glowed as I gawked at her flawless body.

I ran my finger down the artwork along her spine and noted the color from the fallen feathers became faded as I stopped at her tailbone. The intricate bird on her shoulder tilted as it flew away toward the evening sun.

"Aren't you going to ask me what it means?" she mumbled from the pillow.

"No." I retracted my fingers and pulled my phone cord from the charger. She chuckled as she rolled over and let the sheet fall away to expose her bare breasts. Her pink lips parted, and when she caught me looking, her gorgeous brown eyes blinked behind long dark lashes. The thin chain she wore held a cross close to her throat, and it caught the light when she swallowed. The contrast of her skin against the crisp white sheets was beautiful, and I fought the need to reach out and touch her again. But I didn't and wouldn't.

"I wish you'd tell me about this." She reached over to run her finger up my stomach to my chest, but I snagged her fingers, giving them a kiss before I let her go.

"Hungry?" Her voice was all breathy.

"No."

"Of course not." She sighed and swept an arm to clear away her long hair. "The night's over. It's my cue to leave." I simply shrugged, and her head shot back. "Will my payment be left on the nightstand, or will you pay me over an app?" she spat, and I knew her hackles were up. I hated what she said. I didn't want her to degrade herself like that. I knew she had two degrees and worked hard in her family's business.

"Stop," I warned.

"Why?" she challenged.

"Because I said to."

"I see." She rolled her eyes. "Well, if you say so." I sent her a look, and she returned it. "The dangerous Eric Noah doesn't show feelings, huh?"

"They're pointless."

"I beg to differ."

"Then we differ."

"But you have no problem showing me how you feel at night?" She tried to make sense of a senseless situation.

"It's sex."

"Right." I could tell that hurt. "You call me Escaper, instead of my real name. Why is that?" I ignored her question as I thumbed through my emails. "Is it because I'm your escape from the world?"

"No."

Yes.

"Eric," she got up on her knees and crawled over my lap,

"we've been sleeping together for over two years. You come get me, we have sex, I spend the night, then in the morning you can barely look at me. God forbid you should answer a question."

"And?" I knew how I sounded, but it had to be this way. It would always be this way.

"And I'm tired of it." She held her head high, and I could tell she was more than upset this time. "I want more."

"I can't give you more."

"Why?" Hurt raced across her face. When I still said nothing, her eyes glossed over. "You don't just have sex with me, Eric, you make love to me like I'm the only one for you. But the moment the sun comes up, I'm just one of the women out there, just a nightly hook up to…what?" Her eyes blazed. "To blur the pain of your lifestyle?" Her words cut hard, but I remained impassive, unreadable. "You don't use my name, never want to know anything about me, and I'm supposed to be okay with it?" Her soft hands pushed against my chest, and I fought the urge to flip her over and have my way with her again.

"I don't," I pulled her hands up and away from me, "expect anything from you. Just like you shouldn't expect anything from me."

"Wow." She ripped her hands from my hold, dried her tears, and got up. She began to gather her clothes and tripped over her bra in her hurry to get away from me.

Everything inside me wanted to pull her back to bed, but the truth was I wouldn't.

I'd known this day would come. I'd allowed myself to get comfortable with her, and now I needed to hurt her because of who we were. Both of us were wrapped deep in the Cartel. I worked for her cousin, and she worked for her father. Though we were of the same world, we were miles apart. If I publicly dated her, I'd have to answer to more than just her family. I'd have to answer to mine…and that just wasn't an option.

"Don't call me, Eric, because this won't happen again." She tugged her dress on and shimmied into her shoes.

Just as she reached the door, I flew off the bed and whirled her around by her arm to look at me. Her expression carried so much hurt, but there was hope there too, and I knew it was time. I knew she was the one person who could take me down. I'd hurt many women in the past, some worse than others, but the one who stood in front of me now needed to go. I was angry at myself. I'd known better, but I'd been selfish and lazy. I'd grown comfortable with her and didn't want to look for another.

Everything was on the tip of my tongue. How I did know her real name, and I only allowed myself to use it when she was asleep. Or how I was the one who sent her those white roses on her birthday. It was me who sent the bottle of wine and candies a month after Valentine's Day, because I hated that day. I enjoyed the idea of her reaction that some unknown person thought to send her gifts. She deserved the world, but I sure as hell wasn't the one who could give her that.

"I—" I snapped my mouth shut.

Don't.

"Yeah," she sniffed, "I thought so."

I love you, Talya.

She leaned up and kissed my cheek. "I want more, Eric." Her lips brushed over my skin again.

"And I don't," I lied.

"Then this is goodbye." She ducked under my arm and slipped outside the door, leaving me to fall apart in silence.

My phone lit up on top of the white blanket, and I ran a hand through my hair as I retrieved it.

Castillo: Pick up and transport the next payment. 1:30 p.m.

I swiped the message away and zeroed in on the time. I had just under an hour before I had to make the pickup. Beer bottles clinked outside the door, and I closed my eyes and tried not to lose my shit. I hated people in my house, but parties were a must in my world, and I planned to make my way up in it.

"Where're you off to?" someone called out, and I heard a woman laugh as a man called back.

Fuck this. I grabbed my gun, ripped open the door, and fired a couple rounds in the air.

"Get the fuck out!" I yelled and heard the ruckus as everyone scrambled to their feet.

"Alejandro," I spotted my right-hand man, "we leave in forty." I slammed the door shut and headed for the shower.

The spray from the shower beat my face, and no matter how much I pushed away the pain and tried to close the door on Talya, it was impossible. She was the only one I'd ever let inside my tightly closed heart. She'd managed to break down my walls, but only in bed. When we were alone in the dark, I would let my guard down, never with words, just with action. But the moment the sun came up and broke though that protective dark shield, I immediately pulled back and reminded her she was good for one thing. Sex. The lies I told her repeatedly burned at my soul.

I never thought we'd last this long, but shit, it hurt. I knew I couldn't allow matters of the heart to intrude on the careful life I'd built here. I pressed my hands against the shower wall and hung my head back and let the water flow into my nose and mouth until my lungs begged me to move. I gasped in a breath and felt the pain flood through me again. This had to stop; it was a maddening loop. I turned the water off and stepped out. I glanced in the mirror and slicked back my hair to try to get a good look at my face.

I swiped the fog from the mirror with the back of my hand and took in my expression. The tormented face that looked back at me gave me a reason to reach for the jar of pain killers in the cabinet. I swallowed them back with some tequila I kept next to the sink. I saw it was nearly empty as I swallowed and tried not to cough at the burn in my throat. The burn went straight down to my stomach. I tossed the bottle in the trash and headed for the closet.

"You look like shit, boss." Alejandro cringed when I finally emerged from my room. I buttoned up my shirt, rolled my sleeves, and caught the eye of one of my guys. I jabbed my thumb toward my room to let him know to get my place cleaned up. "I told you not to mix the tequila and those pills Filippo brought. That shit messes with your head." His eyes went wide. "I saw dragons last time I done that."

"Yeah." I tuned him out as we headed outside. The heat hit us both like a slap to the face. I never touched any of the product these guys pumped through my party. If I didn't keep a straight head in this business, I was as good as dead.

"Where we goin' today, boss?" He fiddled with the climate control and lowered the blast of cool air that was aimed at him.

"Pick up, drop off." I headed down the driveway and out onto the main road. "Then church."

CHAPTER THREE

Daniel

"Intel has confirmed that the Cartels have started a new movement." Frank lifted his head slightly and adjusted his glasses. They call themselves 'Los Débiles.'"

The weak.

"That's a pathetic play on words. They prey on the weak, but they're hardly weak," Keith muttered.

"Agreed." Frank shook his head. "Los Débiles' purpose is to grab homeless women and children off American streets using soldiers they've hired. They are also targeting the rich, famous, and of course, people like us."

"Just add it to the friggin' list." Mark rubbed his eyes.

I understood his feelings. We were all worn out and tired of the endless fight, and though none of us would ever stop fighting, we needed some fresh blood to join us to help carry the load. All the more reason I knew we needed to recruit some new men.

"The Cartels have made another push into the States and are spreading fast," Frank continued. "The border patrol is adding new agents, police are doubling their efforts in all their border towns, and now, to follow suit, I think, like we've discussed, it's time we added some new people of our own." Frank turned his attention to me. "Cole and Daniel, I've sent over several files on men I've personally handpicked. Some of them are still on active duty, and some are looking to try something new. I want you two to go through their dossiers, but pay some serious attention to Captain Ty Beckett. I've seen what he can do firsthand. I think he should be looked at for team leader." He nodded at me. "Trust me. Read his file."

"All right, Frank." I knew Frank had always been meticulous when vetting anyone, and his suggestions would be seriously close to the mark, so I was very curious to see who he'd recommended.

"The money's already been approved for the new team's salary, so just send the list of what you'll need for supplies, and I'll handle everything else here."

"Frank," Cole spoke up, "has any intel been provided as to possible locations of where the Los Débiles are holding the people they grab?"

"Yes, they have two locations identified." A map popped up on the screen next to his head, and he circled where they were. "We know there are several more places and one main hub. As we speak, we're moving some of our inside men around, trying to understand who the ringleader of the operation is and where the other locations might be."

"Let me guess." Mike spun a bottlecap between his fingers. "We're to sit tight until we know all the locations?" A few of the guys groaned, and I knew they hated to sit still for long.

"I'll make Blackstone a deal." Frank clicked off the map. "I have Eagle Eye watching the borders. Once we bring in a new team leader, you can go in. But I want him to go with you. We don't have time to train on friendly ground, so we'll drop him in the deep end. We'll build the team from there."

"And if any high-profile cases come up?" Mike questioned again.

"That's different," Frank assured us all. "This hold is merely for Los Débiles. Otherwise, it's business as usual." He checked his watch. "That's all the time I have right now. Daniel, Savannah will provide you with the files. I'll be in touch."

The screen went black, and everyone remained quiet, until Mark couldn't take the silence anymore.

"You know, a little poison in their water supply would take care of this entire mess." He shrugged.

"Careful, that might just land you a session with Doc." John chuckled.

"Speaking of that," Cole tapped his coffee cup, "and in all seriousness," all smiles faded, "given the situation here in the house, there's been talk that Doc Roberts will start working with the new team and we'll get someone new." Out of the corner of my eye, I saw Keith shift uncomfortably in his seat.

"What? That's bullshit," Mark blurted. "I mean, it's Doc, he's our go-to person. Why would they suggest that?" He looked over at me, and I knew the change would be hard. Though Shadows was started by my father, then owned by me, and now my son, a huge amount of our funding came from the U.S. Army. In order for us to work together, we needed to compromise on some aspects of the running of the house. Cole could refuse the change, but he also knew and understood that each decision that was passed down to us had been well thought out and carefully executed. If Frank and the team in Washington believed Doc Roberts should change positions for the time being, then we should be open to the idea.

It wasn't easy for any of us to let someone new in. Especially in a role like the one Doc Roberts had held in the house.

"I know, and it's true, but they also think the new team would benefit from Doc Roberts' expertise and experience. Besides, a fresh new psychologist might be a good change for all of us." They all knew if it didn't work out, we could switch back.

"Do we know who'll be coming in, Daniel?" Keith asked quietly.

"No, not yet." I added, "Frank mentioned Dr. Jerry Mayer, but nothing's set in stone."

"He's not horrible." Mark shrugged a shoulder. "He does make a weird clicking noise when he thinks, though."

"He does," John agreed. "Sounds like a pen clicking."

"We know nothing yet, but when we do, you'll know soon after," I assured them all.

"All right, we're training in ten, but first, this." Cole motioned for Abby to put the tray she was holding down in the center of the table. "Thanks, Abby." He handed her a shot, and the rest of us all took one and held it in the air. "To a brother, a great soldier, and one hell of a friend. Raven One to Fox One, happy birthday, Paul."

"Happy birthday," we all repeated as we turned to his picture, then each of us threw back the shot. I held my empty glass a little longer and gave him a nod. We'd retired Paul's call sign out of respect, and it felt nice hearing it again.

"Let's go, boys." Cole knew they would need time to mentally prepare for all these changes.

Needing a mental break myself, I joined the guys outside. I timed their training and tried to give some helpful suggestions to John, who had developed an issue with leg cramps.

"Let me see, John." Mia called him off the track.

"I'm fine."

"That wasn't a suggestion," she snipped back, and I hid my amusement at her tone. The wives never coddled or interfered where they shouldn't. They knew the rules and always respected them, and in return demanded the same from the guys. Mia was a fine nurse and has proven time and time again that she could handle herself in any situation with any loved one. She was a huge asset to the house and never made a call to pull a guy from training unless it was important.

"All right," he huffed, limping his way over to her, "let's just do this."

She dropped down on the ground next to him as his face twisted at the pain.

"How much water did you drink?"

"Double what you told me to drink."

"You've been stretching?"

"Yeah."

She pulled his leg out flat and pressed his toes backward and then forward. She manipulated his leg, and I watched as his calf quivered and tightened. John's head flopped back as the pain finally eased up.

"You're still on those pills for that infection?"

"Yeah."

"Those can cause muscle cramps." She looked him over. "I'd say to change up the meds, but you've only got a week left. Let's keep an eye on the cramps, see what happens after you've finished them.

"Can I still train?" John's face spoke volumes. All the guys hated to miss anything the others were doing. If one was weak, they were all weak. We all knew how important it was to stay in shape. Once you let it go, even a little, it was all that much harder to get it back.

"Yeah, just stop when you feel it coming on and walk it off slowly or stretch it out. You know by now they won't go away if you push it, so don't let it get a hold on you."

"Copy that." He rolled onto his knees and hobbled over to the others.

"Mia?" I kept my gaze on the others but wanted to hear what she really thought.

"I really don't think it's much, but once he's finished with the pills, we can go from there." She grabbed her medic bag from where it lay on the ground. "Maybe if they stopped getting infections, gunshot wounds, and God knows what else, their bodies could actually fully heal."

"Tell that to them." I chuckled as we both watched the guys as they army crawled through thick mud hauling forty-pound sacks up and over the obstacle course. Then lined up to do it all over again. She shook her head and gave a sigh as she turned away.

"Well, you know where to find me." She head-pointed to a seat under a nearby tree where she kept her textbooks to study.

I left the guys to run their next drill and headed back in the house. Savannah had an arm full of fresh laundry as I walked in. Abigail and June normally handled the linen, but I knew June was out, and Abby hadn't been feeling the best.

"Here, let me help you with that." I took the load and followed her up to her old room

"It's strange being in here." She grabbed the corner of the sheet and tucked it under the mattress. "Seems like it was a lifetime ago."

"A lot has happened since then." I nodded.

"I'll never forget the first morning I woke here, how everything smelled so fresh. I remember the window was open, and I listened to all the sounds." She shook her head with a smile. "The first sweet voice I heard was Abby's. Funny to think how scared I was then, and now she's family."

"She is certainly good at working her way into the heart." I smiled.

"She sure is." She smiled warmly back. "This room felt so safe and warm, like no one could touch me here. I really hope the next guest who stays feels the same way." She fluffed the pillows with care.

We'd had many guests stay since Savannah, but they'd never stayed in this room. I wondered if unconsciously we never thought they were worthy of it. Though only one had been a female, and she only stayed the night downstairs on the couch in the entertainment room. I remembered she hadn't wanted a room, nor our help, for that matter. Her father sent for her shortly after she got here, and she went home against our warning. Thankfully, things turned out all right for her.

I wrapped my arm around her shoulders as we walked together into Cole's old room. It felt like yesterday they were still living in the main house and not in the little ones where the other families were now. "Well, they will feel safe and warm because you're here."

"Thanks." Her smile turned into a smirk, and I dropped my hand away and tossed the bedsheets across the mattress. "What?"

"Nope." I pointed for her to take the end and stretch it over the corner. "You and Sue have that same expression, and I know where your head just went." I knew about the times she was in here and slipped through the passageway when they thought no one was paying attention.

"It went nowhere." Her tone shot up, and her face was a dead giveaway.

"You lie, and now we need to change the topic to kids."

"You sure you want to do that?" She made a devious face as I scrambled for another topic. "Fine." She laughed. "Tell me what I can get for Abby at the market. Something to help her with her appetite."

"Sue already grabbed some stuff to make her soup, and she's going to make her some fresh rolls."

"Yum!" She tugged at the blanket to get it to lay just right, and we headed back toward the stairs.

"Where were you?" Mark caught June as she came in the front door.

"Out."

"Clearly you were out." He inspected her clothing. "Where was out?"

"The store."

"You lie." He stood straighter, and I glanced at Savannah, who looked like she was enjoying the show. "Where are your bags?"

"Keith is grabbing them."

"Where's Keith?" Keith came strolling in with a sandwich hanging out of his mouth.

June closed her eyes and cleared her throat. "I was out, and that's all you need to know."

"No." He blocked her path. "I heard you were at dinner."

"I was, alone."

"Oh, her brows went up." Keith egged the conversation along.

"Boys," she scowled at them, "I'm a grown woman who is allowed to come and go from this house."

"Aunt June," Mark nearly stomped his foot, "don't make me ask Abby where you've been."

"Marcus Lopez, I'm not your mother, and you don't need to keep tabs on me." She brushed by, but not before I saw her cheeks had pinked.

"That's it." Mark tossed his hands in the air. "I'm losing control here! Over you, over Mom, over the kids, and don't get me started on Mia. Even Butters doesn't listen to me."

"Calm down, babe," Mia called. "When did you ever really have control?"

"Do you see the emotional abuse I get in this house?" Mark huffed at Keith, who grinned up at me.

"Why we spend money on TV is beyond me." Savi shrugged.

Once I was downstairs, I found Sue in the kitchen. I came up behind her and wrapped my arms around her waist and pulled my beautiful wife in close.

"I was just thinking of you." She wiggled in closer. "Guess who I ran into this morning?" I shrugged. "Tracy Livingston."

"Wow, I haven't heard her name in years." I kissed her neck.

"She's doing great." She pushed back against me. "She's up here for a ski trip with her husband and their three kids. I know she's been living in Texas for the past twenty years. We're going to meet for coffee tomorrow. She was asking about Zack and how you two were doing. We had so many wonderful times together. You two really should come."

"I'd love to. I'll see if Zack's free," I replied with my face buried in her hair. She sighed happily as I pulled away a little, and we both watched the kids play through the window. "Tracy Livingston," I repeated with a chuckle. "She was really rooting for us, wasn't she?"

"She was."

"Who is this Tracy woman?" June came in and buried herself in our hug. We both chuckled and wrapped an arm around her. June was our nanny's younger sister.

"Tracy was my best friend and played matchmaker for me and Daniel."

"I've never heard that story." June pulled away. "In fact, I've never heard how Shadows came about either. Care to spend a little time sharing? I've brought fresh scones from Zack's."

I had a mountain of work to do, but a chance to tell that story was a lot more appealing.

"I can't say no to that." We made a fresh pot of coffee and warmed the scones then settled ourselves in some comfy chairs next to the fire. Scoot, our cranky old cat, was on full display as usual. He insisted on lying on his back to prove his masculinity to anyone who was unfortunate enough to see it.

"Start from the beginning, Daniel." June pulled a blanket over her lap and wrapped both hands around her warm mug. "I want to know everything."

"There's probably a lot you already know."

"Don't skip a thing." She wiggled to get comfy in the big chair across from me. "I could use a good story today."

"Okay, I'll just skip forward a bit after Abby arrived because you know a lot of that."

"Just don't leave any good parts out." She glanced at Sue when she returned.

"Well, if that's the case, Daniel will need this." Sue handed me my father's notebook from Cole's study where I had kept it all these years. I hadn't known of its existence until I was older. Before he died, he'd given it to me. He said he wanted to show me what it felt like when your son was lost to you because of war. He wanted me to know what it was like from his perspective as a father, because one day it might just happen to my own son. Or the son of someone close to me. He thought a little insight from a father who'd already gone through it would be helpful. "It's my father's journal," I informed June. "It's from the time I served in Nam and after."

"Oh, wow," June cooed. "It's amazing your dad did that."

"All right." I smiled at Sue and started to tell my story from the beginning.

CHAPTER FOUR

Location: Vietnam
Coordinates: Classified

DANIEL

We approached the camp on our bellies, using only hand signals. I motioned to the men to freeze as I thought I heard a sound. Every breath, every beat of my heart was calculated because the moment you let your guard down you were dead. We just hoped we could rescue even one more and do some damage before that day came.

I hated this damn place. Mud covered our skin to keep the swarms of mosquitoes from eating us alive. We often had to stop to clean out our boots in fear that we'd get the dreaded flesh-eating disease that had taken the lives of more than a quarter of our men. Food was nonexistent at this point. We were living off the land, which was a joke because this land gave us nothing without a fight, and from what I'd experienced in this country so far, I was more than ready to go home.

We crawled forward to position ourselves to get a better

look at what could only be described as a big birdcage. About seven or eight of our men were inside that thing as it swung ten feet above the jungle floor. Frank crawled up beside Jimmy off to my right, and I saw a shadow on his six. Before I could warn them, I saw a flurry of movement, then Zack's head showed itself. His grin flashed as he motioned with his bloody knife that he'd just looked after the problem.

I caught the attention of one of the men in the cage, and he alerted the others to our presence just as Jimmy signaled urgently, holding up two fingers, and we all strained to listen. I saw Ray freeze at some movement, and I carefully belly-crawled a few feet forward then separated the grass with the barrel of my rifle. I found myself face to face with a young boy who had dropped his armload of wood. I slowly lifted myself up as his eyes stared into mine. He whispered something I couldn't understand, but his watery eyes and the urine trickling out of his shorts told me he was scared. The knowledge flashed through me of other times a soldier had smiled at a child to show a moment of compassion only to have them drop a bomb at their feet.

It was a faceless war that spared no life.

"Kill him!" Wayde hissed from above in the birdcage. "Kill him! They're savages just like the rest of them!"

He was right, most were, but the truth was they were just little kids who knew only violence because of the world around them.

"*Di.*" I flicked my head so he would leave, and he ran like a jack rabbit and disappeared into the jungle.

"Stupid," Wayde muttered down at me.

I held my palm up to him as I sank back into the grass.

"I hope that was wise, Daniel," Ray whispered.

"Me too."

We waited well into the night to ensure the kid hadn't given us away. We listened for shouts or gunfire, but all remained quiet. We had learned the hard way that nothing was what it seemed. Booby traps were everywhere, and underground tunnels proved to be our downfall. It took my unit five months to stop firing at every sound. We'd changed our mindset and learned from the enemy to use stealth to kill or be killed. Americans were being plucked off like flies. There were so many of them, and they knew how to use the terrain to their advantage. There was no way we could win this war. We had been stuck in this nightmare for almost a year with no possible end in sight. We just had to dodge death for a little longer.

"Damn," Frank whispered in my ear as he shook his head in defeat, "does this rain ever stop?"

It always seemed to rain here. It came down in buckets, making it almost impossible to see. When it wasn't raining, steam would rise from the heat of the place and create still another problem for us. I understood his complaint and gave his shoulder a pat as he crawled by me. We both hated this godforsaken country.

I gave the signal, and we shimmied on our stomachs toward their camp. We didn't send any alert that we were here; this had to be slow and quiet. Once in position, I signaled the green light, and like shadows in the night, we attacked in unison. I used a rock to knock my guy off balance then sliced him across the throat before he could scream, and he silently slid to the ground. I used my elbow on the next one then quickly kicked him in the throat to silence any cry for help. Zack finished him off. We picked them off one by one as we advanced toward the cage.

Jimmy blocked a sudden punch from Frank as he got caught up in the moment. "You're good. We're good."

"Yeah, yeah, all good," Frank repeated with a heavy breath, and Ray repeated the words again to check himself too.

Shadows

"Zack." I pointed to the rope for him to give me some slack so I could undo it and release the lever. We worked like a well-oiled machine as we quickly lowered the cage that held the seven men. Ray worked feverishly to untie the door when we suddenly heard a familiar double gunshot. We'd been made.

"Move! Move! Move!" I shouted at the men in the cage as I helped pull the battle-scarred team out of the contraption. Many of them were wounded, one had an arrow in his stomach, and others had bullet or knife wounds. We pushed the strong to keep moving as we carried the weak on our shoulders. *No man left behind* chanted in my head as we retreated through the jungle as fast as we could toward the rendezvous spot where the chopper would pick us up.

My boots slipped on the rocks, and I tripped and put one knee to the ground as I shifted Ben's weight on my shoulder. My muscles burned and screamed at me for relief.

"Leave me, Daniel," he choked out. "Too far gone."

"No."

"Logan, it's too late."

"No!" I pushed on.

Then it happened. In one blink, I had a fellow brother on my back, and then *zip zip zip!* I felt the bullets as they slammed into his body. He went slack, and I lost control of him. He dropped like a rag doll to the ground. I let myself slip for one second and felt the agonizing pain of his death rip through my core. I had no choice. I tore open his shirt, grabbed his tags, and pressed my finger to his eyes to close them.

"I'm sorry." No time for anything else.

I rushed to catch up with the guys as bullets and arrows zipped by as I ran. I waited for one of them to plow into my back.

"It was the kid who told them we were there!" Wayde got

in my face the moment I stepped back into our makeshift base where we waited for the chopper. "There were seven of us, and now it's just Gibs and me!"

"You're welcome." Zack stood, and I reached to pull him low for his own safety. Anger would get us killed, but I knew he was right. Where was our goddamn thanks for risking our lives to save them? We had done our best.

"You want to point fingers. Well, we sure can." I backed up my brother and nodded as Frank and Ray joined us. "Your men were under *your* command, Wayde. *You* got them captured, and *you* got them shot. We," I poked him in the chest, "just saved *your* lives while we carried *your* wounded on our backs."

"You let that kid go! It was that kid who told them. I didn't get them killed," he hissed.

"And neither did we!" I ignored his comment. "None of us asked for this, Wayde. We made it this far, so get your head on straight and act like a damn soldier! We all feel your loss. We all do."

He turned to look at Gibs, who looked like he had mentally checked out weeks ago.

"Their blood is on you, Logan."

I was furious, but I wouldn't give him the satisfaction of knowing that. As I was about to speak, we heard the chopper, and we knew that would also alert the enemy as to where we were.

I signaled for the boys to gather their things because it was time to leave.

"It's not over, Logan." Wayde's bitter words found me. "You didn't win this."

I turned around a few feet away and chuckled with sadness. "At what point did you ever think we would win this?"

Two more months came and went, and we managed to

Shadows

free over thirty more Americans. We learned from each rescue, and each one tested our ability to find new ways to trick the enemy and sharpen our skills. Each day came and went. The sun came up, and the sun went down. We did what we did best until the day we were told to report to a base that was relieving men of their duties.

By the time we set foot in that place, we were different men than when we arrived in Nam. After thirteen months in hell, we had become ruthless killers. We had built a name for ourselves here, and talk of our rescue missions had spread throughout the camps. We were unaware of any of it until we were greeted with a job well done by a well-known commanding officer. I figured we were just doing our job. It wasn't what we had been trained for, but it was what we had learned, and our unit had been damn good at it.

On the sixth day, we got the news we'd been waiting for. With what little we had in our possession, we sat out on some water barrels and waited for the helicopter to arrive to take us out of here. We were going home.

"I don't know if I know how to go back to normal living. You think we can?" Jimmy puffed on a cig as he looked up at the gray sky that hugged the jungle's treetops.

"I don't know what normal is anymore." Zack rested his head in his hands while I fought sleep. I hadn't closed my eyes in forever.

"Normal is not having anyone shooting at us, I guess," I chimed in. "Hey, Ray, you okay?"

"Yeah," he nodded, "just the idea of going back home wasn't something I thought I'd ever be doing. You know? I thought we were goners after what went down with Young's unit."

I fought back the horrific images. Young's entire unit had been slaughtered right in front of us. We'd been delayed and had arrived too late to save them, and we had to witness their deaths. Truckloads of Viet Cong had arrived just before we did. They stood the guys in a line and shot them one by one. They just dropped to the ground like stuffed dolls as we lay silent in the jungle, helpless to do anything for them. Our guys would never get over being too late in our attempt to rescue them. I knew we all had a lot of stuff to get over, if we ever could.

The blades of the chopper could be heard in the distance, and the jolt of adrenaline that lived deep inside the center of my nervous system pushed my fatigue away. Just as the chopper landed, the sky opened up to another downpour, and we grabbed our stuff and raced to the door. It was finally our time to go home.

As my brothers climbed inside and I lifted my foot to leave this land behind, I looked down at the water that pooled at my feet. I imagined it mixed with a heavy red. It didn't rain water in this god-forsaken place; it rained blood from the fallen.

It took over twenty-four hours to get back into the United States, and as we stepped out onto the cool tarmac in Washington DC, it almost felt surreal.

Unlike World War Two, there were no flags being waved, no cheers of loved ones, no cameras in our faces to congratulate us for our service. This was a war like no other, and we were not welcomed home.

What the hell happened?

"There's my son." My mother's voice found me as she wrapped me in one of her famous hugs, and I relished her tight hold. "Thank you, Lord, for bringing my boy home." Her eyes were full of happy tears.

"Hey, Mom," I nuzzled in closer. I had forgotten just how much I needed her warmth. I pulled back and was greeted with a smack on the shoulder.

"I never doubted for a second that you would come

Shadows

home." My dad pulled me in close and patted my back as he gave me a bear hug.

"Is that why you haven't slept through a night since he left?" Mom teased, and my father gave an unsure laugh as he looked around. I bet they were worried I would feel like the world had changed since we'd left. I sensed their tenseness with the greeting we'd had, or rather hadn't had.

"Hey." Zack's voice had me turning around. "You okay?"

I gave him a nod. "Best I've been yet."

"Come here, Zack." My mom and dad took turns checking out their second son, making sure he'd arrived back in one piece, too.

"See you soon." Zack pointed to me as his own mother grabbed him in a hug. "Real soon, okay?" Zack's mom threw a teary smile and a wave at us as we walked by.

The drive home felt strange. Mom and Dad tried to fill the silence while I watched the faces on the sidewalks as we drove. I wondered if they had any clue of the hell we soldiers had been through while they went on with their daily lives. Of course, they didn't. How could they? Any who did know would turn their own haunted eyes away and pretend they were fine. I doubted any would want to talk about it, and fewer still would want to hear about it.

How could a place I called home seem so different to me now? Nothing had changed here, only me. I felt like a stranger in my own skin. I ran my thumb gently over the flag on my rucksack and closed my eyes as I pushed back the disappointment that I didn't feel better about being home.

"Hungry?" Dad found my gaze in the rearview mirror.

"Not really."

"I bet a good night's sleep will help." Mom looked back at me, and I forced a smile. "Back in your room, in your own bed, safe and sound," she said more to herself, and Dad reached over and squeezed her hand. It didn't take much to see they were worried about me. I was concerned about my own mental state, so I completely understood where they were coming from.

I knew when I left it would take a toll on them, and part of me felt guilty for not being happier about being back, but the truth was, I had no idea how to place my feelings anymore. They had been steamrolled by the things I'd seen over there. I wasn't sure how I was going to sleep at night with what I had pushed down inside. I wondered what would happen when it all began to come to the surface.

"Ms. Dorothy dropped off some of her famous bread," Mom started up again. "She knows how much you love her walnut bread."

"That was nice." I leaned my head back and counted down the minutes until I saw our driveway. I was finally home.

I dragged my heavy bag out of the back seat and swung it over my shoulder then looked around at the old place. A few of Dad's crazy, hippy-looking chickens clucked away around my feet. The goats gathered at the fence, probably hoping for a handout. I reached out and patted a few on the head. They said animals could sense people's emotions. I was curious to know what they sensed from me. Most likely nothing, as I was pretty empty inside right now.

"They missed ya. They were always your favorite." Dad nodded at the goats. "I bet they're glad you're back, too."

"Mm." I rubbed one's ears.

"Take your time, son. Come in when you're ready." Dad waited a beat then took my mother's arm and drew her toward the house. I couldn't hear their words, but the tone of Dad's voice and my mother's backward glance told me he was probably asking her to be patient. I hated to hurt her, but I couldn't bring myself to pretend I wasn't tapped out.

I dropped my bag at the step and decided to walk the farm in hopes it would spark some good feelings. The pond was one of my favorite places to sit. I liked to watch the ducks paddle around the water, their butts to the sky in their constant search for food. Bending down, I leaned against the big tree and zoned out. I tried not to, but I glanced down at the one spot that did bring a little surge of something through me, but as quickly as it came, I forced it away. That was a dead end. I couldn't let it in. I was a different person than I was when I left, and I had no right to even pretend I could have it back.

A rabbit jumped out of the tall grass and began to chew on some bushes. When he sensed me, he froze, and his ears gave a little twitch as he looked right at me, almost as if he didn't know whether to be afraid of me or not. I gave a little wave, and it shot back into the grass and disappeared as fast as it came.

"I get that a lot." I gave a little huff.

The sun had started to set as I headed back toward the house. I didn't need to worry my parents any more than I already had by being late for dinner. Mom had outdone herself, as I knew she would, and the meal was very tasty. She had made all my favorites. I worked hard to keep my head on the positive things. Mom's homecooked food was a huge plus. Our farm's cold well water was even better than I remembered. Dad handed me a beer, and I accepted it with a smile. Then Mom served me a huge slice of her apple pie. I was stuffed, but I knew from the hopeful look in her eyes she needed me to have a slice, so I took it and picked up a dessert fork and immediately dug into it.

My parents were the most amazing people a son could ask for. I knew I was lucky to have them. I also knew that some of the men who had come back returned to face empty homes with no one to support them or make them welcome.

"Thanks, Mom. That was perfect." I squeezed her hand

and saw tears well up in her eyes. "I couldn't have asked for a better meal."

"I'm so happy to hear that." She leaned in and hugged me with a sniff. The emotion in the room was as thick as the slice of apple pie.

"It's really good to have you home." Dad blinked a few times and cleared his throat. "Well," he stood, "go get some rest. It's late, and I have the kids to deal with tomorrow." He referred to the animals. "If you need anything, you know where to find us."

"Yes, off with you." Mom waved her apron at me. "I'll clean these things up. I need to keep busy." She shooed me away as I tried to carry some things to the counter.

"Okay. Night, then, and thanks again, Mom." I put the dishes down, gave her a hug, then went upstairs to my room.

Exhausted, I didn't even unpack. I just put my clothes on the chair, splashed a bit of water over my face, and brushed my teeth. I never even turned on a light. I fell into bed and shut my eyes. As soon as I began to drift off, I was carried back into the hell that kept me captive whenever I fell asleep.

CHAPTER FIVE

GENERAL EDISON LOGAN

I knew that look, the demons that rested behind the eyes of those who had fought, killed, and watched their brothers fall. When I returned home from my time in war, we were heroes. We were proud of our service in spite of all we'd gone through, but my son looked like a dead man walking. It made me sick. It was a lot to carry in your early twenties.

"He didn't sleep again last night." Meg glanced over at me from above her reading glasses. She looked just as worried as I did. His nightmares had a pretty good hold on him. Some nights we had to wake him from his screams, but others we let him ride them out. Both of us were unsure which was better. "It's been three weeks, Ed. I think it's time to check in."

"I think so, too." I glanced at the dinner plate that sat in his spot and kissed my wife's head. "We'll get through this, my love. I promise."

"I know." She squeezed my hand. "I know."

I waited for Meg to settle into her usual spot by the fireplace and watched as she cracked open the newest book by her beloved author. I smiled as she sipped her tea and prepared to lose herself in another world, destined to have a happy ending.

I tugged back the curtain a bit and saw the telltale beam of light in the barn that gave up his position. I was determined to give my Meg and our son the same happy outcome her book promised. I slipped on my boots and sweater and made my way across the field, patting the goats as they rushed over for a head scratch.

"Are you watching over our Daniel?" I asked one of the babies as I scratched its knobby little head. "Good boy." I scooted the chickens away from the door and poked my head inside to find Daniel dripping in sweat, knuckles raw and a demon on his shoulder.

He tossed two punches, ducked, and tossed three more, finishing off with a kick. He repeated the moves six more times before he felt me watching him.

"I'm fine, Dad." *Punch, punch, punch.*

"You're not the one I'm concerned about," I lightly joked as I came around and inspected the punching bag. It had seen better days. "You need to get out, see some friends, meet some girls."

"I will, but..." He moved into a different kickbox sequence but was interrupted by a chicken who had slipped inside with me before I could shut the door. He scooted it away from his feet and continued his moves.

"Have you checked in with Zack?"

"Once." *Kick, kick, punch.*

"Frank and Ray?"

"Once," he repeated.

"Why don't you invite them over? It would do all of you good to spend some time together."

His punches became more intense, and I knew that feeling all too well.

"I..."

"I?" I leaned down and scooped the annoying chicken out of his way again.

He dropped his arms and breathed heavily. I could almost feel his mind as it spun and knew he was close to spiraling out of control. I sat the chicken on a hay bale and looked up at the night sky through the open loft doors above us. I took in a deep breath, unsure if he'd hear me in the frame of mind he was in but decided to chance it. I knew it couldn't wait any longer.

"Son, look at me." Slowly, his gaze swung over, and his chest heaved as his lungs gasped for much needed air. "You need to fight this. That darkness inside needs to be channeled in a different way. You're a Logan, and we are fighters. It's in our blood, in our DNA. We're military men, just like your own son will be someday." He gave me a tight nod to let me know he'd heard me. "I got a call from Washington. They wanted me to know what you did over there." I swallowed back a surge of emotion. "You never told me you guys freed prisoners and saved countless lives."

"We went on a lot of missions," he grunted, for the first time speaking about it. "Made our own calls, did our best for those we could. God knows what it meant for the ones we never got out."

I reached up and held on to his shoulder, giving him my strength. I hoped to force the demons away, if only for a moment.

"Those nightmares you're having...what's happening in them?"

"I don't know. I don't remember." He brushed me off, but I wasn't having it. I knew what they could do to a person's sanity. When he caught my look, he squeezed his eyes shut and grimaced. He knew I could be just as stubborn. "It's the same thing. I'm over there." He winced as if talking about it physically hurt. "I'm on my knees, looking for something, and this little boy steps out of the jungle. He's terrified, and so am I, because I know what it means." He rubbed his chest with his eyes locked on the floor. "Guys yell at me to kill him, and I can see the kid's tears as they run down his dirty face, he pees his pants, and bang! A gun goes off, and he falls to the ground."

"Who shot him?" I had to ask, although I knew deep in my core it wouldn't have been Daniel.

"I don't know," his gaze quickly shifts to mine, "but when I look around, I'm all alone, with him at my feet, and I'm holding my gun."

"Nightmares can stem from all kinds of things, Daniel, but mostly they stem from things that are unresolved."

"I never killed that kid." He shook his head. "I let him go."

I nodded slowly to show I knew he would never do that. "Your unit brought a lot of men home to their families." I tried to get him to focus on the positive. "They might never have been seen again. You protected each other, and you made it out in one piece. You helped bring our boys home safe, son. That's what counts. That's what you need to hold on to."

"Did I?" Tears pooled in his eyes, and I saw raw pain appear on his face. "Because we weren't home even four days when Jimmy shoved a pistol down his throat."

"Jimmy didn't have family. He had no help to come home to, and I'm sorry for that, but you have us. Use us."

"I want to do more, Dad." He paused as emotion ripped through him. "I need to do more." He sobbed as he wrapped his arms around my neck, and I held on tight.

"Then we do more." I felt him crumble as he cried out what he had been hanging on to since he'd stepped back on home soil. I had always made it known that there was no weakness in showing vulnerability, and that letting go, no matter how you did it, was what the brain and the heart needed to survive. Without that outlet, that was when the real danger began.

"I hated that place," he whispered. "It took something from me, and I'm not sure how to get it back."

"Time will help you find it." I pulled him back and held his head in my hands like I used to when he was a young boy. "Have trust in yourself to find your way back. The pain and confusion aren't only inside you, son. It's in the others, too. They need you just as much as you need them."

"It's hard to know where to start."

"That's why you have us." I smiled and saw his anxiety drop to a simmer. "You always have us."

The next morning, Meg and I were settled in with our morning coffee and oatmeal, and to my surprise, Daniel walked into the kitchen showered and dressed.

Meg glanced at me, and I used the morning newspaper to hide my grin.

"The wire by the pond needs replacing," he said with his back to me. He nibbled on some toast and kept his gaze out the window.

"There's extra wire behind the henhouse." I turned the page with a smile. "Tools are where they always are."

"Great." He rinsed his plate.

"The mailbox could use a new post, too," I suggested as I realized he needed to keep busy.

"Then you'll know where I am." He went to leave then stopped to give his mama a kiss on the cheek, then he pushed the back screen door open and let it slap behind him the way he used to when he was younger.

"Well, now," Meg beamed at me, "I think today's looking up."

"Indeed." I wasn't going to get too excited yet. Daniel had a long way to go, but this was a start.

——— ★☆★☆★ ———

It was baby steps but as the weeks went on. Daniel continued to find little things around the property to keep himself busy. He even named the damn goats. I secretly wondered if they were named after friends he'd lost. I didn't care. It was just good to hear him talking again.

The chickens were a pain in the butt when it came to doing chores, and there were times when I would watch from the porch as the little cluckers would team up and try to trip Daniel when he was feeding the goats. He cursed them up and down, but a few minutes later he'd be carrying the ringleader under his arm, explaining how things needed to get done by sundown.

The odd time one or two old friends from school would call to see if they'd heard right that Daniel had returned from Nam, but when I would try to get him to take their call, he'd say he just wasn't ready. I didn't blame him. It seemed most people just wanted to forget about what happened over there and ignored what our boys had been through. They couldn't get their heads around a far-away war, especially when they were practicing for a ball game or starting a new career.

Zack came by a few times, and I'd watch them from the study, sitting in the same room together in total silence, both reminiscing internally. It worried me, and I knew it might only be a matter of time before one of them slipped. Though the chores were a step in the right direction, it wasn't improving his overall attitude. I needed to fix it before the worst happened. The beginnings of a plan started to sprout in my head.

"What are you doing?" Meg asked. She was wrapped in

her blue robe, with curlers in her hair and slippers on her feet. I took her in as she stood in the doorway of the garage, still the love of my life. I personally thought she looked adorable but knew if I commented she'd get all twisted up and probably slap me.

"I'm changing things up." I shot her a big smile and hoped my banging around in the wee hours of the morning hadn't been what woke her up. "We need a change, and I think this time around it's my turn to make it happen."

"Should I be concerned, Ed?" Her beautiful eyes so full of concern were part of the reason I needed to make this change a high priority for all of us.

"No, my darlin', you should be thrilled that I've figured out how we're going to save our son. Well, both our sons." I thought of Zack's expression or lack of it last time I'd seen him. Zack was a great young man and a lifelong friend of Daniel's. So, to see them so disconnected when they were together in one room worried me. It wasn't healthy for either of them. Nope, a change was needed.

"Give me ten minutes to get my face on and brew some coffee. Save me a seat at that table."

"I love you, Meg," I called, delighted I'd married that woman. She really was my other half in life.

"Good thing you do," she called back, "because even the goats aren't coming to say hello. My curlers are freaking them out." She laughed all the way down the path that led to the house. When she returned curler free a while later, she was loaded up with coffee and pastries, and I laid out my plan for her. I was beyond happy to see she was even more excited than I was about it.

"This is incredibly impressive, Ed, and what a good use of your time, for both of you."

"It is, but I'm going to have to call in some help for the farm."

"Don't you worry about the farm, you hear me? My sister's boys can chip in. This is exactly what our boy needs, so let's make it happen. I've been on the phone to everyone I know. I've got a lot of contacts who hold some high positions. I think I might just have started to get a few heads thinking."

I leaned over and grabbed her to me and planted kisses on her until she was screaming for mercy. Then we both went to work to make sure we had everything covered.

Later, once all my chores were done, I looked around for Daniel. The cluster of chickens outside the barn doors outed his location once again.

"Daniel?" I went into the barn and found him painting the stalls. His t-shirt was covered in white spatters, and his beloved old, tattered ball hat was jammed backward on his head and had some woodchips stuck to it.

"Yeah?"

"Come with me, will ya? I want to show you something I'm working on."

"Right now?" He held up the paint brush.

"Yeah, right now. Come on." He carefully balanced the brush on the tin, brushed his hands off against his shirt, and followed me out.

We walked across the driveway to the garage where I'd spent many summers teaching Daniel how to tear apart and rebuild the engine of my 1964 Mustang. He was always a quick study and great with his hands.

One of the barn cats whisked by with a mouse in its teeth, but when she spotted Dan, she went to him and dropped it at his feet.

"That's disgusting, Gizzy." He reached down and scooped the sweet girl into his arms. "But thanks for the offer. It's a great dead carcass." She meowed, and I saw a faint smile crease his lips. Daniel had always liked being surrounded by animals, and I was glad there was still a part of him that had never let the love go.

"I, ah, ran into Billy from the hardware store yesterday." I didn't look at him.

"Yeah?"

"He mentioned some girls were curious if you were back in town."

"I'm not interested in girls right now." He set Gizzy on her feet, and, her job done, she ran under the truck.

"Never said you were, but I think you've got some admirers."

"I don't have admirers, Dad. They're just wondering if I'm going to pull a Jimmy or not."

I swallowed back the instant fear and discomfort that brought me. I hated to admit it, but he was right. I was scared about that, too. People always gossiped and knew he and Jimmy had been tight. They would talk.

We went up the steps to the top of the loft, and I pointed for him to stand on the other side of the big table.

"Well, you and Jimmy got me thinking." I started, and he shifted uncomfortably. "Have you heard about what's been happening down in Mexico?"

"No."

"There's this group called the Cartel. They're deep into the drug trade and are making a ton of money. They're ruthless and becoming more and more powerful. Their own government can't seem to stop them. Now they've started to kidnap high profile people, demanding money in exchange for their return. The papers are predicting that the whole situation is about to explode in the next few years, and we want to get ahead of it."

"I'm listening."

"I think we should do something about it."

"We?" He took a moment to digest what I said and ran a hand through his hair as he thought.

"We don't need to make any decisions today, but you wanted to do more, and I think this is just the thing. Look at war and how it ends for the soldiers returning home. You touch down on home soil, and you're expected to go back to a normal life. There is no normal after what we experienced over there."

"Agreed, but I'm not following you."

"Think about it, Daniel. When you boys went to Vietnam, you were basically thrown into a highly charged, dangerous environment where you could have lost your life at any time. You manage to survive. Then when you come home, there's no help for you. You've lost your unit, your whole support system. Then you're stripped of your uniform and told to go back to live in society, get a job, and go on like before. War changes you, changes how you think, how you live."

I stopped for a moment to make sure he was following me. When I saw he was listening, I continued. "Same goes for these people who're being taken. From what I've read, they're stripped of their lives, taken from everything they know, and dropped into a terrifying situation. They're kept in rooms, tunnels, God knows where, and if they ever do get back home, they're dropped back into their lives and have to function like before. It's not realistic. They can't function. So, let's see if we can help."

"How do you think we can help? You want to offer them psych help or something?" He cocked his head and frowned at me.

"Yes, but much more than that, but I'll need that smart head of yours to do it." I leaned back and pulled a paper tube from the back bookcase and rolled it out over top of everything. "Take that end." I pointed to the edge, and then I used a bottle of soda to hold down one side.

"Wow." He admired the drawing of a massive building I'd sketched. "Did you draw this?"

"I did." I laughed at my chicken scratches.

"So, this is like a rescue house or something?"

I leaned back to sit on a stool and crossed my arms. "It will be where our teams will live, train, work, and return from missions with the subjects they've extracted. It will be a safehouse where they can stay until they're ready to go home."

"Or safe for them to go home, too."

"Exactly."

I watched as he thought about it. His finger tapped the table, and his mouth twisted. Then he looked over at me.

"That sounds pretty amazing, Dad."

"I think so." I warmed him up to the subject and tried to contain my own excitement as I went on. "We'll have two teams, yours and mine. I'm getting older, and this is going to be your show, so my team will assist yours." He nodded. "All right, so, I'm thinking three to four floors, sleeping corridors as the team will have to live there, some kind of bunker, and a kitchen."

"Bedrooms up here." He pointed to the top floor and picked up a pencil from the desk and started to lightly write some words. "If we're living there, let's make it nice." He moved around the table, and I saw his wheels as they stared to turn. "Middle floor should be kitchen, living room, and dining room. Maybe an office or two."

"I can see that." I nodded with my hand over my lips to hide my relief at his interest.

We spent the next few days going back and forth, tweaking and adding to our plan. It was a joy to see some life back in our son. Meg often came out to give her opinion, and we both took pleasure as we watched Daniel come to life again.

"You need a bigger kitchen." Meg eyed the drawing measurements. "If you're going to feed an army of men, you'll need an army-sized kitchen."

"Good point." Daniel crossed out the measurements and extended the size. "What else do you see, Mom?"

She glanced over at me, seeing what I saw. Progress.

"Well, let me see. Maybe a garden with fresh flowers. Might seem funny now, but flowers can be soothing."

"I can see that. I'd like to have a boxing ring too." He pressed his lips together. "We need some sort of physical outlet. It would have to go somewhere where it won't be affected by outside elements." He bent over the table and sketched a ring on the bottom floor then looked up. "If you're serious about this Cartel group, we need to be ready in the off chance they ever find us. Because we're going to have a real target on our backs."

"I know." I lifted the paper he was working on and showed him my sketch of the bunker.

"Between the house staff, the two teams, patrol around the grounds, and whoever would be staying with us at that time, I think maybe we extend out here." He drew a line to match the entire length of the floor above. "One entry point, but a hidden way out maybe over here."

"Yeah, I see what you're saying." I moved closer and leaned over the sketch. "We'll need a separate way of communicating, too."

Daniel jotted down some notes, then his pencil stopped. "Dad, where will this be built? Where'd we ever get the money to make it all happen?"

"It'll be built about eighteen miles from here." I rocked in my chair, waiting for him to connect the dots.

"Larry's land?" I grinned for an answer. "I love that place." He grinned back. Larry was my father's best friend and like a second grandfather to Daniel. My thoughts went back to those days. I could remember Daniel playing in those mountains, getting lost in the woods and swimming in the lake. I had wonderful memories of my son's small legs pumping as he ran up the hills as fast as he could go. What better gift could I give him than a place he could once again feel safe to roam free and to be valued once again?

"The best part is Larry's family sold it to me at a reasonable price and agreed to let me keep it in their name so the name Logan would never be tied to it. If there's ever any chatter about what's going on, his grandson Ken will step in and cover for us. There'll be no way anyone can trace it back to us."

"Smart. I know Ken. He's a good guy." This had to be the best kept secret. We didn't need the townsfolk poking around.

"A hundred and twenty-five thousand acres of untouched Montana land. We'll build on the land right next to the lake, so we'll get a bird's eye view of anyone coming or going. Oh, and don't worry about the funding, I've already got a few higher-ups working on that. We just need to lay out our plan for them."

"This is crazy!" He lightly laughed as the whole idea took hold. "Who are you thinking for the team? Johnson, Day, Moore?"

"Yes, and Wildcraft and Jones. Who are you thinking?" I asked curious as to who he'd let in.

"Zack, Frank, and Ray. I'm not sure about the others yet."

"You want us to fight, scale mountains, and get people out, right?" Daniel nodded in excitement that this could really happen. "Yes, you're a damn fine Green Beret, son, and I know Zack is, too. You'll have four spots to fill with the best guys you know. Berets, Deltas, SEALs, Scout Snipers, stack it well."

"Copy that." Daniel threw me a crazy lopsided salute then

caught me in a wild hug. We were on our way. I whacked the floor with my slipper and watched history being made.

——— ⋆☆⋆☆⋆ ———

We broke ground two months later, after our proposal was accepted by Washington. They were on board a hundred percent, and their enthusiasm for our project showed. They saw the storm that was headed our way. Daniel and I threw ourselves into it, and with our focus on the project, we barely noticed the months slip by. I did notice the smile that sat on my son's face each morning when he joined us at the table. He still had his moments when that smile would slip, but we would take what we could.

"Daniel!" I called from the bottom of the stairs. "Come down for a moment, please."

"Yup."

Meg was nervous but equally as anxious to see his reaction. We needed to try something out of the ordinary. It was time to take the next step.

"We're heading into town to Patty's Restaurant for dinner."

"Okay." He turned to leave, but I raised a hand.

"Get ready. We leave in ten."

"Oh," his face dropped, "I, ah," he sputtered, but when he looked at his mom, he swallowed heavily and gave a tight nod. "Let me get my coat."

"Did he just agree?" Meg nearly tore my arm off when she grabbed it.

"I would think so."

We were both happy to get him past the property line for the first time in some eight months. Other than our trip to Washington to present our idea, and visits to the building site, he hadn't set foot off the place. Maybe we should have pushed him harder, but he needed time, and, in that time, he'd made progress. The scar was barely covered over, but I could see the healing had started.

Daniel had been silent on the drive. Meg chatted happily to fill the void when he leaned forward from the back seat of the pickup and looked at me.

"Dad."

"Yeah?"

"What will the name be for the safehouse?"

"Name?"

"Yeah, it should have a name. We can't call it safehouse."

"True." I nodded and looked at Meg, thinking how true that was. "What do you think we should call it?" He leaned back and crossed his arms.

"Shadows." He cleared his throat.

"That's a good one. Why that name?" What I would do for a little look inside his head.

"Because." I looked at him in the rearview mirror. I couldn't see his eyes as they were hidden by the brim of his ballcap. Then he turned and looked out the window. "Because we had to be shadows to survive over there." I felt Meg shift in her seat. We were happy to get some insight into what he'd been through, but it broke our hearts at the same time.

"Shadows it is." I nodded and pulled off the main road into the parking lot of the restaurant. Things were going to be okay.

We hopped out, and I noticed Daniel hesitated. I knew this was hard for him, being back in public, but he opened the door and got out when he spotted Zack.

"Nice to see you, brother." Zack walked across the parking lot. I noted his expression mirrored Daniel's, and I could see that damn demon still perched on their shoulders. "I'm glad you called to meet up." I was happy we'd suggested that Daniel ask Zack to join us for dinner and was even happier when he accepted.

"Yeah, it's great to see you." Daniel took his ball hat off and ran a hand through his hair as he looked around at his surroundings. "I figured the town needed some new gossip about me." He tried to make a joke, but his insecurities about being back in the public eye was obvious.

"Nothing like being whispered about while walkin' down the grocery aisle." Zack matched his dark sarcasm. "Everyone wants to hate the boys who fought the needless fight."

"Daniel?" a female voice called from behind us. "Daniel Logan, is that you?"

"Hi, Tracy." He suddenly looked unsure. "Nice to see you again."

"You too." She approached him carefully, as though he might bite her. "I heard you were back, but we haven't seen you."

"I've been busy." I watched for cues in case he needed me to step in with a story as to why he hadn't been anywhere.

"Sue's going to wig out when she sees you," she whispered more to herself.

Sue?

"Is she here?" Daniel asked as he looked at the ground.

Meg gave me a small smile, apparently seeing what I was.

"She was."

I threw a confused look to Zack, but he shook his head and watched with interest. He obviously didn't know what it was about either.

"When I see her, I'll say hi to her for you. It was really nice seeing you again, Logan."

"Thanks. Ahh, you too." Daniel looked up briefly, and I knew he saw my grin. He looked away, and I knew he wanted to avoid my big smile at all costs.

Did my son have a girl that I didn't know about?

CHAPTER SIX

Daniel

It was another three weeks before I was back in town again. Zack and I were starving after a crazy training day. Frank was on his way, but we had a few hours until we were to meet on the edge of town.

"After you." I held the door to the restaurant open for an elderly lady to pass through. As we entered, the smell of fresh bacon hit our noses in that way only bacon can. I breathed it in.

"Patty!" Zack called out to the owner as she rang in a customer. "Please tell me there's still some bacon left over."

"It's one in the afternoon, Zack. Does it figure we'd still have bacon on the grill?" She scowled.

"It's Montana. Don't pull lack of pig on me."

"Come on, Patty," I chimed in as I took a seat in the back. "You know how this'll end."

"It's true." Zack pointed at me then gave her the slip and disappeared into the kitchen.

I laughed as the waitress handed me a menu with a grin.

"Table for two, please," I heard a familiar voice ask at the front of the restaurant. That voice hit me like a sledgehammer, and my heart pounded in my chest.

"They do have bacon!" Zack dropped into the chair next to me and peeled off his coat. "We need a place that has breakfast any time of the day. Patty loves to pull that on us. I mean, it's break-fast, as in a break for me to eat, and she knows I need my bacon and I need it fast." He grinned, then studied my face and followed my line of sight. "Well, well, well, what do we have here? Is that your Sue?"

"Yeah." I sipped my coffee and watched out of the corner of my eye. They sat two tables away. Sue was in hotpants and a white top.

"I see this going two ways. You tell me how you met that little fox, or I call them over and hear it from her."

I closed my eyes and cursed. I knew he would be relentless if I didn't tell, and at the same time it was nice feeling a sense of normalcy again.

"All right, all right. We met two days before we left for Nam." I lowered my voice as he leaned in with a grin. "I'd fallen asleep under a tree on the side of the property when this sweet voice woke me. She was calling for someone. Turned out it was her dog, and when I saw her standing there in that tall grass—" I gave him a deep, girly sigh, and his hand went to his chest. "She was all sun-kissed skin, big bright eyes, and a gorgeous smile." I wanted to add some drama for him. "It was like I was stuck in a trance as I watched her throw a stick for her dog. She laughed, the most beautiful laugh, as her dog bounced around like a sheep." I stopped to clear my throat dramatically, and he waved for me to go on, but when I didn't answer, he prompted me.

"Did she freak out when she saw you creepin' from the under the tree?

"No." I rolled my eyes, and chuckled.

"So, what, you love this girl? I can hear it in your voice.

Oh, Jesus, Mary and Joseph, you have feelings for this girl, don't you?"

"I don't know," I answered honestly.

"From one look, you might love her?" His jaw dropped.

"I can't explain it." My voice went serious.

"Try."

"When she caught sight of me, her smile didn't fade. It grew. Like she knew there was something there. She felt it, too."

"What is it with you Logans and finding your soul mates?" He gave a chuckle, but I could see he was happy for me that I actually could still feel something other than pain and loss. "All right, so, you had your moment. Then what happened?"

"I introduced myself, and we spent the next two days together. We walked the fields, swam in the lake, just talked about nothing. You know, normal stuff. I'm not sure why I let my guard down with her, but we had this ease with each other. You know? And when I had to say goodbye, she kissed me. Not a passionate kiss, just a kiss. It was perfect." I shook my head as I remembered that kiss. "Let's just say I carried it with me, and it got me through some of the darkest days over there."

"And you haven't called her yet?" Zack shook his head. "Logan, come on. She's gorgeous, easy to talk to, and from what I can see from here, not married." He smirked when he caught my gaze move to her hands.

"I've changed. I'm not going to take her along on this trip." I pointed to my temple. "My head's still not on straight. She deserves better."

"Yeah, that's a load of crap." Zack laughed and waved me off as he leaned his head out of our booth. "Are you two meeting anyone?" he called, and I kicked his ankle and made him yelp in pain. He laughed at my murderous expression as Tracy, the girl who faced our direction, spoke up first.

"Funny, I was going to ask you the same thing."

"Well, this is how I see it." He used the same line he often used on me. "There's two of you and two open seats at our table."

Sue looked nervous, and I noticed she wiped her hands on her pants when they walked toward us. I didn't blame her. I had a feeling Tracy may have hoped we'd be here today and set up this little encounter.

"Nice to know you're okay." Sue eased onto the bench seat, looking unsure what to do. "When did you get back?"

"A few months ago." I kept it vague.

"Oh." She blinked a few times, unhappy with my answer.

"What's the deal with you two?" Zack wasted no time breaking into our private moment. "Were you dating before or something?" I glared at him and hated myself instantly for opening my mouth to him about us.

Tracy looked at both of us, waiting for either of us to speak. We didn't.

"They met for two days, and then the next he was gone," Tracy explained.

"In the field behind my house." I had to say it, but I kept my voice low. I didn't want Sue to think I'd ever forget our short time together. It had meant too much to me. I wasn't sure how she felt about it.

"Months we spent in the damn jungle." Zack shook his head like the shit he was. "And never once did you mention this. Why?"

"Yeah, why?" Tracy played into his shit-giving.

"I'm kind of curious, too," Sue whispered, and it made my chest hurt.

"Let it go," I grunted to Zack, who quickly saw I wasn't in the mood to play anymore. Guilt flooded me.

"Should we order?" He changed the topic, and I noticed Sue's face fell.

I hated to hurt her, but I was a different person now, and I still hadn't figured out who that was.

We made small talk, and all the while I studied the room. I tried to tune out the noises that suddenly made me uneasy. I needed to know everything. One lady at the counter, one at the door, two men in the corner, and a kid was at the gumball machine. Whenever someone would move, my eyes moved to them, and I reset my map of the room.

It was exhausting, and it was one of the reasons I didn't like to leave our property. It was the main reason I didn't feel ready for her. I felt angry with myself for letting my guard down enough to come here again.

"Hey." Sue leaned over, and I noticed we were alone at the table. How did I miss my buddy leaving the table? "Are you all right?"

"Yeah."

"You seem nervous."

"I don't like public places so much anymore."

"Okay." She threaded her purse through her arm and stood. "Then let's go."

I let out a relieved breath and walked her out. I called out a thanks to Patty on the way. Once out in the parking lot, I stopped her.

"Look," I closed my eyes and wished I was better at this, "I'm sorry I didn't call. A part of me assumed you'd moved on."

"We barely know each other, Daniel." I could tell she really didn't think that was true. We may not have shared a lot of deep personal things, but we shared the little things, and somehow those counted the most. "I'm not angry, but can I ask you something?"

"Sure."

"*Are* you okay?"

That was a hard question to answer.

"Most of the time, yes." I went with the truth. "And for the record, I may not have shared you with the guys, but I did think about you every day."

Her lips curved into a small smile.

"Why?"

"Because." I shrugged. "I knew."

"You knew you liked me?"

"Yes, that." I tucked my hands in my pockets, feeling lighter in the chest just being near her. "And you're more than just a beautiful woman. You're smart and caring, and even when we weren't talking, we were comfortable together. That really hit home for me."

"That's nice."

"Would you be up for a date sometime?" I suddenly felt a desperate need to reach out.

"Mm," she eyed me, "I'm not sure you're ready for that."

"We'll never know until we try." My mouth went dry, and I felt a small ball of panic in my gut.

"Look," she stepped closer, and I forced myself to breathe and could feel a flush of warmth with her so near, "the time we spent together, before you left, it was wonderful. Even though it was only a couple of days, it was some of the best times I've had. I heard you were back, and I waited for my phone to ring every night, but it never did. Then I see you here, and you act like you aren't sure you want to see me. Now you ask me out. That tells me that now is not the time. Perhaps in a while, but this shouldn't happen yet."

"I disagree." I swallowed hard.

"Answer me this." Her gorgeous eyes burned into mine. "If we hadn't come here today, would you have called me?"

I broke eye contact and saw her shoulders fall.

"I'm not going to pretend I understand anything of what

you've been through, Daniel, but if we were to start talking again, I just want to make sure it's something you're ready for." Her hand pressed against my chest just the way she had before she kissed me that day many months ago, and I felt her jolt me alive again. "I'm rooting for you, Daniel." She started to walk to the car where Tracy and Zack stood talking.

"I'm rooting for us, Sue," I called back loud enough for her to hear. She stopped but didn't turn around. Still, I caught her nod, and I knew she heard me. I knew I needed to get my head on right and fight for that woman.

"You're welcome." Zack jogged to catch up to me and hit my shoulder as he let out a laugh. I found myself feeling maybe I had something to start living for.

———— ★★★★★ ————

The next day, I pulled on my sneakers, loaded my rucksack, and headed out for a run.

"Where are you off to this morning?" Dad lowered his newspaper and eyed me over the rim of his reading glasses.

"I need to get things straight up here." I tapped my head, grabbed an apple, and headed out the back door. I took a deep breath of fresh air, filling my lungs and nose with the pungent scent of morning.

I needed to get back to some kind of normalcy, and because there wasn't any real structure in my life other than working on the safehouse, I needed to make it happen. One thing I was taught when I joined the army was soldiers needed a routine to keep their head on straight. No matter all the chaos that surrounded you, if could focus on what you needed to do next, you could channel your energy there.

And I needed all my energy to prove to Sue I wanted to be with her. It still baffled my mind that she wasn't dating anyone. She was beautiful and smart, and it made me want to work harder to get her to notice me. I knew I needed that girl in my life, and I was going to do whatever it took.

Over the next week, I found myself restless and often wondered what Sue was up to.

"What's going through your head?" Mom caught me mid-thought as the sheep ate out of the bucket I held. I felt one of them impatiently nibble at my fingers, so I quickly dumped the food into their bin. "Would it happen to be about that pretty young woman you were talking to in Patty's parking lot a few days ago?" I smiled, and she mirrored me.

"Ah, small towns." I shook my head and laughed as one of the sheep tugged at my pantleg. "Would you knock it off." I tried to shoo the little bugger away, but he was relentless. "She doesn't think I'm ready to date," I blurted. I didn't care anymore about not sharing my feelings. It felt good to talk about it. My mom had always been my sounding board, and I knew she missed our talks as well.

"Are you ready?" She hung her arms over the railing.

"I didn't think I was until I saw her." I nudged the damn sheep out of my way before he ripped my jeans and moved closer to mom. "It's just that I've been waiting for that horrible ache in my chest to ease a bit, and it has, thanks to you and Dad and the safehouse. But when I saw Sue, it was different. Like something let go, it let some kind of warmth fill the hole. You know?" I took off my ball hat to cool my head, then put it back on.

"I can't stop thinking about her, but what if I'm not ready? What if I mess it up? I still have some dark places that my head goes to, and I'm worried I'll pull her into them and scare her off." We both moved outside and closed the gate. One of the baby goats demanded my attention. "Ugh, what do you think I should do?"

"Honestly?"

"Yeah, Mom, just give it to me. Don't tiptoe around me."

"I think you need to turn off your head and ask yourself what you really want."

"I want her." I didn't miss a beat.

"Then you know what you need to do."

"Any suggestions?"

She used her finger to trace the splits in the wood on the fence for a bit, then she smiled. I could tell she was thinking of Dad and knew that was the kind of relationship I'd want with Sue.

"When we were first dating, your dad would often leave me a flower on the front step in the morning on his way to work just so I'd know he was thinking of me. After that, he started showing up at random times where I was to make sure I saw him. He was persistent in all the right ways. There's a balance in picking up social cues. Sometimes you might ignore them, but sometimes you need to act on them." She looked over at me.

"From what I know about Sue," she raised an eyebrow, and I chuckled and knew she'd done a little digging, "she's smart, Dan. She's lovely and apparently refused to date over the past year." She eyed me. "That tells me she's been waiting for you. I may be wrong. Perhaps it's wishful thinking on my part, but when a girl takes herself off the market, there's a reason." She cocked her head to make her point.

"Maybe." I smiled and hoped she was right.

"Now get that darn bucket moving. There's more animals to feed." She gave me a push.

"I love you, Mom."

"Love you, too, sweetheart."

Once I finished up my chores, I jumped the fence and knew what I needed to do.

I flipped through the pages in my notebook and ran my

finger down over my messy handwriting until I found her number. I dialed and waited for her to pick up.

"Hello?"

"Hey, Tracy, it's Daniel Logan."

"Um, hi, Daniel." She had a right to sound confused. "Not to sound rude, but where did you get my number?"

"Zack." I kept it short as I wanted to get this conversation moving in the right direction fast. "Look, Tracy, I need a favor."

"Well, that depends."

"It's to do with Sue."

"Oh, yeah." She chuckled. "I'm totally in on that. What do you need?" I kicked my feet up and explained my plan, happy to have her on my side.

Taking a page out of my father's playbook, I spent the next week working to get Sue to notice me. I slipped the odd flower into the side of her mailbox where she'd see it as she left for work. Thanks to Tracy, I got the inside knowledge on as many things as I could.

"What are you doing?" Mom peered over my shoulder as she saw I was all thumbs with the ribbon, glue, and paper bag.

"Trying to be romantic," I huffed. "I'm fantastically failing at it."

"No, you're not." She set the fresh lavender she had picked on the counter and moved to stand next to me. "You're doing just fine, but sometimes a simple gesture is much more romantic than an over the top one. Here, let me show you want I mean." She separated half of her flowers and brought them to the table. "Placing her favorite candy, with a small sprig or two of lavender, will mean so much more than a bag full of lollies." She used a piece of twine, gathered some sprigs of lavender and the lollies together, and made a sweet little bouquet. "Women read into things, so let her mind soar with this." She held it up, and I looked at her, confused.

"It's much prettier than what I did but what am I supposed to read into it?"

"Well, they say to plant lavender for luck, and it's well known the scent is supposed to relax your body, and the candy means you think she's sweet."

"Ahh, I see what you did there." I admired her handiwork. "And it's her favorite candy, too, so she'll know I did my research."

"Well done, Daniel. Don't forget you're a Logan. You men know how to sweep a woman off her feet."

"That's the plan." I kissed her cheek and hurried outside. I wanted to drop it off before she got off work.

If it could be said that a guy skipped, that was what I did on the way there. I was so proud of my gift to her. As I reached for the office door, it swung open, and I just managed to catch it with my hand and step aside in time to avoid a collision with a delivery man's dolly.

"Oops, sorry." He tipped his hat to me, and I threw him a smile as I rushed inside to the receptionist.

"Let me guess, you're Daniel Logan?" The receptionist beamed up at me as she placed the phone in its cradle and eyed the candy bouquet I held with a grin.

"I hope it's a good sign that you know who I am." I flashed her back with one of my killer smiles.

"So happens you've been the major topic of conversation around here lately."

"Details would be much appreciated." I winked and leaned my head down toward her in hopes she'd spill.

"She said you were charming." She blushed, and I knew I had my in. "Let's just say I haven't seen Sue's face light up like it has lately in quite some time. "Now, before I get into trouble, shall I call her up?"

"I'd appreciate that…" I waited for her name.

"Jenny." She shook her head and fussed with the phone cord as she made a quick call. "A tall, very handsome man is standing in front of me asking for you." She giggled. "Get up here before Victoria spots him."

I played along with a laugh, but truth be told, I only had eyes for one woman, and she was now walking my way.

"First flowers on my mailbox and now an in-person delivery?" Sue looked gorgeous in her knee-length skirt and light blue blouse. I shamelessly gawked at the beauty in front of me. Jenny let out a dreamy sigh at the two of us.

"I just figured it was such a gorgeous day outside I should head into town, and would you look at that, I ended up here." I grinned as she rolled her eyes, but I could tell she was pleased to see me. "Seems about right. It's a pretty kind of day, you're a pretty woman, so it only makes sense that you should have a pretty bouquet." I held up the lavender and twisted the bouquet to show her the lollies. "I even included something sweet."

"I think I just got pregnant." Jenny dramatically flopped on her desk, and Sue broke into a smirk.

"Okay, Mr. Logan," Sue's eyes sparkled, "I will say this is a pretty nice gesture."

"I'm glad you like them." I leaned forward in a little bow as I mentally checked off another day. I was wearing her down one day at a time. I reached for her hand and kissed the back of it. I wanted to press for a date, but I knew Sue needed me to show her I was ready for it first.

"Thank you. I adore lavender." She took the flowers and inhaled the scent. "You just made my day."

"That was the hope." I tucked my hands in my pockets because the urge to pull her to me and inhale her as deeply as she did the flowers was painful.

"I should get back." She stepped back.

"Of course." I gave her a nod and watched her smack Jenny on the shoulder as she walked by her desk on her way down the hall.

"Daniel?" Jenny broke me from my spell as I watched Sue's adorable butt as she disappeared down the hall.

"Yeah?"

"She goes to lunch every day at eleven."

"Thanks, Jenny." I whisked out the door and got to planning.

At dinner that night, I nearly bounced around the kitchen as I filled Mom in on all that had happened. Dad gave me a thumbs up from the table and shared a few stories about some dates he'd taken Mom on. If I could get even a quarter of my parents' happiness, I'd be set for life.

"I'm proud of you, son." Mom squeezed my arm. "You keep that up, and she'll soon see you're ready."

That following Monday at eleven, I stood outside the stairs of her work with a cloth bag in my hand. Sue laughed when she spotted me and slowly came down the stairs and folded her arms. She wore a white open-neck blouse tied in a bow at the waist with a pretty pair of yellow plaid seersucker skirt. Her tanned arms and legs looked great with her outfit, and her hair made me want to reach out and touch it. I was glad she didn't dress in those crazy hippie clothes girls were into these days.

"Mr. Logan, surely you have something better to do with your time than stand here outside my work at lunchtime."

"The only thing I want to do with my free time, Sue, is spend it with you."

She bit her lip to try to stop her smile, but it broke free, and she shook her head. "What's in the bag?"

"Spend your lunch break with me."

"Is it food? I'm a girl who needs to eat."

"Good. I'm a man who likes to provide. I also like to eat." I grinned, and she playfully huffed and tried to stall.

"Fine." She reached to try to snatch the bag, but I held it close to my chest, and she gave a big belly laugh as she swung her hips to check mine. "It better be yummy."

I chuckled and took her by the arm and led her over to a bench that was shaded by a huge pine tree. We sat beside each other, and she watched with interest as I draped a big napkin over her skirt, then pulled out a couple of plastic containers and two forks and handed her one of each.

"That smells positively amazing." She took the fork and speared one of the cheesy penne noodles and popped it in her mouth. She moaned as she closed her eyes, and I stilled with fascination. "Where on Earth did you get this, or did you make it?"

"No, I didn't make it," I lifted my fork, "but it's one of the perks of having a friend who can cook."

"Zack made this?"

"Yes." I swallowed and wiped my mouth on a napkin.

"He should be a chef."

"That's his dream. He and his brother, Alex, both cook, so they are looking to open a restaurant someday." She nodded, and we chatted comfortably as we ate our tasty lunch.

After a while, she got quiet, and I could tell she was thinking about something. "What is it, Sue?" I asked.

"What about you, Daniel? What do you want? What are your dreams?" She took another mouthful then dragged the fork slowly out of her mouth as she looked at me. It took great effort to force my gaze from her mouth up to her eyes. I swallowed hard and took a second to answer.

"Dreams and wants are two vastly different things." She waited for me to go on. "My dream would be not to have ever left for Nam. My want is to make a difference. To change things for the better somehow." I skirted around my secret about the safehouse. "To have both, a career and a family." I added.

She nodded and took a few more bites, and I could see the wheels turning in her head. I knew that look. It seemed everyone had the same look on their face when they thought about the war in Vietnam, and I was starting to despise it.

"You can ask," I whispered.

"What was it like over there? I don't mean the worst of times, just the day in and day out."

I wanted to choose my words carefully because my gut reaction was to shock and give the gory details. It often worked to make people stop asking. But I didn't want that for Sue. I wanted her to see I could handle the ugly that plagued my life even if it was a challenge to do so.

"Have you ever been to the lake at night?" She nodded. "Ever swam down deep and then look around, and for a hair of a second you get confused as to which way is up and which way is down? Your lungs burn, and panic begins to idle, then it suddenly gets a green light and bursts through your core and takes over your head." I took a breath to slow myself down.

"I do, actually."

"So, imagine that feeling on my best day." She stopped chewing and placed her fork down on her napkin. "We had to be monsters there, and now we're monsters here. Go figure." I shrugged.

She leaned back and tucked a piece of hair behind her ear then covered her mouth. It was subtle movement, but it told me she'd heard what I said. I hated people when they overreacted and overplayed the sympathy card. I wanted nothing to do with that.

"That must have been incredibly hard. What kept you going?"

I held her gaze and watched as her eyes softened then

fluttered down, and a smile turned up the corners of her lips. Then she took the bag and tucked her dish and napkin in it. I added mine and rolled the top down. Neither of us spoke, and as if on cue, we both stood.

"I should get back inside." She brushed off her skirt. "Thank you for that delicious lunch, and be sure to tell Zack how much I loved it." She smiled then placed a soft hand on my arm. "And Daniel, thank you for sharing that with me." I nodded and walked with her the short distance to the steps. "I…" She stumbled for something else to say.

"I'll see you tomorrow," I said a bit firmer than I intended.

"Tomorrow?" She looked like she was missing something.

"Yes, for lunch."

"Oh," she chuckled, "is that so?"

"Yes, have a great rest of your day, Sue." I kissed the back of her hand like the gentleman I was and left with the biggest grin I'd ever had on my face. She hadn't said no.

I wanted to run like I used to as a kid, arms beating at my sides, legs burning with heat, mouth gaping open catching flies as I ran to tell my best friend I had a date with a girl. I wanted to tell him it was a girl I was totally smitten over, but not today. Instead I relished my high and just enjoyed the sun as it shone brighter than ever. I steered toward Zack with a happy grin.

"Oh, that face tells me my meal sealed the deal?" Zack tossed a tea towel over his shoulder as he leaned his hip against the doorframe while I hopped up the steps.

"It helped." I hit his arm as I whisked past him. I held up the container from today's lunch and wiggled my brows at him. "My charm did the rest. So, what's on the menu for tomorrow?" I lifted the pot that was simmering on the stove. "Now, that smells good."

"Of course, it does. I made it." He came up behind me and pushed a spoon into my hand. I dove in and took a mouthful of the pineapple sauce. "You should learn how to cook, Daniel. The ladies love it."

"Why would I want to cook when I have you?" I took another spoonful, and he glared at my double dip. "Besides, imagine if I cooked. Would you really want the ladies looking at me more than they already do? Don't do this for me, Zack, do this for you."

"Done?" His mouth drew up on one side.

"I am now, yes." I smirked. "Sue loved the dish. Thanks for that. We have another date tomorrow." I began to clean the container I had returned.

"Well, in that case, since you obviously like it..." He opened the fridge and pulled out a container. "Take some of the pineapple rice and pulled pork. All I ask is honest feedback."

"Always."

That's how it went, off and on, whenever I could, for the next couple weeks. She'd find me at the bottom of the stairs with something yummy made by Zack, and we ate and talked about anything. Between seeing her, and our work on the construction of Shadows, I was kept busy and was happier than I'd been in a very long time.

Things were moving along well at home, and it was time to let the other guys in on the plan. I found myself waking up excited to get my day going. I couldn't wait for the others to experience this feeling. I knew they needed it as much as I did, perhaps even more.

Then one Friday I decided it was time to make my first real move with Sue. I figured with the high I was on that day, it was a now or never moment.

"You put up quite the fight, Mr. Logan." Sue took two steps away from me then turned around.

"So do you." I played back. "Sue," I took her hand and

hoped to God she wouldn't reject me, "I'd like to take you out on a real date."

"Daniel." She looked unsure, but I saw her lips twitch.

"Look, I'm all for a picnic lunch and being the object of your co-workers' entertainment," I smirked and pointed my chin at the window where I knew eyes were watching us, "but you deserve a real date."

"I don't know." I could see I was wearing her down. When she didn't bite, I tried a different tact. "A friend of mine is flying in today, and tomorrow we're having a barbecue at Barry Lake. Why don't you and Tracy come? Keep it strictly friends getting to know one another some more."

She held a hand over her eyes to shield them from the sun and looked up at me. Her pretty pink lips twitched as she thought.

"Bring Jenny and Tracy if that makes you more comfortable."

"What time?"

I laughed as unexpected jitters raced through me.

"Five thirty." Zack popped out of nowhere to answer for me. "Did you know this guy comes across town every day with a huge-ass smile on his face when he meets you for lunch?"

"Oh, really?" She beamed at me.

"Don't you have somewhere to be Zack?" I glared, but he knew I wasn't mad. He always had my back. Even now.

"I'll be right over there when you're finished." He slapped my shoulder and waved goodbye to Sue.

"Big smile, huh?" she teased, and I gave an unapologetic shrug. "Okay, I'd like that. I'd like to bring something tomorrow, though. Do you have anything to suggest?"

"Daisies from the Miller farm." I figured I wouldn't protest, as I was gaining ground with her. "Pick a lot. They're Mom's favorite."

"Oh, so, I'm going to meet your parents?"

"Yes, as my flirty friend." She laughed, and I knew I'd hooked her.

"I appreciate the inside information." Her smile grew as she headed up the stairs. "I'll bring Tracy, but I'll leave Jenny here. I'll need a good story for Monday."

"I'll be sure to make it a good one, then."

"I don't doubt it." I almost ran up to open the door for her as she juggled her water, purse, and sweater, but even as I thought it, something told me Sue appreciated how I didn't ignore her independence.

That was a major turn-on.

"I'll be your wingman anytime." Zack lifted his hat off as if to take a bow, then placed it back on with a chuckle. "That was fun."

"I invited her and Tracy to the barbecue." We both walked toward the truck.

"You're my favorite, you know that?" Zack grinned and slapped my shoulder.

"See, when you cook for me, good things happen. With your food and my charm, it's a win-win."

We raced toward his truck and headed for the highway. The trip to the airport was long, with my best friend running over any possible details from my first date with Sue.

"I still can't believe you didn't call that girl when you got back. She's gorgeous."

I slammed the truck door closed and held up a hand to stop traffic as we hurried across the road.

"My head space was compromised when I got home, but thanks to the safe house, I feel like I have a reason to be living again."

"Well," he turned after we spotted Frank, "it's a good thing this is all working out, and look, our buddy is here."

"Not a word." I shoved a finger in his face.

"Hey, boys." Frank shook our hands with his duffle bag over his shoulder. "Any word from Ray?"

"Not yet." I knew Ray took Jimmy's death the hardest. They had grown up together, but his sister assured me he just needed space. I disagreed but respected their wishes. "I'll go over and check on him soon."

"Good." His smile changed to a happier one. There was a sense of peace having us all together. Almost like we could breathe again. "What's new?"

"Well," Zack gave me a smirk, "Daniel has a new girl."

I turned around and punched him in the shoulder as Frank's face lit up.

"Looks like we have a story for the road, boys."

We took the winding back roads of Redstone almost to the top of the mountain before we veered off, taking a hidden road through the thick trees.

"Has anyone questioned the construction up here?" Frank was a numbers man. We'd been damn lucky to have him with us in Nam, as he could calculate impossible distances over sprawling terrain within a few yards. We would have blindly followed him anywhere.

"No." I rolled down my window to get ready to demonstrate something. "We spread the word we're doing construction for the Cuttingham family. They just made their first million in the green air industry. I know their son, Ken, well, and he even got their family to donate toward what we were doing."

"Smart." Frank seemed impressed as I slowed down.

"There will be three checkpoints, with armed soldiers, one starting here. You'll have to show your ID to move on, and so on and so on. This will be the safest place to be."

"Holy…" Frank moved to lean out his window as we approached the house. "That's massive."

"You have no idea." Zack hit my shoulder with excitement.

After the tour of Shadows, which was almost finished, we took some beers out to the patio and looked over the lake, dreaming of what was to come with our newfound freedom.

We were going to pave a new path with the Army and change lives for the better.

CHAPTER SEVEN

Daniel

Barry Lake was cool, and the sun was hot, so it was the perfect place to gather to enjoy our day off. The construction of Shadows was hard work, and, despite the hired help provided by the Army, who used a heavy NDA clause, we all pitched in wherever we could.

I flipped the burgers and listened to Zack fill Frank in about how we are going to use the elements around us to train. Since the lake wasn't overly busy, we were free to talk about the safehouse without a worry.

"We'll use the mountains, the water, the helicopter, the woods, everything that each of us has a background in," Zack went on. "We'll all train as a team, one solid unit."

"This is ridiculously perfect." Frank laughed, feeling the same excitement I felt. "I can't believe I was shoveling shit at some local farm waiting to hear back from my uncle on a possible job at Army headquarters, and you two were here figuring out a new way of fighting a war. And I'm only hearing about this now?"

"Daniel didn't want to say anything until he knew it

would happen." Zack shrugged. "We all know how disappointment can trigger shit for us if we're not careful."

"No hurt feelings on my end," Frank smiled into his beer, "just pleased to be a part of it."

"Me too."

"So," Frank looked around, "when do we start?"

"Not sure yet. Edison says maybe a week or two more. I know he's looking for a psychologist who will not only work with the people we've retrieved but also us."

"Smart. I think we can all agree that to keep our shit together is…"

"She's for sure coming?" I faintly heard my mother say as I tuned out my buddies.

"Yes," Dad assured her.

"I'm so excited to officially meet her. I know she's very pretty and very well-spoken." Mom nearly squealed. "You're sure she's coming?"

I held up the flipper. "I can hear you."

"If he said she's coming, she's coming." Dad ignored me.

"Of course, she's coming. Look at him. So handsome and strong."

"Thanks, Mom," I huffed through a laugh.

I handed a plate of burgers to my cousin, who fed the kids first.

"He's got the Logan charm. She'll come." Dad kissed Mom on the cheek when she rolled her eyes. "Come on, you know you can't resist me."

"I certainly can." She pointed the baby oil bottle at him. "I just choose not to."

"Right, because of my charm."

"Your three," Zack whispered as he walked by.

I looked at my three o'clock, and there she was. My stomach twisted into a happy knot of excitement. She wore short shorts over her one-piece bathing suit. She had a beach blanket tucked under one arm and held a huge bouquet of daisies in her other hand.

"Oh, I see my boy has the same swagger as I do," I heard Dad say behind me.

"Would you look at our son's face?" Mom cooed, and I ignored them with a chuckle.

Sue waved and pointed to an open spot on the sand, asking if it was okay to take it. I gave her a nod and made a beeline for her.

"I'm glad you came." I picked up one side of the blanket and helped her smooth it out. "Are you hungry?"

"Starved," Tracy piped in. I hadn't even greeted her, as I'd only had eyes for Sue. I quickly made up for it.

"Hi, Tracy. I'm glad you could come. There are tons of burgers on the table. Please help yourself."

"Thanks!" She raced off, leaving me alone with Sue. She gathered up her long brown hair in her hands and twisted it into a ponytail.

"Where's your friend you said was coming?"

"Oh, that's Frank." I pointed to him. Frank stood and seemed to be having a serious chat with my father, but I knew they were both watching us.

"Army guy, too?"

"Yeah." I moved my gaze over to the water. "He was in Nam, too."

"So, what you're telling me is he has some good stories on you to tell?" She giggled, and it lightened the mood and stopped the dangerous slope I was heading toward. I still found it hard to control, and I knew I had a lot of work to do there, but Sue made everything easier. Even something as simple as breathing.

"Oh, yeah." I laughed, thinking about just how much shit we actually did have on one another.

I hopped to my feet and offered her my hand. She took it

with a confused look.

"I want you to meet my parents."

"Oh, yes. All right." She leaned back and scooped the flowers she had brought. "Lead the way."

"Mom? Dad?" They both stood grinning. "This is Sue, the girl I was telling you about."

"Lovely to meet you, Sue." Dad offered a hand, and Mom nearly fell over her feet trying to get closer then enveloped her in a big hug.

"We're so glad to meet you, Sue. Please call us Edison and Meg. Our son has told us a little about you, but I'm curious to know more." Sue smiled at her, and I was grateful to know they were so interested in getting to know her. As I expected, Sue didn't put on at all. She was just as she was with me. She never tried to impress. She didn't need to because she was who she was, warm and friendly.

"Well, that works out great for me," Sue looked up at me, "because I have a ton of questions about this guy, like was he always such a romantic?"

"Oh, Sue, I'm not sure how to tell you this, but that kind of charm only comes out when a Logan has fallen."

"Mom!" My mouth dropped open. "Dad, can you help here, please?"

"I would, but it's true."

"Oh, I wonder what else I can get out of them." Sue, to my surprise, rubbed her hands together and made my dad laugh.

"The three of you are just dangerous." I held up my hands and stepped back.

"Oh, Meg, I picked these for you."

After my mother thanked her for her thoughtful gift of the flowers, my father gave me a knowing grin. I had to grin back, and he slapped me on the back.

We ate, swam, and built a bonfire for later that evening. We did all the things I'd forgotten I'd even missed until now.

"Where are you living?" Sue asked Frank, who had joined us. He and Zack had been tossing the football around near the water's edge.

"I'm in Washington at the moment, but I think I might just spend some time here in the Montana mountains." Frank leaned back on his arms and watched us.

"I bet that'll make some people happy." She smiled at me.

"It's strange not seeing the guys every day," he admitted, and Zack gave me a look. We might not talk about it, but we all felt the same way.

"Interesting how war can still divide people even after you've left it." Sue brushed some sand off her arm, and us three all looked at one another. It was amazing how Sue just understood things without even trying.

"Well, I won't speak for the rest of you," Zack leaned back and propped a leg up, "but I haven't felt this put back together since we left that shit storm."

"Did any of you go to Jimmy's funeral?" Frank asked the one question that still stung like crazy. Zack looked at me, and we both hung our heads. "Yeah," Frank tossed a stick in the water, "it was just too soon."

"We had a drink for him," I whispered. "It was about all I could handle at the time."

Sue remained quiet, but she did reach over and cover my hand with hers. Just that simple action provided more comfort than she'd ever know.

That evening, while the others played a game of water football, Sue and I settled ourselves next to the sand pit near the fire. I was impressed she had made the effort to get to know my family and friends. It told me she was interested in who I was and where I came from. I hoped I could do the same with her family at some point.

"Thanks for coming," I smiled down at her, and she gave me a warm smile back, "and for giving me another chance."

"You always had a chance, Daniel. I just needed to make sure you were ready."

"I am."

"I see that now."

"I kind of admire the fact that you made me work for it," I confessed. "Can I ask you something?"

"Yes."

"Why didn't you date during the time I was away?"

"How did you know that?"

"Mom did a little digging." I smirked. "She wanted to know if I had any competition."

"That's kind of sweet." She chuckled. "I wish I had thought to do that."

"You'd have gotten the same answer."

"Really?" She seemed relieved.

"Yes, well, as much as I love my war brothers, I don't date family," I teased.

"Okay, so they're not my competition." She played along.

"Nope, totally safe there." I chuckled then watched as her smile fluttered away as she lost herself in a thought.

"Call it silly," she rubbed a stone between her fingers, "but when I met you that day in the field, it was as if everything just made sense. I spent a lot of time sitting under that tree wondering what you were doing in that exact moment. If you were alive or not. If I ever made it into your mind." Her hair fell and blocked her from my view, so I reached over and tucked it behind her ear, and she looked up at me. "Then when you didn't come see me after I heard you were back, I wondered if I was right about what I'd felt."

"What did you feel?" I leaned in, and her gaze dropped down to my lips.

"I was afraid I'd maybe built up what we had together in my head, and it was really nothing at all."

"I'm so sorry."

"Don't be. Within moments, I saw the truth."

"You're an incredible woman, Sue." I pressed my lips to hers and savored our connection. I wanted to prove to her that she was all I wanted. She was warm in my arms, and I could feel her heart pound through her chest against mine. I pulled away then. I didn't want to push myself on her. I wasn't going to risk what we had gained by moving too fast. This wasn't the time or the place for that. I knew we had plenty of time to get to know one another in private. It was something I instinctively knew, that one day I would want to look back at this time and savor every moment of getting to know her.

We sat there together, stuck in time, eyes on the fire, fingers laced as we both relaxed and enjoyed the night. I kissed her fingers, and she put them to her lips as if to seal the feeling inside.

"I would sit in our spot and wonder what you kissed like," she confessed, and her lashes fluttered over her big brown eyes as she looked at me. They were half closed as she blinked in sleepy contentment. She smiled then and shook her head to bring herself out of her lazy spell.

"And?"

"And I wish we were alone."

I chuckled deep to show her I felt the same way then watched as one of the kids got flipped out of their innertube by Frank. He laughed and picked the kid up and tossed him out into the water. I was nice to see him having a great time.

"Frank seems really nice." She wrapped her arms around her legs and rested her chin on her knees.

"He's a great guy." I nodded, thankful that Frank hadn't gone down a dark path when he got home like some guys did. Thankfully, like Zack and me, he had a supportive family to help him through it.

Shadows

She made a noise, and I looked over as she pressed her lips to her knees and closed her eyes.

"What?"

"Nothing." She made a funny noise and a laugh slipped out. I laughed, too, but was curious what was so comical. "I promised I wouldn't say."

"Say what?" I glared at my buddies, wondering what story they'd told her.

"I just think it's cute that you loved your goat that much to take its photo all the way over there."

Son of a bitch, Frank was going to die.

I hopped to my feet, but she blocked me so I couldn't get by.

"No, you can't. I promised!" She could barely talk through her laughter as her warm hands pressed against my arms. I felt a rush of love and the will to deliver some payback. So, I played dirty. I hooked her hands, pulled her in like I was going to hug her then snagged a huge towel from the sand and tied her arms around her body. All the while, she laughed, unable to save herself.

"No, Daniel," her words were slurred from laughter, "they're my only source of good stories besides your parents!"

"It's true!" Dad called from somewhere, sending Sue into an even harder fit of tears.

"You're next," I winked and tore off toward the water.

"Frank! I'm sorry!" she called, trying to warn him. Frank suddenly tuned in to us, tossed the kid, and ducked under the water. I dove in after him.

We wrestled and shoved each other under. It was great fun, and then Zack got the kids involved, and suddenly we were being attacked by little humans who used us as mountains to climb. It felt amazing to just let loose again.

"You think you can stop us?" I roared, making the kids

scream with excitement. "Just try to stop us!" Frank, Zack, and I started grabbing a kid at a time, tossing them over our heads, only to have them come back for more.

Finally, when we were exhausted, and the kids had no doubt swallowed half the lake, we came in to fuel up again.

"Who knew kids like to be knocked around so much?" Frank grabbed a leftover burger and downed it in two bites.

"I think one of them bit my neck." Zack felt around his skin, and Frank and I smirked. "Savages."

I glanced at Sue talking to Mom and Dad at the other picnic table.

"She seems to fit right in." Zack wiggled his eyebrows. "She really is something special."

"Yeah, she is, isn't she?" I hoovered some fries, washed them down with water, and headed in their direction, but not before hearing…

"I'm really happy for you, Logan." I smiled at Frank's warmth before starting to gather my things.

A while later, our stuff was packed up and the lake looked as if no one had a party.

"Sue seems really nice." My father found me later as I returned with some dry towels from my truck. I dropped them on a rock, and we enjoyed our first moment alone since he'd met Sue. "I haven't seen you laugh like that in a long time. She must be special."

"Dad," I turned to face him head on, "I know I barely know that girl, but I'm gonna marry her. You watch."

"Like father, like son. When we know, we know." He grinned around his cigar. "I can't tell you how good it is to see you like this."

"I can't tell you how much I missed being normal."

Famous last words…

CHAPTER EIGHT

Daniel

"I've got steaks, I've got bacon, I've got sides, I've got it all." Zack burst through my front door with a massive cooler.

"You got beer?" I looked up from my pathetic attempt of trying to fit my sleeping bag back into its ridiculously tiny pouch. Whoever thought up the idea to make a nearly impossible pouch to carry a sleeping bag in should be taken out back and taught a lesson. I never could understand why things that came out of a package so easily could never be put back in the same way.

"Hello, boys. Your hero has arrived." Frank came in behind Zack with two cases of beer held high in the air.

"Nice." I let go of the pouch to slap his hand, and the bag sprang back out. "Screw this." I tossed it on the chair and grabbed my army one. "I should know better than to stray."

"What is that?" Frank looked at the bag in disgust. "Did you get it from the local hardware store?"

"Yeah, and the only thing it has in its favor is it has a hole so you can get into it." I kicked the nylon heap.

"First, you should be ashamed, and second, I have a friend who'll get you a decent one. Just toss that abomination to the curb before someone sees it. In the meantime, I've got a spare one with me you can use."

I rolled my eyes but knew Frank had a valid point. Most of the average sleeping bags barely breathed at all and were either too hot or too cold.

"Are we doing this or not?" Zack tossed me the keys, and we headed outside where I zipped up my jacket against the crisp mountain air. I reached out my arms and gave a good stretch. When I exhaled, I could see my breath.

It was perfect camping weather.

We tossed our stuff in the back of my truck and secured everything.

Zack whistled for Watcher, his German shepherd. He hopped happily in the back seat with a whine of excitement, and his tongue hung over his lower jaw. I could totally relate. This was just what I needed. I looked around the property out of habit. I wondered if and when the need to watch my back would ever leave my subconscious.

"Go ahead." Frank waved me off. "You have my word I won't tell your little secret."

"Huh?"

"They're waiting for you, you know."

"Who is?"

"The goats. You know you want to." He pointed, and sure as anything the little buggers were waiting for their head pat. Frank knew they were my weakness.

"You think you're funny?" I raced after Frank as he took off at a run then circled back to the truck. Zack beeped the horn a few times to add to the fun. "I dare you to close your eyes at night." I laughed as I jumped behind the wheel, and Frank ducked to avoid my swat as he hopped in the other door.

"The only one you're hurting here is them, Daniel."

"Remember, Frank," I shifted the truck into first gear, "I know all about Woobie."

His face flinched, and he shut up real quick while Zack and I laughed all the way down the driveway.

Our destination was on the other side of the lake from Shadows. The terrain was rough, and when we turned off the main road, it got positively ruthless. Like Shadows, you had to knew the area and what route you had to be on, and even then, it was easy to get completely turned around. There were holes that could take your tires off and rocks big enough to break an axle. You could never get through with a regular vehicle. Our trucks were set up high and designed for this kind of terrain. Grandpa and his buddy had done an amazing job of breaking a track through the mountainside. It was a huge job, and it constantly awed me that we could drive through here at all. You just had to hope you wouldn't meet anyone else because there was only room for one vehicle on this trail. Thank God, this was private property.

Finally, after a backbreaking drive up then down around the mountain, we came to the clearing. It was just big enough and flat enough for a tent, a fire pit, and three long logs to sit on. The lake was a stone's throw away and gently lapped at the shoreline.

"Listen." I closed my eyes and listened to the crickets and frogs that chatted with each other.

"If this is what nights at Shadows are going to be like," Frank stood shoulder to shoulder with me and took it all in, "you wouldn't have had to say much more."

"Looks like a full moon." Zack stepped into view, and we all admired the moon's glow over the ripples of the water. "I think this is the sound of our new freedom."

"Just took us a war to get us here," I muttered.

We stood there for a few more minutes in silence.

Watcher came to sit next to Zack. His intelligent face scanned the lake, and I was happy Zack had brought him along. A good dog was invaluable in so many ways. Their sixth sense had saved more than one of our buddies over the years. Their companionship and loyalty could never be questioned either. Once Shadows was up and running, I planned to make sure we had a K9 unit. The guys who guarded the house would appreciate their help. Shadows was deep in the woods, after all, and there were a lot of different animals around. A dog would alert us to anything nearby.

"Well, we should get our stuff out." Frank headed back to the truck, and he and I set up the tent and prepared a fire, while Zack unpacked the food and got things squared away.

Once the fire was hot, Zack put the meat on the grate, and lay the foil-wrapped potatoes on top of the coals. We popped a beer and settled back to enjoy the night.

"Feels kind of strange," I whispered as we all stared into the fire, "being here."

"Yeah." Zack poked the fire with a stick, careful not to jostle the potatoes.

"I still can't believe all three of us made it back alive, let alone got a chance to sit here like this." I shifted on the log as the guys murmured their agreement.

"Endless nights of sitting in that hell. And that damn rain that never seemed to stop," Zack added.

"I thought I'd never get home again, sure not in one piece, anyway. Figured a part of me would be left over there to rot." I shivered as I spoke and felt like I should knock wood and reached for a stick.

"That blast," Frank spoke up, "the one when we were in the gully, I still can't get that memory out of my head. I thought that was it for me. My body was going to be blown to bits, and every inch of me would rot there forever."

"For me," Zack's throat contracted, "it was when we ran

out of our rations." He gave us a look in case we laughed over his love of food. We knew running out of food would be his worst nightmare. We didn't laugh; nothing about our time over there was funny. "Trying to live off a land that no one prepared us for terrified me. I was so thirsty that I drank the rainwater from those leaves we used for bedding."

"Jesus," Frank cut in.

"It frigged with me in more ways than one. It messed me up. Here." He pointed to his head. "Ya know?" We all nodded. "And I was so damn sick after that I actually wanted to die. It let you know that it wasn't only who we were fighting that could kill us, but everything else too." He rubbed his head. "I know I've said it before, but thanks, Daniel, for looking out for me while I battled that. It sure as hell wasn't pretty."

"I think it's why we're here," I nodded, "because when one was down, the other was up."

"Yeah, maybe." Zack looked uneasy as he added another log to the fire. I felt like it was my turn to share my weakest moment. I figured I'd go for it and get it off my chest, too. Maybe it would help release some of the pain I carried.

"I'll be honest, I gave up hope once when we were there." I felt Frank turn and look at me, and I kept my own eyes on the fire. I needed there to be no secrets between us so we could be free to lean when we needed to. "It was a day I felt so damn miserable. I was wet and tired and hungry, and I could hear the screams of someone being tortured. I guess I just figured it was going to end like that for me. I couldn't face the idea of it. I remember I just wanted to do it clean and have it be over."

"I think we've all had those moments, Daniel," Frank said, and I looked at him. Zack nodded as well. "But we didn't give in to it." We all agreed and sat in silence as the fire snapped. Zack flipped the steaks, rolled the spuds over, and placed another tin-foil pack beside the steaks then sat back down on his log.

"I still see that kid." I began to talk again. They all knew who I meant. "His hands were too small to carry much of a weapon. His feet were all torn up from walking without shoes. I mean, he must have had to go night after night with no choice but to do what he was told. That kid was only trying to survive. I know the others looked at me as weak because I didn't shoot him, but he was just a boy, someone's kid. I still to this day don't believe he told anyone where we were."

"I don't think so either," Zack agreed.

"We survived that place for a reason, guys, and now," I turned and looked over at them and held my beer out toward where the construction was happening across the water, "I think I know why."

"To fighting a new war together." Frank held his beer up, and we all tapped our cans to seal our secrets and become that much closer as brothers.

Zack handed me a plate of steak, lava hot potatoes, and bacon-wrapped asparagus.

"Only you would bring a five-star restaurant to the middle of the woods." I laughed while I cut into the mouth-watering hunk of meat.

"Shit, I'd pay you to cook for me in Washington." Frank folded an entire asparagus spear in his mouth.

"Dad did say they needed a new cook for the mess hall," I added.

"Nah," Zack sprinkled a bit of homemade seasoning on his potato, "you wouldn't find me in a kitchen like that. I want a place where I can greet everyone make them feel like they're invited into my kitchen, like family. I want to get to know the regulars and win over the newbies. I want to decorate for the holidays, make a place for people so they feel warm and welcome even if they're away from their own. I mean, we've all felt what it's like to be away from family."

"True, true." I thought about what he said. "But for the love of God, have the odd night where we can dance, listen to some good music. This town could really use something other than that western bar," I begged through a mouthful of food.

"I know we really do." Zack grinned as I shook my head, trying to understand why we needed to shove tacky cowgirl bars down tourists' throats. Redstone was better than that.

"We need a *Zack's*." I pointed my fork at him. "Keep it simple and to the truth."

"I like that," he smiled, "Zack's. I'm sure my brother will love that."

"I think when he hears your sales pitch on why you should call it that, he'll get it." Frank smiled.

"He's not wrong." I shrugged.

"Daniel, I'm never wrong." He playfully shoved my shoulder.

We spent two more nights in the woods. We talked of old times and more about rough times. None of us knew until it happened just how much we needed it. A lot was shared, and we laughed and cried and hiked and fished, and laughed some more.

It was like old days again when we were younger and less scarred by life. We found ourselves with big grins and lighter chests. There was even a point where I felt that the demons that had sat heavily on our shoulders were gone, or at least they were there less than before. I only hoped it would last.

I leaned back against a tree on the last night we were there and thought about the progress we had made. Maybe, just maybe, we could actually be whole again now that we were really home for good and had a future we could aim for. I sure hoped so.

The next morning, we woke to a glass lake that reflected the mountains and sunshine like a painting. The truck was basically packed, but we couldn't resist going out one last time.

We climbed into the canoe and paddled out into the center of the lake and cast our fishing lines. Watcher sat perfectly still at the nose of the canoe and only whined when we reeled in a fish.

"Hey, Zack, move that Black Ghost around more." I watched his black and yellow fly as it sat on the water.

"Stick to your nymphs. I know what I'm doing." He moved his fly with a little flick.

"You two'll never agree on how to fish." Frank shook his head. "The proof's in the catch." He eyed the pail beside him with three good-sized trout in it.

"Dad showed me the Silver Nymph he tied. He swears by it, so I tied myself a couple. Seems to be doing okay." I pointed to my own two fat trout and went back to fishing.

I let my mind drift as I relaxed, and I glanced across the lake. It was good to be able to see our hard work at Shadows from this prospective. It was important to learn every inch of the land around our safehouse. Zack and I had the advantage over Frank because we'd grown up and played there as kids, but there was still a lot of unexplored land, and things had grown up a lot since then. The more we hiked and explored, the more knowledge we'd have, and that knowledge could save your life.

"So," Zack grinned as he sipped now cold coffee from a stained Snoopy cup, "Daniel has Sue in his sights, but what about you, Frank? Anyone catch our *number guy's* eye?"

"Nope."

"Bull!" Zack saw what I did. A lie flickered across Frank's face so quickly that it was almost missed. "Come on, spill it!"

"Whatever." He drew his line in and cast again so hard the

canoe rocked. We waited impatiently for him to go on. "Okay, okay. I was in Washington a few weeks ago, and there was this woman who caught my attention. And before you try to drill it out of me, her name is Heather."

"Would that be Mia's mother?" I spilled my secret with a sly grin. I felt he deserved it because he'd run his mouth to Sue.

"Wait, who's Mia?" Zack looked between the two of us. "If this is a secret, I need answers, guys."

"Ah," Frank tossed his fishing rod at me, "fine. Let's keep the score board even." He growled as I grinned happily at Zack. "All I said was if I ever had a daughter, I wanted her name to be Mia."

"Come again?" Zack questioned.

"I don't know what the big deal is. I mean, women often pick out names for their kids when they're younger. Why is it strange for a man to do it?"

"It's not," I added to show I wasn't making fun of him for *that* reason.

"Why Mia?" Zack tried to follow.

"Because," he glanced at me, and I welcomed his answer to the world with open arms because it was funny as shit, "because any man who might try to hurt her will have to deal with me and will be missing in action."

"MIA," I added for the full effect. Zack's lips pressed together as he tried everything in his power not to laugh. That lasted about three full seconds.

"I'm not laughing at the name, honestly, brother. It's more the explanation of the name." Frank punched Zack, which only made him laugh harder.

"Okay, okay," I held a hand up in an attempt to stop the teasing. I didn't want to be too cruel to our friend, "let's just be happy he isn't going to name her after his blanket Woobie."

"You're such a bitch tit, Logan." Frank glared at me. Zack tried to keep his seat while he belly laughed in the wildly rocking canoe. Watcher licked his face as he tried to catch his breath.

"I promise our secrets at the lake stay at the lake," I said to Frank in a very serious voice with my hand over my heart. He snatched his pole from my hands and suggested we should start back.

CHAPTER NINE

Daniel

We trained, we worked on Shadows, we ran errands in town, and repeated. That was how each day went. Every spare moment I had, I spent it with Sue. She never asked what I was up to. She just seemed to know I was doing something I needed to do with the guys, and that was enough for her.

"That's really pretty." I admired her bracelet as it caught the sunlight. I flicked on the blinker as we were about to pull off into the grocery store parking lot. I was pleased to have a day off with her. When I stopped the truck, I lifted her wrist to study the bracelet more closely. The flat oval stones were smoothly polished, and when you studied each one, you could see the small, intricate grain that ran through each stone.

"Thank you. My mother gave it to me." She held it up. "I love black stones, so this was perfect."

"Blackstone," I repeated and thought how perfect that sounded for a team name. I really liked the sound of it and also knew it would always remind me of Sue. "Thanks for that."

"For what?" She zipped her coat.

"Nothing." I kissed her hand and let it drop back to her lap.

"Are you flirting with me, Mr. Logan?"

"I am." I gave her my best smile, the one she'd commented on to Tracy. I was lucky Tracy had ratted her out to me about it, because I planned to turn it on whenever I felt it was needed.

"You think you're pretty charming, don't you?" She tried to play it strong, but I could see she was falling deeper into my hold each day by the way her cheeks pinked up.

"Only with you." I winked and picked up the list of food I needed for tonight's dinner. "Let me grab that for you." I raced around the side of the truck to help her out onto the icy sidewalk. Since our night at the lake a few months back, I'd mostly started thinking ahead instead of backward. There were a few times the guys or I would slip up for a moment or two and let our heads go dark, but we worked together as a team and fought our way out of it.

If I was told before I'd left for Nam that I'd be where I was today, I would have laughed. Who would have ever thought I'd be helping to build a safehouse on Larry's land? Yet here I was, doing just that. The big difference was we trained to fight a different kind of war now. One I never would have imagined. One I planned to fight, but this time with the world's most wonderful woman next to me.

I took Sue's hand, and we headed into the store together. I was proud to show she was mine.

"That's a pretty long list." Sue studied the list I held up. "Why don't we start here and just weave up and down each aisle?"

"Lead the way."

"I see you need a lot of apples. Have you tried Pete's?"

"Pete's?" I looked at the giant rows of apples from local suppliers.

"Pete has one of the best orchards in Glen Haven. It's about an hour from here."

"Was he the guy who bought Cliff's old farm?"

"Yeah, about six years ago he sold to Pete, and now he's got the best produce for miles. Story is he built up the soil with a concoction of nutrients. It's a big secret, and everyone's dying to figure it out. He's not tellin' either. I know he's lovin' the whole thing." She chuckled as she rubbed an apple on her jeans to shine it up then handed it to me. "Try it." I took a bite and let the taste burst over my tongue. "See, much better than those ones."

"I'm sold." I handed her the bag of apples I'd picked up, and she put it back, then we loaded up on Pete's. "Here." I handed her the list. "You seem to know the best local stuff."

"All right." She pulled the list from my fingers and began to show me the ropes. That was one of the many things I loved about Sue. She always managed to amaze me even in the smallest ways. Truth be told, the best part of walking shoulder to shoulder, plucking items off the shelves, was it felt so normal, like we were a real couple doing real couple things. I made sure to take a moment to soak it up.

"What?" She'd just carefully selected some corn and put in the cart. Her expression told me she seen me watching her.

"It's just nice."

"What is?"

"Being here with you."

She leaned on the front of the cart as she thought about what I said.

"We could do more things like this since you seem to enjoy it."

"Oh, yeah?"

"Mhm." Her eyes lit up. "I need to order some firewood for Dad this afternoon. Maybe you can help me with that."

"If that means more time with you, then I'm all for it. "

With a cart full of food, enough to feed an army, she laughed at me as I pushed it toward the truck. Then we came to a dead stop.

"Oh, my God!" Her hands went to her mouth, and I saw the windshield of my truck had been smashed and the words "child killer" were spray painted along the side of the door. I cursed ever putting the Army sticker on my truck. I knew it was a target on my back.

I heard the footsteps as they raced up behind us, and I instinctively slipped into Army mode and shoved Sue aside as I whirled around. I thought I was going to meet a punch, but instead I got a bucket full of pig's blood splashed over my chest and down my front.

Three teenagers ran toward a yellow Volkswagen van. It had a huge peace sign painted on the side of it with *make love not war* crudely written under it. One of the two guys still held a pail that dripped red. The girl, dressed in some sort of long dress with fringes on it, screamed something over her shoulder as she ran. I couldn't make it out. Her brightly colored beads bounced around as she urged the boys to run faster. It was obvious they weren't from around here. At a safe distance, close to their van, they stopped and turned around. The girl jumped up and down in her excitement.

"Go back to Nam, baby killer!" the boy with a military jacket that had been ruined with black marker yelled with his hands up to his mouth like a megaphone.

"You should be ashamed of yourself," the girl wildly screamed at me as she twirled and danced like some sort of crazy doll.

"You're a disgrace to our country." The military jacket guy suddenly came at me in a full run. Sue screamed for help. "To our flag!" he yelled. And just like that, the past sucked me backward and I could see that little boy's terrified eyes and his urine-soaked pants. How many times had that vision come to me and woken me sweaty and panting from a dead sleep as it raced to the surface of my memory?

"You're wrong," I said through clenched teeth as I easily blocked the two-handed shove he threw at me. I held back. I sure didn't want Sue to hear anything about some of the dark moments I'd had there. "You have no idea what it was like over there!" I glared at him.

"Dan, are you okay?" Sue quickly handed me something to wipe my face clean of the disgusting blood that had already started to dry.

"How can you be with someone like that!" the guy hissed at Sue and took a step toward her.

"Get away from me." She lifted her hands and quickly glanced at me.

I saw black.

I drilled my elbow into his jaw, forcing his last words back down his throat. Then I reached down and grabbed him by the front of the jacket and pulled him up. My fist drew back to drill him in the face, but at a sound from Sue, I looked up and saw her wild eyes on me as she processed what I was about to do. That stopped my fist immediately.

"Daniel!" she cried.

"It's okay, it's okay." I tried to sound normal, but my head had slipped back to the jungle. The smell of the steamy earth and the buzz of mosquitoes filled my senses at the smell of the blood. I tried to fight it, and the urge to vomit stung the back of my throat. I blinked a few times and shook my head desperately to fight back the memories and the need to kill. I dropped the kid with a thud, and he jumped up and gave his head a shake as he touched his jaw.

"Get in the car," his buddy yelled. "We need to get out of here!"

"I know your face." He pointed at me. "I'm coming back for ya, and it won't be just my fists."

"What fists?" I challenged as I removed my soaked jacket, tossed it aside, and stepped toward him. He quickly weighed his options and turned and raced back toward their ridiculous van. They peeled out onto the road with the girl screaming obscenities from the window.

I barely remembered Sue's cries or when Zack came out of nowhere with Tracy.

"You okay, buddy? We saw the last of it. What the hell?" Zack's voice sounded off in the distance, and I didn't answer him. All I could think of was thank God Sue had been there, because if she hadn't, I'd probably have ended up in prison.

"Daniel?" Sue's voice found me. I stood there a moment on shaky legs, and when I turned around to face her, I grabbed her and slammed her to me, using her as an anchor.

"I slipped back!" I repeated a few times. "I'm so sorry."

"Is he always like this?" Tracy's voice came to me, and I looked over at her and tried to focus.

"We're all like this," Zack replied grimly. "You have no idea what Daniel did to keep us all alive over there. Unlike those little shits who have zero understanding of the hell we went through." He waved a hand at the car. "No one could if you weren't there."

"Jesus," Tracy breathed, "who are they?"

"Stupid hippie protestors," was all he offered.

With Sue held tight in my arms, I mouthed a thank you to Zack, who nodded back at me to show he understood.

"We should go before the cops arrive," Zack advised as he grabbed our grocery cart and started to load up the bed of his truck. "I have an extra coat in my duffle, Dan." We all pitched in and emptied the cart then quickly urged the girls into the truck, and Zack started the engine. "Give me a quick sec. I'll run inside and call your dad. He can come and get your truck." Zack locked eyes with me, and we both understood what could have happened.

Sue linked her arm in mine as we sat in the back, and I glanced at my bloody jacket as it lay in the parking lot. When Zack hopped back in and we peeled away, I hoped to hell it would be the last time I'd ever lay eyes on those people. I wondered what the fallout would be from it all. I'd seen them on TV with their crazy clothes and long hair, their fingers up in the V that once had meant victory but now had become an anti-war symbol.

We could never have imagined what kind of godforsaken war we had been dropped into, and now the world hated us for even going there. We were all just damaged goods that no one wanted to see.

My mind suddenly went to my buddy, Ray. His sister had insisted he was fine when we went to check in on him a few months back, but we hadn't actually seen him. His place was empty the time after that, and when we asked his sister where he was, she'd said he'd taken a trip to visit their brother on the west coast. I suddenly had a bad feeling, especially since he never returned our calls. Why hadn't I pushed it? Had she been told by Ray to keep us away? I couldn't live with myself if something happened to him. This time we weren't going to be put off, and we weren't going to call first. A sudden urgency flooded me.

"Zack." I broke the silence. "I think we should make a stop."

"Yeah, agreed." No question, we were on the same wavelength.

When we arrived at 424 Russet Lane, the house looked dark and cold. Just like before and the time before that. The only difference was his sister's car wasn't in the driveway waiting to intervene. I knew Ray well enough that he would have sold his sister on some story that would make her lie for him. They were tight, and she would do anything to protect him, even though protecting might mean letting him slip off the rails. She wouldn't get it, but we did.

"Doesn't look like anyone's home." Tracy warmed her hands with the truck vent.

"Maybe he's out?" Sue added. I glanced at Zack, and we both knew this was how it always looked. Cold and empty. We all got out of the car, but I pressed a hand to Sue's chest to tell her she should stay there. Tracy came around and stood next to her.

"There isn't any smoke coming from the chimney." I pointed feeling the need to explain each observation out loud. "It's winter, yet there's no fire going."

"The car's got a few inches of snow, and that was last Monday. No tire tracks." Zack echoed my tone.

"Okay, Hardy Boys." Tracy chuckled, but it died quickly as I glanced at her. I saw Sue take her arm.

"Zack, stay here with the girls, keep the truck running. I'm going to check it out."

"Copy that."

"Dan," Sue grabbed my hand again, "maybe we should call someone?"

"He's our friend. I just want to make sure he's okay. Promise." I shot her a smile as I moved toward the house. I could see my breath as it puffed in the chilly air.

The snow crunched under my boots, making it hard to hear any signs of life around me.

I did my normal sweep. I checked the perimeter, then looked for any open windows or signs of movement. I even checked for possible signs of a break-in as I cautiously headed for the door. The walkway hadn't been shoveled, the blinds were drawn, but the door was unlocked when I tested it.

I signaled to Zack I was going in.

"Anderson!" I used his last name first. Nothing. "Ray," I called and wished I had a weapon, "it's Daniel. I'm coming in."

No response.

"Anderson." I made a bird call, the same one we used in Nam. "It's Logan. Check in."

Nothing.

That familiar chill came on. My sixth sense had me in survival mode, and it told me I wasn't alone.

"Ahhh!" Ray screamed then came in rushing with a long pair of barbecue tongs in his hand and a pot on his head. I dodged his charge but got a swat across the cheek with the tongs as I tried to step back into position. I shook off the sting and took in my surroundings. The place looked like one of our camps back in Nam. There were dirty sheets, and branches and old pieces of wood hung from the walls as if for cover. Empty bean cans and wrappers littered the floor, and my friend looked like he'd lost complete touch with reality.

"Hey! Ray, it's Logan!"

He whipped the tongs around like a sword and tried to kick my thigh. His face ran with sweat and camouflage grease paint.

"Where are the rest of 'em?" Saliva pooled at the corners of his mouth, and I could tell he was on something. I just didn't know what. I knew a lot of our soldiers had learned about marijuana over there, and a lot of them used it. It was easy to get. But I also knew none of my guys had ever touched it. We'd all stayed clean the whole time we were there.

We had a purpose then, but the trouble was we were back

home now with nothing but messed up heads and an uncertain future. I knew a lot of guys had turned to drugs after they got back. That, along with alcohol and suicide, took a lot of them after they'd made it home *safe*. That was a joke on us if there ever was one. We were ignored—shunned, really. We were called baby killers and murderers and left to feel ashamed of our service. No one seemed to remember we hadn't asked to go; we were told to go. The awful words people used were triggers for us. Some poor guys did whatever it took to take away the pain of it, the shame of it. Anything just to make it go away.

"We're coming for you!" He dropped the tongs and raced toward me, grabbed me around the waist, and slammed me into the wall. He sent punches into my sides while I just held on. I couldn't bring myself to hurt him. When he pulled back a fist to drive it into my jaw, I blocked it and turned my body, twisting his arm not enough to break it, but enough so he'd have to submit. He wasn't exactly in top form; he'd lost weight and strength. When he fell to the ground, I went with him.

"Hey!" I smacked his face and hoped the adrenaline he was riding would finally fizzle out. The drugs in his system had given him a surge, but I knew he couldn't keep it up for long. "Ray, stop. You're home, buddy. You're in your house. It's me, Dan." I reached for a bucket of water he probably kept for drinking and dumped the icy liquid over his head. He jolted and yelped and swung blindly. "Come back to me, Ray!" I screamed at him.

"Where-where am I?" He blinked and looked around, and I knew I had him back. Then a horrific sob ripped from his chest as he leaned forward and jammed his head into my chest. I wrapped my arms around my friend and held him to let him know it was all right.

"I can't do this." He broke and held his head like it might explode. "It hurts so much."

"I know."

"Jimmy," he cried out for his best friend.

"I know, I know." I hated how much it hurt to even hear his name. "It's unfair, all of it, but Zack's here with me. It's okay now, Ray. We're gonna help you. We aren't going to leave you alone. Come on, Ray, if Zack, Frank, and I can move forward from this, so can you. We'll help you."

"I can't." I knew how close he and Jimmy had been. I couldn't help but think how I'd be if anything had happened to Zack.

"You can," I insisted and waited for him to look at me. "That voice that's on your shoulder, it taunts all of us every day. It dares us to do unspeakable things, but it's because we feel like we don't belong here anymore. But we do." I leaned my back against the wall next to him. "If you'd returned my calls, you would know why I wanted to talk. We need each other now more than ever."

"Marijuana's easier," he confessed.

"I'm sure it is." I shrugged, not wanting to scold him for getting to this point on his own, for not reaching out. "But, buddy, you were wearing a pot on your head." He let out a laugh as he dried his eyes, and I joined in to let the fear drain out of me. "You played your sister well. She wouldn't let us see you."

"I know." He covered his mouth, trying to hide his quivering chin. "When you came last time, I just couldn't see you. I wasn't ready. I saw you out the window. You both looked good, but I still hadn't showered, couldn't eat. I just can't keep my head straight. I keep slipping between there and here. I couldn't face you."

"We're far from good, Ray. We both still have trouble, but we keep in touch, help one another. It's why we came to see you. We didn't want to you to be alone. Especially not after what happened with Jimmy."

"I know," he dropped his arms, "but it was easier to hide and lie. I feel bad. I didn't help him, and it just made it worse. Maybe if I'd just reached out to Jimmy, he'd be here right now."

"If it helps," I rubbed my head, "we all feel that way."

We sat in silence, both taking another moment to heal.

"Your place looks like shit." I looked around and spotted more crap.

"It looks how I feel." He let out a heavy sigh. "I didn't think we'd come home to this, after what we did. What they asked us to do."

"None of us saw that coming." I nodded and knew now was the time to make things right with him. "Ray, you don't belong here."

"If I don't belong here," he let out a long shaky breath, "where do I belong?"

"With us. You belong with us. Me and Zack and Frank at Shadows."

"Where? To do what?"

"To do what we're meant to do." I got to my feet and tugged him up. "Get your crap. You're goin' with us. Zack's outside with the truck."

I kept a close eye on him while he grabbed his duffle bag and started to blindly stuff some belongings inside. When he wasn't looking, I unloaded his handgun that was on the counter and tossed the bullets in a cereal box. The idea the friggin' thing was loaded and close by the entire time made me shudder. I knew we'd probably been days away from losing another brother. I shook my head as I tried to get my head around it all.

"Grab your gear." I pointed to his fatigues and boots. "You're gonna need all of it." I scribbled my number on a note to his sister and explained that Ray was going to stay with me for a while. If she needed him, she could reach out at any time. I used the magnet that was shaped like the state of Montana to stick it to the fridge.

When we stepped outside, I found Zack by the door. He'd come to check on us and seemed to have a good handle on everything that had gone down. I nodded at him, and he stepped forward and gave Ray a slap on the shoulder then hauled him in for a hug.

"Lean on us." His voice was muffled by Ray's shoulder. "You're not alone."

They had a few more words, and I stepped back to give them some privacy. When they were finished, Ray's worn-out gaze found mine, then we all walked to the truck together. Sue stood next to Tracy by the open door. She looked worried but relieved.

"You must be Ray." She smiled at my buddy and offered a hand. "I'm Sue, and this is my friend, Tracy." Tracy nodded at him with an uncertain smile. "Why don't we get you something to eat?"

"Anything but beans." He managed a chuckle.

"Zack filled me in, and he's kept an eye on you both," Sue whispered as she pushed up on her tiptoes and kissed me. "You're a good man, Daniel Logan."

"I'm trying." I leaned in and kissed her again, happy she'd embraced Ray. She was a damn good woman, and I appreciated every inch of her.

Once Ray was settled in front, his things stowed in the back, Tracy jumped in beside us and we left for my parents' house.

Zack let me know he'd called ahead from the neighbor's phone and told my parents what was going on.

When we arrived, a police cruiser was parked in the driveway, and I glanced at Sue, who elbowed Tracy.

"Oh, great, my big brother's here." Tracy rolled her eyes as she grabbed her purse and hopped out of the truck.

"They're not here for me, right?" Ray tried to make a joke, but I could see him second guessing coming with us.

"No, that's for me." I was careful to avoid a patch of ice as I helped Sue down from the truck.

"You in some trouble, Logan?"

"I hope not, Ray, but at this point I don't overly trust what might've been said about me."

"There were witnesses, Daniel," Sue urged me toward the door, "plus Travis is good people even if he's a mess of stress all the time."

"I'd be too if I had to watch over this whole town with just four guys to help me." Zack carried an armful of groceries into the house. We'd keep everything here until we were cleared to take it all to Shadows.

"Hey, Daniel." Officer Travis leaned against the counter with his notebook open. He looked a bit uncomfortable as he flicked his pen between his fingers. "Can I ask you a few questions?"

"Yeah." I waited for the others to leave, but they didn't. "Go ahead."

Travis made a face at his sister, and she gave him a wry look, then he turned to me and went on to ask about what happened at the store. I gave him the details as I saw them.

"Honestly, Travis," Sue moved to stand next to me, "it was self-defense. That guy was out for blood."

"That's what some of the customers said, too. You're in the clear here, Daniel. I just had to do my part and get your statement. I'll make sure your description gets passed along. We'll get them if they come back, but I doubt they will." He turned his attention to Sue. "Were you hurt?"

"No." She looked at me, and I suddenly wondered if they'd dated before.

"You sure?" The way he looked at her had my eyes slit.

"Yes, Daniel made sure I was all right." I felt Sue lean into me, and I wrapped my arm possessively around her waist.

"All right." He let it go, and I heard a little hiss from Tracy. "If you need anything, here's my card. I'll do my best to help where I can."

"Thanks." I nodded at him. He held out his card, and when I didn't take it, he put it on the table and left.

"I'm surprised Travis had the time to come all the way out here." Mom tucked his card into a drawer. "I know they're extremely short staffed."

"He only came because he wanted to see Sue." Tracy scoffed, and Sue hit her arm.

Called it.

"What? It's true." Tracy glanced at me with a grin. "He's had a crush on her since she got boobs."

"Classy, Tracy." Sue flushed pink.

"All right, then," my father came to her rescue, "let's focus on moving forward. Now, Ray, why don't you get showered and changed while Meg prepares one of her home-cooked meals? That'll fix you right up."

"I don't remember the last time I've had a real meal." Ray rubbed his face.

"Well, you're home now, so follow me and I'll get you set up." Dad led the way, and Ray gave me a thankful glance and followed him. I could hear Dad's voice as they walked down the hall. "You won't be hungry again, believe me. Now Meg's got her eye on you." He chuckled.

"Come on, Tracy, let's get the rest of the stuff from the truck." Zack held out a hand to her and they slipped out. I pulled Sue out onto the porch.

"It's wonderful that your family will take Ray in like that." Sue looked up at me. "They have so much love."

"I'm a lucky man to have them, too. They're the best. I

hope I never take them for granted." I leaned down and kissed her.

"You never would, Daniel. You're a part of them. Ray's a lucky man to have you as a friend." She hugged me.

It took a few days for Ray to settle. He needed time to get the drugs out of his system before he could really get his feet under him. But after a week of hot showers, clean clothes, and a full belly, he was back to the old Ray I knew. We knew he'd need some psychological help, and Dad already had things on track for that.

"Daniel?" my mom called to me from the study. I pried my eyes away from the blueprints of the new weapons barn I was reviewing and went to find her.

"I think you should take this." She pointed to the phone, and I rushed over to answer it.

"Hello?"

"Daniel?" Ray's sister sounded frantic. "Is he still with you?

"Yes, he is."

"I just got back into town, and I thought…" She started to cry. I gave her a moment. "I saw your note. I'm so sorry about lying to you." She sniffed. "I was just so relieved he was home, and I only wanted to do what he asked. By the time I saw he was slipping, it was too late. I had so much going on. There just wasn't—"

"It's honestly okay," I assured her, "truly. I think what he needs right now is to be here with us. You know, guys who understand what he's seen. We have some idea of how to pull him back when he gets in a bad way. It isn't easy, but there's ways to do it."

"It's really not," she agreed.

"Look, I'd really like Ray to stay with me and my family for a bit, get him back on track the way Zack and I did. I might even have something that should help to keep him focused, you know, to channel the pain."

"I can figure out some money for him." I felt terrible she even went there. I knew that since their parents died, she'd done everything to help Ray, even at her own family's expense.

"Nah, he's been more than helpful around the farm. He'll earn his keep and then some."

"That's kind, Daniel. Thank you."

"I'm not doing it to be kind. I'm selfish and want my friend back to normal." She chuckled at that, and I caught Mom's glossy eyes as she pretended to read her romance novel. "Just do me one favor."

"Anything."

"Call every few days and talk to him. He needs to know he still has his sister's support."

"You got it."

I hung up and felt good about being able to relieve a little of her stress. I was really gaining some insight into what it was like for the families of the guys who came back. They were lost on what to do. Their pain was as real as ours, just different.

"I love you, Mom." I hugged her, and she grinned as I left the room.

"I'm pleased to say I think Ray is ready for your next move," Dad said as he came in the door.

"Really?" My excitement made him happy, and he smacked me on the back.

"Yeah, really."

I hurried back to the kitchen and called Zack to share the news that we'd got the green light to share our new life plan with Ray.

CHAPTER TEN

DANIEL

"Where are we going, exactly?" Ray took the front seat of Zack's truck and rubbed his hands together with excitement.

"Just trust us." Frank hit his shoulder, and we headed up the windy Montana mountain road. Chuck Berry's *Maybelline* bounced from the speakers as we climbed to a higher altitude where the air was crisp and cool.

"Wow." Ray shook his head when we finally reached our destination. He ran a hand over his face. "This is really impressive."

"It is, isn't it?" I looked over what he saw and smiled back at him. It really was impressive, I thought, and felt my chest swell as I took in my father's vision of how we were going to improve our lives, not to mention the lives of countless others.

Frank handed out bottles of Highlander, and we each popped the caps on our favorite cold brew.

"To making history." Frank tapped his bottle to ours.

"Hey, fellas?" Dad stood in the main doorway and waved

us in. We followed him inside, and he led the way to the living room where he handed me a stick. "Part of making history is marking history." He bent down and wrote his name in the six-by-twelve space of wet concrete that was right in front of the fireplace. "Your turn, son."

I did the same, and one by one, the guys wrote their names and ranks, and when we finished, Dad wrote the year.

"Have you thought of a name for your team yet?" Dad asked as he took a seat on the patio near us.

"Eagle Eye?" Frank spoke up first.

"Mm," Zack shook his head, "what about Red Stone? Like after our town?"

"So, we're offering up our location along with our name?" I joked and took a sip of from my bottle. "What about Blackstone?"

"Ohh," Zack nodded along with Ray, "I like Blackstone. Where did you get that name?"

"Somewhere special." I grinned behind my bottle and glanced at Dad.

"Team Blackstone." Dad smiled at me. "That's good."

"So, no to Eagle Eye?" Frank waved us off. "Whatever, I'll form my own team later."

"Whatever." I laughed. "Although wouldn't it be amazing to have brother companies all over the US someday? I mean, teams fighting an organization that's quickly expanding all over the world isn't the craziest of ideas."

"Yeah, and my team will be called Eagle Eye." Frank huffed playfully.

"Maybe even Canada could get involved," Dad said, deep in thought. "No one would ever suspect our friendly ally to the north."

"I've always wanted to go there." I sighed.

"You should." Dad sipped his beer. "We should plan a trip sometime."

"Now, that's something to work toward." Zack banged the table, making us all laugh.

We spent the night giving each other shit and planned out what the next steps should be.

A week or so later, I met Dad in the newly finished kitchen.

"Congratulations, Dad!" I tapped my shoulder to his. "Look how far you've taken us. We're that much closer to our dream."

"It's incredible, isn't it?" He shook his head as if in disbelief. We both couldn't get our heads around it. Things were finally coming together.

The fridge was fully stocked, and two massive dishwashers, which had to be specially made, had just been installed and were already performing a test run. I even had a friend make the house logo out of copper wire. It was an upside-down triangle with a break halfway down where the word Shadows was written through it. An outline of our beloved Montana mountains was outlined along the top. Mom and I had come up with it, and I was pleased with the outcome.

"They sure did an amazing job." I ran my hand along the countertop and admired the beautiful craftsmanship. Dad hadn't skimped on a thing. It was top of the line all the way.

"Yes, they did." He looked at his watch, and I knew I hadn't been asked to be here today just to see the final touches on the house.

"What's going on?"

"Washington's been interviewing psychologists for the house, and I think we've found one who will work. I've spent some time with him, but I want you to meet him. Just because I like him doesn't mean you will, so I need to see what you think before we make the final call."

"Great. I'd be happy to." I was pleased he wanted to involve me in the decision making.

Shadows

"Good, because he's getting set up in the room by the stairs, next to the big office. He's just here on a trial basis. We haven't firmed up anything with him yet. Why not go in as a new client and see how he works?"

"Okay, sure. Should I call Zack and Frank and see what they think?"

"Already thought of that. They'll be here in a few hours." He pulled some files out of his bag and placed them on the island. "When you're done, I'd like to talk to you about the latest on the Cartel. We need to speed up our training. There's been chatter from Washington, and they're anxiously waiting for the green light to deploy us to Mexico."

I quickly looked interested.

"Apparently, there's a southern politician who got himself in trouble while visiting Tijuana with his family. They found a few local guys who'd said he was poking around on stuff that wasn't for him. They had Cartel connections. According to the guy's wife, he's been missing for the past two days. They want to send a team over and gather intel before they make any moves." He flipped open the folder, and I scanned the information on the missing man.

"Geez." I fingered the awful photos. "Yeah, if these are photos of what they'd do to their own people who cross them, imagine what's happening to this politician as we speak. Jesus, they even killed the dog." I threw down a photo in disgust. "Imagine what they'd do to us," I added.

"Speaking of dogs, we got the funding you wanted for the two K9 trainers. Figure out where you're getting the dogs, and let's get that buttoned up sooner rather than later."

"Copy that."

"I'm not gonna sugar coat this, Dan. I've got a pretty good idea of the things you've been through. So, I know you can handle this."

"Sadly," I pushed some of the photos around as I studied the gruesome murders, "this is nothing I haven't seen before."

"So, let's make sure these animals are stopped." Dad pulled the photos away from me and nodded at the door. "The doctor awaits."

I gave my head a shake to clear it of the images I'd just seen and walked down the hall, curious to meet the man who was going to mess with our heads. I stopped at the open door and took him in. He had a distinguished look about him. He didn't wear a white coat but did have on a rather stiff white dress shirt. His pants had a military crease, and his shoes gleamed with polish but looked expensive. He had his legs crossed and swung one foot as he studied the notes on his lap. He was younger than I expected but oozed poise and education.

"You must be Daniel Logan." He looked over with a friendly smile as he adjusted his glasses on his nose.

"I am, and you must be Dr. Roberts."

"I am." He gestured toward the big, comfortable chair in front of him. "I can tell by your hesitation you thought I'd be older."

"Was I that obvious?"

"No, I just get it a lot." He grinned than looked at my file. "I'm just a few years older than you." Interesting. "Would you care to get started?"

"Sure." I sat down and rubbed my hands over my thighs and thought how strange it was that in all the time since I'd been home from the war, I was only now about to get some help, and I knew I had my own father to thank for it.

After some brief "get to know you" chat, he jumped right in. "Daniel, if you could describe your time in Nam, in sequence, and in just a few words, what would they be?" Well, that certainly ripped the Band-Aid off. I drove my heels hard into the floor to stop the images those words brought.

This was what I needed, just do the session.

"Shock, bewildered, horrific, brutal, hopeless, hell." I swallowed hard.

"Powerful words." He looked me in the eyes and held them a moment then slowly looked down and jotted something on his notepad. "When you were over there, did you think much about home?"

"Of course."

"All right, same question, but describe what it was like when you came home. No limit on the words, just try to put them in sequence as you did before. How you've felt since you've been back."

I forced my mind to think about the plane ride home, the belly of the aircraft opening once we landed, and the sunlight that burst over us along with the knowledge we were home. Then the shock of our lack of welcome. Even though we had an idea of it, it was still a shock.

"Relief, exhaustion, confusion, broken, anxious, demons." I rubbed the back of my head and took a moment to think, then added, "Safe, light, happy, love, difference."

"Good." My eyes were drawn to his pencil as he drew a curved line and started to make little ticks along its arch. "Do you allow yourself to remember what happened over there?" He caught me staring at his pad but didn't move it.

"I try not to, no."

"Why?"

"What would that accomplish? Looking backward, I mean."

"Do you feel bothered when you think back? Do you have dreams or nightmares about being over there?"

"Yes." I knew he would already know any guy who'd been to war would have nightmares about it, but I understood he needed to ask, so I kept my voice even and gave him the answer.

"How often?" he shot back.

I answered without thought. "Maybe three times a week." It was an honest answer.

He crossed his legs then gave a little stretch, and I followed his lead and rolled my head to relax the tension in my neck. I wondered if he'd done that to keep the session relaxed.

"It's a misconception that soldiers think they have to push all the bad stuff aside when they get home. Show how tough they are and all that. I mean, don't get me wrong, I know you have to be mentally strong to be able to do your job when you're there, and it's hard to let your guard down now. You've seen things over there that were horrific."

I nodded and broke eye contact.

"Yet, in order to move forward, you have to be able to take that horror over here," he moved his hands out to his side and made a circle with them, "and now you've finished your assignment, and you're back safe and sound, you need to bring that over here to the forefront." He moved his hands to the center as he spoke. "You need to do that, Daniel, in order to deal with it, or those demons you mentioned earlier will always be there waiting for you in your sleep, or maybe the next time something triggers you. They'll eat away at you for the rest of your life."

"Okay," I nodded in agreement and saw his point, "I'm open to help. What's the first step?"

"Acceptance of what happened." He rubbed his chin and gauged my reaction. "You never asked to be a part of that war. You were told to go, and you did. You survived and returned home a different man. Screw what you see in the media, screw the dirty looks from the person behind the checkout counter, you did what you had to, to get yourself home." He paused. "Let go of all that, and I can help you with the rest."

A slow smile tugged at the corners of my mouth, and I sank down deeper into the chair.

"Okay."

"Well let's get started." He smiled.

By the time the session was over, I walked out of the room lighter than I'd been since I got back. I found Dad in the living room elbow deep in Cartel research. When he heard my footsteps, he removed his glasses he looked up and took a hard look at me.

"Well?"

"I think we'd be crazy not to hire him."

CHAPTER ELEVEN

Daniel

Debbi wore a bright yellow t-shirt with a cat on the front that read, *You're not drinking alone if your cat is in the room.*

"I think we should make a quick call to Zack, give him our coordinates." Frank gave me a creeped-out face. "Because if we don't return, Debbi did it." I hid my laugh by faking a cough.

Debbi led the way down a hallway and eyed me as she unlocked the door to a giant room filled with seven-foot-high fenced-in cages. A lot of eyes blinked back at me as I took in the place.

"Um, Daniel…" Frank squinted and plugged his ears at the deafening sounds that bounced off the concrete walls. Excited barks and whines bombarded us and drowned out Frank's words. I swallowed back the smell of soiled pads and desperation.

"One call, and I can get you the best of the best from the military police." Frank's voice was loud and close to my ear.

"No," I shook my head and looked around at the desperately unhappy pups behind the fences. The neighborhood pound held way too many dogs who needed someone. "They need us as much as we need them. Let's give this a chance first," I yelled back in his ear then bent down and reached through a cage and patted a border collie's head. He whined as he soaked up the attention.

After a few minutes, the dogs settled down enough that we could actually hear each other, and Debbi leaned in.

"How many do you want?"

"Eleven."

"Eleven?" She tucked a piece of frizzy hair behind her ear, only to have it pop back out. "What do you plan to do with them?" Her face became suspicious.

"Well, Debbi," I flashed her my biggest friendly smile, I hoped it would put her at ease. "I plan to give them a life. One outside a cage."

"Fine." She shook her head and shrugged like I was crazy. "Use these to mark the ones you want." She handed me a handful of yellow scarves. "Come find me when you're ready, and in the meantime, I'll get the papers drawn up."

"Thanks, Debbi," I called loudly. I was determined to make her like me.

"I say veto that one." Frank pointed in the corner at the little Chihuahua. "His beady little eyes pierce my soul."

"I'm not entirely sure a Chihuahua is what we're looking for." I chuckled.

"Yeah, well, just be happy Sue isn't here. She'd want them all."

"And that's exactly why she isn't." I grimaced and split the scarfs up and handed half to him.

"Okay, Logan, where do we start?"

"I think," I resisted the urge to take them all, "we go with our gut."

Several hours later, we had weeded out some dogs I felt

could be worked with. I knew we needed dogs who weren't nervous or snappy. They had to at least look trainable. We needed intelligence and strength too, but that would show itself in time. We just did our best and tried to harden our hearts to those who obviously wouldn't work. I was happy the border collie made the cut.

After all the paperwork was done, and Debbi was satisfied with our motives, we had our new K9 Trainees ready to go. We arranged to pick them up in a few days after they all got their proper shots. We headed back to Shadows.

"I need a shower." Frank attempted to brush the dog hair that covered his shirt when he stepped out of the truck.

"Me too."

"No time for that," Dad called as he approached us. "We've got training to do."

———— ★★★★★ ————

"You four looked exhausted." Sue laughed as she reached up to rub my back when I sat down next to her at Patty's. "You look like zombies. What've you been up to?"

"Work," Zack muttered and leaned his head on Tracy's shoulder as if too tired to hold it up. The two of them had been hooking up of late, and I was happy for him.

"Is that dog hair?" Tracy plucked a few long hairs from his wool jacket.

"Don't ask," he huffed.

I had to smile at him. I knew we both thoroughly enjoyed these times with the girls. It gave us a chance to let ourselves relax a bit and have a bit of much-needed fun. I sat back and enjoyed the conversation between Tracy and Sue about their week. I tried to pay attention to Tracy's story but found my mind drifting.

Shadows

We'd spent the past few weeks cramming our heads full of as much information as possible on the Cartel. Dad had brought in a few speakers who had inside knowledge of what to expect from them and how they operated. It was a whole different world from what we were used to, and each rescue would be totally different. We needed to cover every possible contingency, and that meant a lot of work.

We kept ourselves in tip-top shape with a daily run, followed up by a couple circuits on a tough obstacle course we'd set up. Between all that and the fact we were nearing the completion of Shadows, our brains were full and our bodies exhausted.

"So," Sue's hand ran over my thigh and instantly brought me back to her, "can you come by for lunch anytime soon?"

"Are you asking because you want to see me or because you know Zack just made the best pumpkin soup known to man?" I teased.

"Both." Her eyes lit up with excitement.

"I'll see if I can get away."

"All the ladies love the best friend's cooking, Dan." Zack used a piece of bread to soak up his leftovers. "Once you accept that, we can all co-exist. A foursome."

"Aren't I lucky?" Tracy snickered, and Zack scooped his arm around her shoulder and pulled her in for a hug. "Anyway, so, Sue, here's what happened the last time my boss came in…" I tuned her out when I spotted a man helping his dog into his car.

Now that our dogs had arrived, most were making great progress in their training. The K9 guys had done exceptionally well with a few of them. I was pleased to see the border collie was adapting fast and seemed to love it even more than I'd hoped. I couldn't help but feel proud of her; she was a natural. Adding to all of that was the excitement of the arrival of our new helicopter. We were mentally and physically riding a wave, but all of it took a toll on us. Sue had hit the nail on the head; we were mighty tired.

I thought back to yesterday when the last of the speakers had finished. We'd all sat there in silence and wondered what the hell was wrong with the human race.

"Edison," Ray spoke up as we gathered our belongings, about to go to the kitchen for some much-needed food, "I've been doing some digging of my own on the Cartel, and aside from the import and export of drugs, weapons, and people, they are as heinous a group as I've ever heard of."

"They are." Dad nodded. "It's why I'm trying to prepare you for the worst. The Cartel are incredibly violent and thrive on fear and never hesitate to use torture over words."

"So, that being said, we do have permission to use deadly force, if need be, correct?" Ray glanced at me. "I mean, we aren't supposed to try to spare any Cartel lives here, right? Because I want to be honest with you, if it comes down to me or them, it's me." We'd all spent a great deal of time with Dr. Roberts, trying to reprogram our mindset after Nam, where it was kill or be killed. He'd helped all of us get our heads on straight, and although the good doctor had given us the green light to head back into combat, we didn't want to ruin what we'd managed to repair, with his help, in a spray of bullets. "I just want to make sure our orders from Washington aren't to be peacekeepers, because there's no peace when dealing with these people."

My father waited for the room to quiet down and placed a hand on Ray's shoulder as he spoke. "Men, our orders are to extract our mark with whatever means necessary. You be sure it's always you, never them who comes out on top. Understood?" Dad then glanced around the room. "I know all of you have worked with the doc and are doing well, and I want you to know he will be speaking with each and every one of you after every mission. We don't want you to take any steps back."

"Copy that." Ray let out a heavy breath, no doubt relieved with the answer he got. It was one thing to survive in the jungle that was Nam, with no real support and in constant fear, but it would be quite another thing to work directly under the Army as an elite team. We would be under a microscope and would be given every possible thing we would need to keep ourselves in the right headspace. I knew we all still felt the pressure to prove this was a good idea, and that rested on all our shoulders.

"I'm going to just say it." Tracy pulled me back from my thoughts, and I tuned in to her and ignored Sue's warning to be quiet. "What is it that you guys really do? Construction? Because, if it's that, then why can't we see what you're working on? Why is it such a taboo thing to talk about?"

Before any of us could try out our lie, Sue piped up. "They work for a secret agency." She kept a straight face, and I smirked at Zack, thankful she didn't jump on Tracy's insistence on knowing the truth. She dropped her voice and widened her eyes as she talked. "Didn't you hear that Area 51 is actually Barry Lake?" Tracy rolled her eyes and stuck her tongue out at her. "It's true. Remember when we were there, and you noticed those big lights that flickered above you?"

"No," she huffed, unsure.

"That's because they wiped your memory." Sue shrugged. "They did other things too, but we're not allowed to talk about it." She made the whole table burst out laughing, and we joined the fun and started to give Tracy all kinds of shit about what the aliens might have done to her body. Soon Tracy forgot about her question and was laughing with the rest of us.

When we were saying our goodbyes at the truck later, I

pulled Sue away from the rest and figured I should address it with her. I hated to lie, but I wasn't sure what else to do.

"Um, so, about Area 51." I smiled, and she looked at me with her head cocked to one side. "Even though we're back from the war, we're still kind of part of the military." The truth was we did get some funding from the US military, but it could never be said we worked under or directly for the military. That part was left murky. I didn't care because I knew we would be doing what was needed, and the government might just want to look the other way. They recognized the need for us. Who knew what might happen in the future if this whole operation panned out? "And with that some things that can't be shared. Believe me, you would be the first person I'd want to share things with, but orders are orders, and—"

"Daniel Logan, you're a great man," she interrupted me, "with a great family and friends, and if you don't or can't share what you're up to all day long, I'm okay with that right now. Just if it's nothing illegal or you've got another family hidden away somewhere..." she joked.

"Never," I promised her.

"Then it's okay."

"Okay?" This seemed too easy.

"Yes, for now, it's okay." She kissed me. "I love you, Dan, but I also know you have your military life during the day and me at night. For the moment, that works."

"And when it doesn't?" I felt a wave of nausea with that question.

"Then I'll let you know, and we can go from there." She gave me a smile, and I saw such trust and confidence in her that it took everything inside me not to blurt the truth.

"For the record," I drew her in closer, "I'm unbelievably in love with you, too."

"I think we both made our feelings quite clear the other

night." She gave me a hungry look. "But you better be in love with me, Mr. Logan, because I'm not giving you up. Ever."

"Like I'd ever let you."

"Seriously," her hand cupped my face, "you seem even quieter than normal. Is everything okay?"

"Yeah." I kissed her again and wished I didn't have to let go. While I loved my time with her, these little visits were wearing on me mentally, not being able to share with her. "I just have a lot on my mind."

"If there's ever anything I can do to help…"

"You do help, Sue. You help by just being here, even if it's only for an hour. I need my Sue time."

"Let's go, lovebirds!" Tracy called. I reluctantly let Sue go, and she slipped out of my arms to join Tracy in her car. "Seriously, you two are attached at the hip."

"Don't be jealous, friend, be happy." Sue scowled at her.

"I am." Tracy waved at me and slipped behind the wheel of her car.

"I'll call you about lunch." I waved at Sue and felt my buddies watching me.

I glanced over and saw Frank, Zack, and Ray all staring at me with big-ass smirks on their faces.

"Do you hear that, Frank?" Zack pretended to listen.

"Yup," Frank played along, "I do believe that's wedding bells."

"Shut up." I laughed. "Let's get back."

———— ★☆★☆★ ————

We ate, trained, researched, planned, and learned how to speak Spanish. Maybe not enough to pass ourselves off for long, but enough to get by. Thankfully, we were able to pick it up fairly quickly, as we all had a basic grounding in learning languages such as French and Vietnamese. It helped, anyway. A good soldier used whatever he could as a survival tool. We would never cower and run away from a situation when in the field. My team would use whatever resources we had and never stop taking advantage of every chance we could to learn something about the enemy. It allowed us to turn the tables and use it against them later. We learned as much of the language as we could from the ones we held hostage, used their own fighting techniques against them whenever we could, and never let something catch us off guard a second time. If you didn't take advantage of every opportunity to learn about the dangers you faced, you were as good as dead.

"Here." Dad handed me a knife, and Mom held up a camera as I crawled into our brand-new helicopter and carved our team's name under my father's then etched in the year. I heard the shutter on the camera go off a few times. "Let's make it a tradition that when we have a new team join our family, the team leader will come aboard to carve their name into the skin of the chopper. This guy," he patted the side wall, "gets us home." We all cheered at that. "And it never hurts to have a little lady luck." He smiled at Mom, who kissed her fingers and pressed them over the words.

I handed Dad back the knife while Mom snapped a few more photos of our two teams. The excitement was high as we looked forward to our first flight out.

Later that afternoon when the fun died down, I leaned against the deck railing with my notebook and practiced the words I struggled with. The boys and I spoke Spanish whenever we communicated with each other these days. It was imperative that we could understand each other as well as the enemy. We had to be able to know what was being said if we got in a position to hear the Cartel as they spoke to one another in person or over a radio.

"Dan?" My father stepped through the sliding glass doors,

and he looked serious. "Gather your team. We've got orders." He couldn't hide the excitement in his voice, and my heart leapt in my throat. A mix of excitement and anxiety of the unknown shot through my body as well. "I'll take the lead on the mission today, only because of how quickly this came about, but from the moment we leave, you'll be in charge. Blackstone will lead, and Team Tracker will be your backup."

"Understood." I nodded. My dad had named his team Tracker after a dog he'd saved back when he was in Germany. My heart swelled with love for him. The fact that he had provided this new life and position for me made me realize once again how lucky I was. I knew my father was a great man, but he was an even better husband and father. So, for just one second, I allowed myself a moment to appreciate it.

I rushed back inside and used the intercom to communicate with the guys. It wasn't long before my Blackstone team gathered in the situation room along with Team Tracker.

"We got our orders from Washington." Dad jumped right in, and you could hear a pin drop as the men waited to hear what he'd tell us. "I've been on the phone with our liaison. It seems we not only have information on our mark but have confirmation on where he's being held." He put two photos up on a screen. "These were sent over, so take a good look. Dan, your Team Blackstone will take the lead, so you'll need to make contact and confirm he is indeed there. Tracker," he addressed his team, "we're the eyes and ears and will move in or distract the enemy away from Blackstone if need be." He pulled down a map of the US and Mexico and used a marker to show our route, and backup plans were discussed in case something went amiss. Dad was clear and concise and gave each of the men lots of time to ask questions and made sure everyone knew his role and was okay with it.

"Our orders are to use whatever means necessary to get

this guy back, but my main concern is that I want you all back alive and in one piece." My father checked the time. "Pack your bags, boys. We leave in one hour."

Zack looked at me, and I saw the rush that sparkled in his eyes as he hopped to his feet and ran off to get ready.

As team leader of Blackstone, I knew I was the one responsible to get my men home in one piece, as well as our mark. As hard as it was to put my head back into combat mode, there was a sense of comfort in the control I felt. It was something I'd never experienced before. I knew it was because I'd had a direct part in the planning of it all. I'd also helped develop other contingency plans in case things went differently than we expected. That assurance that I knew exactly what would happen and when gave me the confidence I needed. I was ready for what was ahead.

"You set?" Ray asked as he tossed his black duffle bag by the front door.

"Yes, just need to make a quick call." I rushed down the hallway to my office and partially closed the door so I could keep one ear on my team.

I waited for three rings. All the while, I rapidly tapped my shoe against the floor and stared out the window. I let out a quick breath when Sue answered the phone.

"Hello?"

"Hey, baby, how are you?" I asked.

"Better now." She sounded all breathy, and I felt the warmth.

"Did you have a good day at work?" I asked and tried to find the words I'd need next.

"I did, and I finished two projects that were due, so," she paused, "I was thinking what if we had dinner at my place tomorrow night? How about pasta?"

I hesitated a beat and rubbed my forehead as I wondered just how this conversation was going to go over.

"I'm sorry, but I won't be able to make that." I kept my voice even.

"Okay, well, what about the next day?"

"Um," I cleared my throat and knew I shouldn't string her along, "actually, I wanted to tell you that I have to go away for a few days, for work."

"Oh…" Her voice trailed off, and I felt a kick to the gut. "When will you be back?"

"I'm not sure yet. Hopefully, we should only be about four days. So, maybe we can plan something for the weekend or into the next week?"

"Dan," something in her voice sat with me funny, "please be careful."

Where does she think I'm going?

"Of course, I will." I tried to lighten the mood, but even I found it strange that she went there. "It's just a quick trip."

"Promise me something?"

"Sure."

"Promise me when you get home, you'll call me right away?"

I paused and realized she intuitively knew something. I let the lightness I had strived for drop from my tone.

"I promise, Sue. I love you."

"I love you, too. Be safe." The phone disconnected, and I slowly hooked the receiver back on the wall. I couldn't shake her reaction. Maybe she could hear the worry in my voice, but I'd practiced a few times before I called her.

"Dan?" I found my mother in the doorway of the office.

"Hey, Mom." I leaned against the windowsill, wishing the conversation had gone a little differently.

"May I give you a piece of advice, son?" She stepped farther into the room and waited for me to nod for her to go on. "Never promise something you don't have control over. Broken promises are a lot worse in the long run, if things don't go as planned. Happy surprises are much better to go with."

"Okay." I could see what she was saying. Our job was unpredictable, and our word was everything.

"How'd she take your leaving?"

"I swear it's like she knows or something." I huffed and rubbed the back of my neck. "I've never even hinted at what we do, other than it's Army related, and I'm not allowed to share, but it's like she just knows."

"She's smart. She's most likely put two and two together that it's something important and dangerous. It's a good sign, you know."

"What is?"

"The fact she's not digging and is still supportive means you two have a good relationship. One built on trust and love. That's hard to find these days."

"She's a pretty amazing person."

"All the more reason to come home in one piece." She leaned in for a hug.

"That and my mom's cooking." I pulled back and flashed her one of my smiles. "I'll promise you this. I'll be as careful as possible."

"See, now, that's one promise I know you can keep."

"Dan, the chopper's here." Frank popped his head in and waved politely at Mom.

"You boys be each other's eyes out there."

"We will," he assured her. "I still think Eagle Eye makes more sense for a name," he grumbled from behind me, and I smirked.

I hurried outside with my bag over my shoulder to where the helicopter waited. As we lifted off the ground, I took one last good look down on our new home and marveled once again at what we'd accomplished. Then I slipped into Army mode and began to review the plan in my head.

CHAPTER TWELVE

Daniel

It was a long trip, but we made it to Mexico without incident and left the chopper then transferred to a Bronco. The moment we crossed the border, everyone suddenly went quiet. The hum of the big motor seemed to calm our heads and helped prepare us for what we needed to do. We were going back into battle. I would have preferred to have gone in by chopper, but since we weren't sure exactly what we would be dealing with, we figured it was best to travel by vehicle. Getting the lay of the land was critical since this was our new war zone.

I caught Zack's expression, and I knew he was fighting the past. I leaned over, took his hand, and got him to run his fingers over the single black stone that was tucked in the mesh pocket of our vests. We would never give the Cartels any information on who we were, but that didn't mean we couldn't bring a symbol. We'd become a bit superstitious in Nam, and now it carried over to Mexico.

Zack nodded and clapped his hand against my shoulder, and I knew he was back with us again. Frank muttered something, and I knew he'd be doing some mental math to soothe his head. I checked on Ray, and he seemed to be holding up just fine.

"Blackstone One, we are good to go." I used the radio to check in with my father.

"Copy that. ETA ten minutes out."

"Masks down," I ordered my team. We had blackened out our faces to seal our identity from whoever we encountered. We swayed in our seats as we turned down the street and bounced around on the uneven pavement. We were here. It was where the last known sighting of our subject had been reported. Our hired driver parked where we'd instructed him, just a few houses away. As a unit, we slipped into the shadows and moved quietly through the alleyways, clearing them as we went. The night was young, and a heavy stench of garbage and rotten food filled the air. Rats raced across the powerlines and over the tops of our boots as we moved.

We relied heavily on our hand signals in fear someone would hear us. Part of being unseen was being unheard.

We stopped at the building we'd been told to look for. It had bars on the lower windows, but the one higher up had a piece of cardboard in place of glass, with tiny lookout holes poked through it. I signaled to Ray that this was the place.

Zack bent down, and I used his knee for a step, then his shoulder as I held on to the wall for balance. He stood and lifted me higher so I could gain access to the window. I used the tip of my gun to push the cardboard back in one corner to see inside. Frank and Ray scanned the buildings nearby, as their windows and rooftops would have made perfect perches for a sniper.

I pulled a marble from my pocket and tossed it inside, I heard it hit the floor, but it didn't bounce or roll. I strained to hear voices, but all was quiet.

I removed my flashlight and scanned inside. There didn't

seem to be any Cartel in there, at least I hoped to hell there wasn't. There seemed to be a lot of dust particles in the beam from my flashlight, and it made it difficult to see clearly.

The wind changed directions, and I gagged on the smell that shot up my nose and down my throat. As my eyes watered, I focused in on what looked like a pile of dead bodies against the far wall. Arms and legs seemed to be oddly out of place with the torsos like they'd been thrown about. Between that vision and the sound of the flies, I was shot right back to my first night in Nam.

Focus.

Then I spotted the chains, I moved the light farther down and saw the tops of handcuffs, but because of the angle I couldn't see anything else.

Shit.

I signaled to Zack I was about to climb down. He lowered, and I hopped off.

"Well?" he asked.

I fought the urge to gag again and leaned against the wall and swallowed hard a couple times. I knew what we needed to do.

"I didn't see any Cartel in there. I couldn't see anyone alive either. I didn't get eyes on our subject, but he could be directly below where I was. We'll need to get a better look to know for sure."

"Copy that." Frank eyed me, and without me saying it, knew we were about to face something bad.

Slowly, we made it around the building to the door. I quickly checked in with Team Tracker, who stood the ready to move in if need be.

"Blackstone One to Tracker One, do you copy?"

"Ten-four, Blackstone, we hear you loud and clear."

"We are entering the building on the south entrance."

"Copy that."

I used my fingers to count down, then we slipped inside and were hit with what could only be described as a human landfill. We quickly broke cigarettes in half and stuck them up our noses, the filters helped with the smell of rotting flesh. We waded across the tacky floor and tried to ignore the buzz of the insects who all wanted a turn to eat. It explained why the marble hadn't rolled. Ray used the toe of his boot to slide a severed leg out of his way as he led us over to the window I'd used earlier.

"Sick sons of bitches," Frank muttered and moved to my right with his gun held high.

Countless dead eyes stared up at us with a silent plea to be returned home for a proper burial.

"If one of them blinks," Zack hissed, "I'm out."

"Focus," I whispered and scanned the dark corners not touched by our light. I slipped into the mindset of someone being hunted. Where would I hide, and when would I shoot?

We moved slow and steady. Even our breaths were in unison, and I swore we shared one heartbeat. Voices filled my head when I took in the lifeless faces. What did they do to deserve such a ruthless, violent death? I made the mistake of focusing on them too long and spotted a woman who must have only been in her twenties. She had bruises all up and down her legs and arms. I squeezed my eyes shut and fought the urge to curse loudly.

"Don't carry it," Zack reminded me, and I opened my eyes and pushed the thoughts aside.

Finally, we made it through the body maze and came up to the pipe that held the handcuffs.

"Dammit," Zack cursed when he shone his light on the handcuffs. All that was left was a hand that was severed just above the wrist, the hand only had three fingers left on it, "where's the rest of him?"

"I think right there." Ray moved his flashlight to a mangled heap of a man without a hand.

I dropped to my knees and searched his jacket, but it was picked clean. His face was unrecognizable, but his expensive suit told me the chances were high that this was our subject.

"Frank, fingerprint the hand. I'll do this hand to see if they belong to one another."

"Copy that," he pulled out his kit and did as he was told. I did the same, pressing the cold fingers into the ink and onto the paper. Just as we finished, I heard my father's voice.

"Tracker One to Blackstone One, you have company. South entrance."

Our flashlights went out in unison, and Frank and Ray moved quickly to get between some racks while Zack and I pressed ourselves against the wall behind a group of oil barrels. I didn't want to think what might be inside of them.

I eased to my knees and craned my neck to see four men came into view. Each held a flashlight. One yelled in Spanish to look for the body. I clicked my radio four times indicating how many men were there.

We watched in horror as they used machetes to clear their paths through the bodies like they were just brush in a forest. The smell didn't seem to bother them as they kicked, slashed, and tossed human remains around, cursing at the mess. They were savages.

"*Él está aquí!*" the ringleader shouted as he flicked his rifle butt against the handcuff that hung above the body we had just fingerprinted. The other guy picked up the hand from where it had dropped and held it up and waved it around. "*Moverlo!*" He ordered the others to move the body but suddenly stopped the man who held up the hand. He moved closer and shone a light on the fingers, and he saw the ink on the thumb.

Dammit.

He put a finger to his mouth and snapped his fingers for one of them to hand him his gun.

We could take them. I had no doubt about that, but where there were four cockroaches, there were a billion more waiting to disperse. The last thing we needed was to out our location. I knew my team would stay put unless I gave a signal, so as the ringleader unknowingly approached us, I slowly slid my knife from its sheath, and Zack did the same. If we were going to add to the body count, we were going to do it silently. Frank and Ray would back us up with their weapons, ready to kill quickly if I gave the sign.

"Who's in my house?" the guy spat in broken English then laughed like he got a sick high from the situation. "We were wondering when you were going to come. We found your informant." I closed my eyes for a second, wondering which informant they'd killed. "Do you feel that?" he asked his buddy in Spanish. "That's warm American blood."

"Soldier blood." His buddy laughed.

"Our blood now." The ringleader's steps came closer as we pressed ourselves lower and slid deeper between the barrels. As he got close, his light caught the toe of my boot, and I steadied my breath and waited for the bullets to rain down.

Nothing.

"You think you can come onto our land and stop what we do?" He stopped right next to me, and my fingers flexed on the handle of my knife as I lifted my arm. "You have no idea how big we really are."

Slowly, I inched my weight to my hip, drew my legs upward, and was just about to pounce when a flash of light tore through the holes in the cardboard on the window and was followed by an ear-shattering bang. As someone who had used that tactic before, I knew it was team Tracker creating a distraction. I jumped to my feet with a shout and rammed the knife into the ringleader's neck. Frank shot two bullets over my shoulder, and Zack shot two from between the barrels.

"Move!" Ray yelled as we headed for the door. It wouldn't be long before the police or other Cartels arrived. Frank took the corner hard and lost his footing and landed on a pile of bodies. I didn't think as I hooked my arm on his vest and scooped him up as I raced by. We untangled from each other as we slipped outside and raced in the opposite direction from the way we'd arrived. Sirens and squealing tires could be heard as lights suddenly lit up the side streets. They helped to alert us of where not to go. Suddenly, one of our Broncos pulled up next to us and our hired driver waved for us to get in. Once inside, he tore off down the street. I caught an occasional glimpse of another car that held some of Dad's men.

"Everyone good?" I tugged at my vest, feeling restricted as my chest pumped with adrenaline.

"Yeah! Whoo, man, did I miss the action." Ray laughed more out of relief than anything else. We joined in as we relished the old feeling of living on the edge. However, it was short lived as we settled in and mulled over what our new enemy was capable of. Silence once again filled the steel box on wheels, and we zoned out as we processed the nightmare we'd just walked in on.

"They're ruthless," Zack murmured as he stared out the window. "If darkness had a home, it was that warehouse."

"Agreed." Frank nodded from the front seat. He sounded a million miles away. "Given the number of Cartel members and how quickly it's growing, this could get out of hand real fast if the US isn't ready."

"That's why we're here, to let them know we aren't to be played with." I felt a whole new surge of anger flush through me.

An hour later, we were out of the city and in a field where we met up with Team Tracker. Dad's face slipped a little when he saw me, and I knew he'd been worried, even though we checked in.

"Thanks for the distraction." I slapped his shoulder.

"More of them were coming our way. I'm not sure if they had a chance to let them know you were there. There wasn't much time."

"I didn't see any radios, but that doesn't mean anything."

"Well, what did you see?" His team gathered around us as we quickly filled them in on what happened.

"Do we have any new information on where our possible mark would be?" I hated the idea to go home and potentially leave our mark in the hands of these savages.

"No, which leads me to believe you boys found him."

"Maybe we wait out the night and—"

"Our orders are to return to the US." My father stepped closer. "Trust me, son, when that sun rises, and we lose the protection of the night, we'll be sitting ducks. Our mission is to get in and get out."

"Understood." He was right.

"Let's go back home and get those prints off to Washington. We'll soon know whether or not it's him," Dad advised.

We piled into the cars and headed out. I wondered just what we'd set in motion on this night. Clearly, they'd found our informant and knew we were coming. I couldn't help but feel like we'd just kicked the world's most dangerous hornets' nest.

"Frank, you friggin' stink." Zack coughed and plugged his nose, and I smirked as I remembered what Dr. Roberts had said. *See the humor where you can.*

CHAPTER THIRTEEN

Daniel

We returned home to Shadows after the assignment, and after such a short, intense trip, it did wonders for my head. If this was how it was going to be, I knew I could do this job and do it well.

"Are you all back in one piece?" Mom called as she raced over to the helicopter as soon as the engine was cut. The wind whirled her hair around her head as she peered in the door, but she didn't care. She needed to know.

"We are." I hugged her quickly and made sure she saw Dad was fine, too. She made her rounds and inspected each one of us as we stepped out of the chopper. We were all her own. Of course, Zack ate up the attention and wrapped an arm around her shoulders as we walked down toward the house together. I noticed all of us tapped the spot where our team's name and date were etched into the chopper.

"It was dicey, but we were well prepared and will be even more so the next time we leave." Zack filled her in. He knew Mom loved to know all the details.

The moment I got inside, I dropped my bag and raced off

toward my office. Frank's teasing voice about my being whipped by a woman could be heard behind me. I didn't care if I was or not. I kept my promises.

I dialed her number twice, as the first time my mind and my fingers refused to work together as one.

"Hello?"

"Hey, baby."

"You're home?"

"I am."

"Oh." She went quiet, and I could tell by her sniff that she was relieved. "When did you get back?"

"About six minutes ago." I caught my smile as it reflected back at me from the window. I looked like a kid about to open a gift at Christmas. "And it takes six minutes to cross the property and head straight inside the house to call you."

"You sure know how to make a girl feel special."

"That's the plan, Sue. I want to make you feel special every day from now on." I tapped my finger against the receiver as I soaked up her happy chuckle. "I want to see you."

"I want to see you, too."

"I need to do a few things here, but I'd like to spend the night with you. Are you all right with that?"

"More than all right. I'll leave the key under the red flowerpot, so if you run late, you can just come in." She paused. "You'll know where to find me." My chest burst with happiness and anticipation. I had never been this happy with anyone before. She was everything to me.

"I won't be late, so be ready because I'm about to show you how much I missed you."

I hung up and raced up stairs to shower and was on my way once I hugged Mom and declined dinner with the family. She just smiled and waved me off with a laugh.

An hour later, I gently pulled back the blankets and

slipped underneath to wrap my arms around the most precious thing I've ever cared about. I felt my love for her fill me and did my best to show her without words.

The next day, after I dropped Sue off at work, I drove to the new packing and shipping store that had just opened in Redstone. We'd been expecting a shipment of fatigues, and Dad had just gotten word they'd arrived. He called Sue's house and asked me to pick them up before I came home. I removed my hat as I stepped inside.

"Hi, Ezra," I greeted the owner as I inspected the place. "I hear there's a package for me."

"Yes, it arrived last night." He disappeared out back and returned a moment later with the box. "I just need your signature there and there." He pointed to the blank lines.

"All right." I scribbled my name. "What's been new with you?"

"I asked Pamela to marry me." He grinned, and I shuddered. Pamela was definitely not my kind of woman. She flirted with any male who so much as looked in her direction and always had her breasts on display. It was darn hard not to look down at them.

"That's nice, Ezra. Congratulations."

"Thanks. We're excited to start a family as soon as possible." He wiggled his brows, and I again shuddered at the thought of their offspring.

"I hope the best for you." I forced a smile.

"Did you hear the latest news?" He changed the subject when I turned to leave.

"What news is that?"

"Did you hear Wayde got himself in some hot water? Figured as he was in Nam with you, you might have already heard about it."

"Nope." I answered, but I turned back to hear what he had

to say. I always wondered if he would find trouble once he was home.

"He was on the news." Ezra practically rubbed his hands together.

"It's Redstone, Ezra. Even a cat makes it on the news." I let my tongue drip with sarcasm. "What happened?"

"Wayde was arrested. They showed the police putting him in a patrol car. Guess he assaulted someone at a bar."

It was only a matter of time before Wayde spun out too far, but I was glad he was in jail and not six feet below. He needed help, and it really brought it home to me again how many guys went off to fight then came home in a mental mess and were left to fend for themselves. It made the job we were doing at Shadows that much more important and urgent.

"I'm sorry to hear that, but I think it needed to happen."

"He's crazy, is what he is." Ezra shook his head. "I know you guys saw stuff over there, but bringing it back here and messing with the folks in town isn't okay."

I swallowed back the lash that was about to leap off my tongue. No one could know unless they'd been there.

"Well, some of us weren't lucky enough to escape the draft." I gave him a pointed look to show I knew he'd got an exemption because of a bum knee. "Some of us saw things that will forever warp our minds. It's just a shame we didn't have any support from you all when we returned home."

"He's better behind bars," he grunted and ignored what I said.

"Let's hope." I gave him a polite smile, tucked the box under my arm, and headed back to my truck.

When I got back to the house that afternoon, the delicious smell of chicken pot pie drew me toward the kitchen. I dropped the package on the counter and breathed deeply. My stomach was going to have a real treat tonight.

Shadows

"I'll look after these." Mom picked up the box, and I grinned and rubbed my belly as I looked toward the oven. She laughed and let me know it would be ready soon.

As I neared my father's office, I could hear his disappointed voice, and I slowed as I got close to his door. I heard him say goodbye, then he pushed back his squeaky chair.

"Dad?" I eased the door open and took in his perplexed expression. "Is everything all right?"

"Hey, son, I didn't realize you were home. How's our Sue?"

"She's good. She's glad I'm back." I couldn't help but feel warmed by that. I never thought about finding love before I met her, and now it had become wonderfully consuming. "She's a lovely distraction with everything else going on."

"I get that." The corners of his mouth rose, and I knew he was thinking of Mom. "I'm happy you have that."

"Me too." I waited a beat to allow him a moment, but now that we'd gotten the small talk out of the way, it was time to get down to business. "What's going on, Dad?"

"Did you pick up that package?"

I stared at him for a second and noticed he avoided eye contact. "Yeah, the fatigues are being washed as we speak."

"Good, good." He ran a hand over his mouth, and I was more than curious to know who was on the phone.

"Dad," this time he looked over at me, "you said this house was mine to run. If there's something going on, I can handle it."

"I know you can." He rubbed his face. "I just wish it had turned out differently for us the first time out."

"Oh." I realized what happened. "Why don't you fill me in, and then I'll call a meeting to let the guys know." He smiled at me, and I leaned my head slightly to stretch the cords in my neck. "What are you thinking?"

"You just never cease to amaze me." He handed me the file and took me through what he knew.

Thirty minutes later, Blackstone and Tracker were gathered in the conference room, and I started the meeting. "Okay, men, I'm not going to sugar coat this. It isn't how the Army operates, and it isn't how we're going to run things here either." I took a moment to let it sink in. They already knew the news wasn't going to be good.

"The results came back from Washington. Thankfully, his prints were already in the system, which made everything much easier. Unfortunately, the man with the severed hand was indeed Tod Thomas, South Carolina's politician, a.k.a. our mark." The room stayed silent as we took a moment for Mr. Thomas; at the very least, he deserved that. "If we can take anything away from this, it would be that we gave his family closure."

Frank cleared his throat. "What now?"

"Now we wait for our next call, and we go in even better prepared than before. Every mission we come back from, we'll analyze. We'll learn from our mistakes and grow from the things we did right." I took a breath and looked around at their faces. I made eye contact with each one. "I wish our first mission had gone better, but it's the reality that they won't always go the way we planned. We need to put this one behind us and move on."

They all nodded, and I pushed aside the file. We were all in this together, and I knew each man would spend time mentally going through everything again and again.

Zack spoke up. "Something we could work on is our response time from when we get the call to when we actually ship out."

"Yeah, I think we should always be on call." Ray joined in. "Maybe have a bag packed that stays in our closet and have gear stored closer to the chopper pad so we aren't having to haul it up the hill?"

"That would improve our time by about thirty percent. Maybe we could put up a small building near the pad. With hooks and lockers for each man." Frank started to scribble on some paper, and I saw his brilliant mind start to take off.

"We need to find out how they made our informant," Frank added. "That should be priority number one."

"Our contact in Washington is on that."

A few of Tracker's men had some good insight as well, and as the guys collaborated, I felt the pride build inside me. I glanced at Dad, and he gave me a nod then he slipped out of the room. This was what we needed, to talk things out, to give every man a chance to give his input no matter how small, to learn and to let go so we could move on. That was what would give us the mental strength to continue to do our job well. We spent the next few hours tweaking the mission and came up with more productive ways to cut down on time.

I was mentally and physically exhausted but happy with everything by the time we all headed to the kitchen for that pot pie. It was all I'd hoped it would be. I enjoyed the talk around the table as the guys made sure they kept things on a positive note and fired off lots of compliments for the cook. Mom took a bow, as it was a family recipe and she loved nothing more than to share it with all of us. She laughed with everyone as she took the credit, and her smile beamed brightly as each plate was mopped clean with her homemade rolls. After managing a big slice of mom's chocolate cake, a few buttons were loosened and groans of appreciation could be heard around the table as the plates were pushed back.

"Mrs. Logan, that was indeed a meal that would do any man's mama proud." Zack rubbed his belly with a sigh.

"Get away with you, Zack." Mama blushed as she shooed us all from the kitchen.

Later, on my way up the stairs to my room, my mind went back to the previous night with Sue. I couldn't help but wish she was on my bed right now waiting for me. I grinned as I opened the door then stopped short when I noticed a familiar red box sitting on my bed where I'd wished Sue would be. I went over and picked it up then turned and sank onto the bed. Memories of how much I had loved my Nan flooded through me as I ran my fingers over her small memory box. She'd been a real feisty woman with lots of good advice to give, whether you wanted it or not. I chuckled out loud at the thought. She'd fallen ill way too early in her life and had left us within only a few days.

I lifted the lid to find not the expected little trinkets and pieces of memorabilia Nan used to keep inside but another even smaller box. It held Nan's simple gold wedding band, and her engagement ring lay next to it with a traditional round cut diamond on top. I could tell it had been buffed and polished and made ready to be worn by someone special.

"She would have wanted you to have that," Dad said from the doorway. "Life tosses us some highs and a lot of lows, but when you least expect it, it'll surprise you with the greatest gift of all, love. Whenever you're ready, your mom and I will welcome that wonderful woman into our family with open arms and love her like our own." He smiled warmly, and I wondered if Mom was around the corner, listening.

"This means," I cleared my throat of emotion, "everything, Dad, but how do I make it work? I want to ask her, but I can't figure out how we'd do it. Do we live in separate houses? Do I disappear for days at a time and just expect her to live with my absences without proper explanation?"

He came farther into the room and rested his weight against my dresser. "I wanted all this for you, but I sure never intended it to become an obstacle when it came to love. There are always ways around these things, though. Perhaps it's worth asking her and just see where it takes you. She's been great about everything up to this point."

"She has, but if we get engaged or married, now suddenly it's like a deal breaker." I shook my head with all that brought me.

"Okay." He stood and put a finger to his chin. "She knows you work for the Army, correct?" I nodded. "Well, why not give her something? Why don't you share that you work for the Army and you sometimes have to leave on highly classified missions? Missions that you aren't allowed to talk about. If she can accept that, it might be enough for her to understand that it's your career."

"Maybe?" Sue was an understanding person, but I wasn't sure just how understanding she would be when it came to our building a life together while I disappeared for days at a time without much notice.

"I could talk to her as well and assure her that what you say is the truth."

"That might help, yes."

"Well, that aside, the one and only thing I do suggest is you ask her father for his blessing. I've always said that respect for family is key, and so is consistent communication. I know it seems like a dilemma when you can't tell her about your missions, but in every other aspect of your life, it's key."

"Thanks, Dad, and I certainly planned to talk to her father first."

"Good, so, go plan something romantic, and when you're ready, go get your wife."

"Wife," I echoed, and something shifted inside that assured me this was what I needed to do.

CHAPTER FOURTEEN

GENERAL EDISON LOGAN

I held Meg's hand as we walked through the house. We stopped to admire the mantel that still needed a second coat of paint. We hoped it would one day hold pictures of generations of soldiers who wanted to make a difference in the world, even if living here meant they'd have to accept the biggest sacrifice of all. If Shadows was to be a safe haven, it had to remain a secret. An oath of trust and loyalty would have to be taken by all who came here.

Meg filled me in on her phone call with Dan. "He picked her up from work and told her he had made dinner plans for the two of them. She had no idea where they were going until he turned down the old road behind our house. I guess she was speechless when he parked on the edge of the field and she spotted the picnic he'd set up under the tree where they first met." Her voice grew more excited. "He got down on one knee, opened the red box, and explained how he sees the world now and can't imagine another day without her in it, with him." She paused to gather herself while I smiled to know that we'd raised quite the gentleman. "Of course, he followed that up with the fact that her father had already given his blessing, that seemed to woo her further." She jiggled her head. "Of course, she said yes! Oh, then she kissed him, and they enjoyed a beautiful, yet chilly evening together." She laughed.

"That's great to hear." I let out a happy sigh of relief and allowed my mind a moment to wonder about the grandbabies who might be in our future.

"It is. But, Edison, I'm worried the arrangement they have won't be enough." She turned to face me straight on. "When you came up with this idea, it was a good one, but we didn't think far enough ahead. Yes, we gave our son and the boys something to live for, but part of living is finding love. They're all good men who will make wonderful husbands one day, but being a part of this house eliminates them from having it all." She placed a hand on my chest. "I think we should bend the rules for Dan's sake and let Sue in on what's happening here. He's the first one to find love, so I think we'll have to let him be our trial run. These boys are our future, too, and they all need to be a part of the decision. This all needs to be addressed so everyone fully understands the situation."

"You're right." I covered her hand with mine. "We need to have a serious discussion with everyone and figure it out as a family."

"We only want what's best for them."

"We do." I tucked her under my arm.

"It really is stunning here, Ed." She wrapped her arm around my waist as we looked out over the property, admiring the fresh snow-capped mountains and the lake below.

"Then why do you sound melancholy?"

"Because our son is engaged to be married, and I only hope she'll be able to deal with such a big secret."

"She's strong, my love." I hugged her to my side then leaned down and kissed the top of her head. I knew what she was feeling because I'd felt it many times myself. We got our boy back, and we wanted only the best for him.

I promised her I would deal with it, and that was just what I did.

I made some calls and had both teams gather around the conference table a short time later. I knew they were wondering why I had called a meeting without Daniel present.

"Before you start," Ray held up a hand, "and for my mental health, can you tell me if this is about the Cartels or not."

"It's not. This is about Daniel," I reassured him with a smile and watched his shoulders sag with relief. "I won't drag this out, mainly because I need to be on the road to town here shortly. I think it's fair to say that Daniel is in a really good place." Everyone nodded. "He's gone over and above to make sure we have everything we could possibly need."

"Question?" Zack held up a hand. "Is this about Sue and Daniel?"

"Ah." I was caught off guard. "Yeah, it is, actually."

"I can save you the time and let you know we get it and think she should move in here. We were talking the other night," he pointed to Ray and Frank, "and if anyone deserves to have a wife move in, its him."

"Yeah, she's really good people, and I think she could bring a lot to the house." Frank played with a pencil.

"I'm pleased you feel that way, but what about the rest of you?"

"I'm in no hurry to find someone." Zack shrugged. "I want to do this and keep working toward getting my restaurant off the ground."

"Ray?" I raised an eyebrow at him.

"I'm way too messed up to be getting involved with a woman." His honesty showed on his face, and I was happy to hear it.

"Frank?"

"Truth," he looked around the room, "I don't see myself being a lifer here. I have plans to someday work at military headquarters in Washington, but until that day comes when my knees are tired and my back is fried, I'll be here chasing tail, but nothing serious."

"What about Heather?" Zack piped in.

"She's focused on her schooling." He shrugged. "Time will tell, but if that day comes, I'll be fine to step away."

"Agreed, Edison," Zack nodded, "if or when I find someone, I'll be okay moving on. This is great for now, but we only have one set of joints, and I can feel mine already." He laughed.

"I hear ya on that," I laughed, "and I get it." I rubbed my shoulder and thought about how much I hated it when it rained here.

"Daniel's different." Frank tossed the pencil back in the cup. "He's a lifer. He should start his family here. Lord knows, poor Meg could use some female company."

"All right, then." I couldn't contain my happiness. "You're all good men." I nodded at them then gave a wave, checked my watch, and headed upstairs for my keys. I had somewhere special to be.

With a lightness in my chest, I drove down the mountain road thinking about the changes that were to come. I parked in my normal spot and waved at a neighbor as they bumped passing by. Patty's place was quiet, as the Sunday lunch rush was over. It made it easy to spot Sue where she sat in the corner of the restaurant nursing a glass of soda.

"Good morning, Ed." She leaned in and gave me a hug. I loved that she treated me like family already. I always wondered what it would have been like if I'd had a daughter of my own. I guessed now I kind of did.

"Hey, thanks for agreeing to meet me."

"Of course." She smiled as she watched me remove my jacket and waited patiently while I gave my order to the waitress and took a moment to ask how her day was going. "I bet you're wondering why I'm here." I gave Sue my full attention.

"Is it something to do with Daniel's birthday or the fact that he proposed so soon?" She smiled.

I chuckled and thought she wasn't so far off the mark.

"One thing you should know about us Logans, we have a history of long, happy lives with our spouses." I poured some sugar in my coffee and stirred it absently. "Also that it takes only one look for us to know." I tapped my heart.

Her eyes widened as she fiddled with the diamond that used to sit on my mother's finger.

"That's incredibly romantic."

"We do have a certain level of charm." I winked and made her laugh.

"That you do. So, then, why are you here?"

"The fact that you said yes means that Daniel shared the details about his career with you and you accepted all that comes with that."

"Yes, there'll certainly be a lot of challenges, but I know we can make it work." She lifted her chin as if I was challenging her on something. I placed my hand on hers, and she settled.

"Sue, we couldn't be happier about you marrying Dan. You know that. Anyway, Meg and I have made a rather large decision. We feel it's only right that you two get a proper chance at a real life together, and the only way to do that is have you move in with him, at the safehouse." I stopped and waited for her to question my words, but her face never changed.

"You mean Shadows?"

"Ah, yes." *What?* "Did Daniel tell you about that?"

"Not really. No." She shook her head. "Ed, your son doesn't sleep well. He often talks or even yells in his sleep."

"He struggles a lot," I muttered and thought about how many people were plagued with the horrors of what they'd seen over there. They still had so much in their heads long after they came back from war. Even though Daniel was getting help now, I knew it could take a long time and a lot of help to ever be free of it. I only prayed that one day it would go away completely.

"I know Shadows is a secret, and I think I can imagine why. I love your son, and I plan on spending a long, happy life with him, too."

I eyed her over my mug, completely flabbergasted with this amazing young woman. My son had made an excellent choice. The fact that she had never breathed a word about Shadows to anyone meant a lot.

"How long have you known?"

"Since he was attacked at the grocery store. I believe those hippies may have triggered something in him."

"How much do you know?"

She leaned her arms on the table and looked at me dead in the eye. "How much do you want me to know?"

"You're spending way too much time with Meg."

She tossed her head back and laughed.

"My mother-in-law to be and I are a lot alike." She took a moment, and her face grew serious. "I know enough to understand that if anything got out it would be incredibly dangerous for all of you. As much as I appreciate Dan's need for secrecy, it means a lot that you would bring me in and allow me to be a part of it."

"We welcome you with open arms, Sue, but there's one thing I need you to know before we decide what comes next."

"Of course. What's that?"

"Do you know who we're fighting?"

"Someone in Mexico?"

Wow, Daniel really did talk a lot in his sleep.

"Have you heard of the Mexican Cartel?" Her face dropped, which proved she had. "So, you know what we're doing is very dangerous." She nodded, so I went on and filled her in on a few things to make sure she knew the risks. "So, the people we're fighting with can cross our borders at any time and without anyone being aware of it." I didn't want to scare her, but she needed to see the whole picture. "So that means if you're going to live at Shadows, you could be considered a target. Can you live with the fact that you might need to follow rules, maybe have an escort at times, and live in a house buzzing with soldiers? It's rarely quiet, and there aren't many women. There's still a lot we'll have to figure out."

She fiddled with the sugar packet while she thought. I wished I could see inside her head to know if I'd gone too far. Maybe it was too soon to bring up something like this. I began to sweat and tugged at my collar.

"I've got a pretty good head on my shoulders," she finally said. "I graduated top of my class. Who knows, maybe I could be of use to you."

"Oh, my dear." I grinned with delight and knew she'd fit right in with the rest of us. I could only have hoped she'd take me up on an offer to work at Shadows full time. "I'm one step ahead of you on that one."

"Good." She seemed to like that comment. "Are you and Meg thinking of moving in at Shadows, too?"

"No, we couldn't leave our farm and animals, but we'll be there a lot."

Shadows

After breakfast, I called Meg to get Daniel to the house, and we headed in that direction with a fun little plan to let everyone in on the news that we were about to break rule number one.

The Army had engrained in me that rules were meant to be followed, but there was an equally strong pull in me that my son deserved this.

"I thought this land was being developed for some bigshot millionaire guy." She leaned forward to see out the windshield.

"That's the story we planted when people started asking questions. We knew the build would be widely seen, so we had to come up with a cover story."

"Wow, well, if it counts for anything, it worked." She chuckled. "No one so much as blinked an eye at it."

"The back road on the other side of the mountain helped, too." I figured I could start filling in some gaps for her since she was part of it now. "There are three checkpoints. This is the first one." I showed my ID and was waved in. "We have security throughout the entire property and sensors in places we don't. I'll let Daniel fill you in on the rest, but I do have one last thing I'd like to go over."

"Of course." She turned to give her attention to me.

"This whole thing is somewhat new to us, too, so if you see anything that could be improved or if someone steps over a line, you must tell one of us. Communication is key here."

"You have my word." Her face was a picture of amazement as I pulled into the roundabout driveway in front of the massive safehouse.

"Ready on my signal?"

"I am."

"Be right back."

I jogged inside and found Daniel in the kitchen.

"Dear God," he boomed, "this is the biggest fridge I've ever seen. Have you really stopped and studied how far back it actually goes? I know there's pickles in there somewhere." He reached behind him. "Someone hand me a ladder. I'm going in."

"I picked it out myself." I chuckled. "Dan?"

"Dad, I hope I'm not the one who has to grocery shop for that thing." I nodded absently at him. I was glad to see he was wearing the new fatigues we'd bought. The ones we had were quite ratty. "Maybe we should start a rotation of us guys to do it," he continued. "Maybe only have to do it every other month. I know I have a hard enough time just finding the baking soda in a store, let alone—"

"Dan," I said louder and caught his attention, "I want you to know I did something."

"Okay." He closed the fridge door, folded his arms, and looked at me.

"I've never broken a military rule before, but in fairness, you broke it first." I couldn't help but smirk at my blame game.

"What?"

"If you're going to start a new life with someone, you need to do it right. You deserve it."

"I'm having trouble following you here, Dad."

I took him by the shoulders and walked him out front. As I gave a wave to the car, Sue opened the door and stepped out.

"Hey, you."

"Oh, my God." He shook his head at me, no doubt trying to understand what was happening. "How...I mean, why? Dad." He raked a hand though his hair. "What will the guys think?"

"We had a meeting. They understood and feel the same

way, that she should be here. You've proven time and time again you're a leader, so be the leader of your family too."

"Co-leader." Sue lifted an eyebrow at me.

"Co-leaders. Forgive me, dear," I corrected myself. "But." I held up a finger. "This is a one-time thing, not something that will happen again. The guys have agreed that when love comes into the picture for them, they'll step away from Shadows. They can choose to stay on, but they can't live here at the house. I can't see how this business and family can co-exist. Add in a bunch of little ones running around…" I rolled my eyes and laughed.

"You sure about this?" Daniel took her hand. "This is a huge secret and will be a big change in your life."

"It is, and maybe I would be a little more apprehensive if I hadn't known about Shadows for quite some time now."

"Wait, how?"

"You talk in your sleep."

"I do?"

"Mmhm." She chuckled. "It's why I know you love your goats so much, too."

"Hey, they're cute, and they don't judge. Unlike the chickens."

They both laughed, and he picked up Sue and gave her a big kiss while I reached for my keys to give them some privacy to explore the house together.

CHAPTER FIFTEEN

Several months later
D<small>ANIEL</small>

Sue's wedding dress flowed like a fountain and puddled at her feet in what Mom described as a Casablanca fit. I had zero idea what that meant, but I didn't care one bit. All I knew was that when she stepped through the doors and began to come up the aisle, my heart stopped and I couldn't swallow.

The music started, and the guests got to their feet while I stayed focused on her. Her arm was linked with her father's as they slowly made their way toward me. I vaguely felt Zack bump my arm to snap out of the trance I was in as she approached.

My soon to be wife stopped in front of me and looked up with the most gorgeous smile I'd ever seen on her face. What I saw in her eyes was my own love for her reflected right back at me.

They said you should stop and take a moment during your wedding to soak up the memories, so that was just what I did. I stopped to admire her. I knew that kind of rare beauty and pure heart was impossible to find, let alone capture. Sue had that and more, and she was about to be mine.

I looked at the wildflowers that sprang up from her bouquet. The pretty pinks and greens really stood out against the stark white of her gown. I knew how much she loved pink, and it made me smile as I brought my eyes to those soft pink lips of hers as she smiled up at me.

Her gaze stayed on mine as a lovely blush came over her cheeks, and the tip of her tongue ran over those lips, and I had to clear my throat to stop my grin from spreading. If I was to die in this moment, I would die a lucky man.

She settled herself on the platform next to me. Our fingers linked, and I gave her hand a squeeze. She squeezed mine back then gently pulled her hand away to hold her bouquet.

"That's a change from the fatigues." She chuckled quietly.

"Some things are worth the discomfort." I smiled, and we turned our attention to the minister.

We listened to his words, we agreed, and once we exchanged the rings, I barely waited for permission as I leaned in, wrapped my arms around her, and drew her warm lips to mine. We had kept it short and skipped on writing vows. Neither of us wanted this part to be long. It was hard not to let loose and show her just how excited I was that she was mine. I managed to behave and gave her a long, simple, closed-mouth kiss. The rest had to wait for later.

"Oh, my goodness, we did it!" She squealed as we waved and mouthed a thank you to everyone.

"We did."

Everyone clapped as we walked down the aisle hand in hand. Rice was tossed at us as we descended the stairs, and I helped her into the town car my father had provided for us.

We waved happily at our family and friends as the driver pulled away from the curb.

I wrapped my arms around my wife and stared down at her.

"Well, you behaved." She laughed and grabbed my lapels to pull me in for another kiss. "Let's say we skip out on the party and just jump right into the honeymoon."

"God, I love you!" I kissed her again and then sat back with a deep, happy sigh.

"Dammit, Logan," Zack caught me as we came into the reception room, "why'd you have to keep it in your pants! I just lost twenty bucks."

"Bet him again. Say I won't last the dinner."

"Really?"

"Really." I smirked at Frank and shook my head. He tilted his beer at me.

"Thanks for the twenty." He chuckled.

"You guys are comical." Sue rolled her eyes playfully but soon was swept up in the decor that Mom had done. It was all about wildflowers. The same colors from her bouquet were used on every table, and there was even a sprinkle of petals around the edges of the dance floor. Mom kept it simple but gorgeous, just like Sue wanted.

We lasted a whole forty-five minutes after dinner before I danced her out the door. I figured everyone was having too good of a time to even notice we'd left. Everyone but Zack, who flipped me the finger as Frank collected his cash.

We made it to the stairs before Mom and Dad caught us. They stepped out in front of us, grinning like they'd known our plan all along.

"What gave us away?" Sue laughed holding on to my hand.

"Well," my father rubbed his chin, "like father, like son, hey, Meg?"

"Yes, we pulled that one, too." Mom laughed hard. "Before you go, we want to give you our present."

"Oh?" I thought their present was the wedding they held for us.

"Here." Dad handed me some keys.

"Oh, my God, Dad, what on Earth?" I admired the leather keychain.

"You're married now, and that means grandbabies might soon be on the way," Mom said and patted me on the shoulder.

"You need a family vehicle for around town, and you have your truck for driving these mountain roads back and forth from Shadows," Dad added. "Sue, you will need a car."

Sue gasped. "Ed, no, that's much too expensive."

"It's not, and you need it. Now," he pointed to a 1974 Chrysler Town and Country Wagon with wood grained sides, "I've moved your luggage from your truck to the back of this one. I'll drop your truck off tomorrow."

"Dad, thank you." I couldn't believe it. "Thank you, Mom," I hugged them both, and Sue did the same. We raced off toward the car, and I started the engine and listened to her purr.

Sue ran her hand along the dash, admiring the interior.

"Ready for the rest of our lives?" I shifted the gear in drive.

"Ready!" She grinned at me, and we waved out the window at my parents as we drove down the street toward our weeklong honeymoon.

CHAPTER SIXTEEN

DANIEL

"Daniel?" I turned to find a familiar face smiling back at me. "Daniel Logan, is that you?"

"Trix?" I tucked my keys in my coat pocket and leaned in for a hug. "How are you?"

"I've been great, thanks to you." Her smile wavered. "Seriously, what you did for my brother made all the difference for me. It certainly helped my marriage."

"Ray is the best. He just needed a little help."

"Yeah." She nodded, then her gaze fell to my hand. "I heard you got married. How long's it been?"

"Just over a year."

"Wow," she beamed, "does time ever fly. Doesn't seem that long ago I remember Ray getting the call to ship out."

"Seems like a lifetime ago." I checked my watch and knew I needed to get home. "Sorry for cutting this short, Trix, but I really need to get home."

"Of course. Give baby brother a hug for me."

"I will." I headed back to my truck and drove home. Home. I still loved the sound of that.

A few months ago, we were granted another wonderful addition to our lives. Sue found out she was pregnant. We soon made the decision to buy a home of our own, outside of Shadows. We wanted a chance to live like a normal family. With a baby on the way, a secondary home just made sense, as life at Shadows was far from the way we had both grown up.

"Honey, I'm home." I chuckled as I closed the door to our new house and breathed in the smell of freshly baked cookies. I hooked my coat on the tree rack in the hall and kicked my boots off on the mat. We'd closed on our house three weeks before, and Sue had worked hard on making it homey ever since.

Mom called it *nesting*. It was something to do with her being pregnant. Whatever it was, I was glad it involved yummy cooking. My stomach grumbled as I went into the kitchen to find a stack of chocolate chip cookies on the counter. Two bites later, the cookie was gone, so I went in for a second. I knew I'd burned off enough calories that day that I could eat the entire stack. We'd run drills up and down the mountain until my legs ached.

"I thought I heard you." Sue waddled into the kitchen with a heavy load of laundry.

"Whoa!" I quickly took the basket from her and sat her in a chair. "Sue, you can't be carrying things this heavy." I poured her a glass of water and took in her sweaty face. "Don't make me send Mom here to supervise you."

"I'm fine." She waved me off, but I was legitimately concerned for her and wondered just what she had been up to during the day when I was gone.

"You're six and a half months pregnant, re-doing a new house, and apparently doing an army load of laundry. You need to be resting."

"We need to be ready for this baby."

"We are ready." I looked around and pointed out that we were more than ready. I was thankful that my team had appeared the week before to set up the nursery. My mom had basically set up the kitchen by herself while Sue had to sit under her watchful eye, and my dad and his team had set up pretty much everything else.

"I just still feel unprepared." She let her emotions show, and I could see she was beyond exhausted and a little nervous.

"Oh, darlin'," I bent down in front of her and took her hands, "even if we aren't totally ready for this, we have so many people who will step in to help. When our baby comes, you're going to be so tired, so you need to rest now. We both do, because I hear there are a lot of sleepless nights ahead of us. Everything will fall into place, I promise." I kissed her fingers, and she let out a heavy sigh. "Now, I'm going to run you a bath, and while you two soak, I'm going to make dinner."

"No, Dan, you worked all day." She stood and put her hands against my chest, and I could feel her belly press against me. I captured her hands, then turned her around and marched her into the bathroom and sat her on the closed toilet seat.

"I promised to take care of you." I turned the water on, pushed the plug in the hole, and poured her favorite bath salts all around. "And that's what I'm doing."

I unzipped her dress as the tub filled then handed her an elastic. She gathered up her hair and tied it on top of her head, then she let me help her into the tub.

"Thank you." She sighed as she slid low into the bubbles so only her belly with its new outie button was above the waterline. I leaned down and smiled at our baby inside, then gave it a kiss.

"You look adorable." I grinned and lit a few candles then turned off the overhead light.

"I'll come get you when dinner's ready."

"Dan?"

"Yeah?" I held on to the handle of the door.

"You asked me what name I'd really like for a boy."

"I did." I smiled, loving that she'd thought some more about it. Up to now, we just couldn't come up with one we both liked.

"What about the name Cole."

"Cole. Cole Logan." I tested the name.

"No." She shook her head, and I looked at her with a question. "Cole Edison Logan."

A smile broke across my lips while I tested the name again.

"I love it."

"I do, too." She rubbed her tummy. "I think we have a Cole in here."

I turned back and sat on the floor next to the tub and reached over to pat her bump.

"So, if it's a boy, Cole, and if it's a girl, Emery." I was happy we had names now; our minds were made up. To me, that was the most important part and made it more real.

"I love you, Dan."

"I love you more." I drew a circle around her belly and rested my head on the side of the tub. Dinner could wait for a few more minutes.

I had to keep a watchful eye on Sue as the months drew on. She was a stubborn mother-to-be and was determined to have everything perfect before the due date. A few times, I tried to get her to sit and relax, but that didn't go over so well. I had to get creative, so I'd make up little tasks that needed to get done, and while she was busy on those, I did the bigger jobs. Even Mom got in on the creativity and often made up reasons Sue needed to go places with her. It was a struggle, but when our baby finally decided to make an appearance, I wanted Sue rested and ready.

CHAPTER SEVENTEEN

DANIEL

Our son Cole was brought home wrapped in a camo blanket given to him by his grandparents. I figured why not. He might as well have a head start, as he was about to grow up in a world that was flooded by all things military. To say I was proud to have a son was an understatement, but there was no doubt in my mind if we'd had a daughter, I wouldn't have changed anything about the way she was raised. The Logans were born leaders and fighters, and I was determined to make sure our son would be brought up the same way.

Little did I know how friggin' stubborn Private Cole would be. *Sue Junior, for sure.*

"Sue! Suuuuuuue," I called out. I knew she was somewhere in the house laughing at me. "He hates the peas. I mean, I don't blame him. They're nasty, but he *really* hates the peas."

"He has to eat them."

"Well, his mouth is shut, and he won't let me get the spoon in there!" I shouted over my shoulder and then looked my son dead in the eye and tried to distract him with a funny face. It didn't work. "Listen, Cole," I bent down to his level in the highchair, "I was in Nam. I stayed alive in a jungle for a year, managed to dodge serious diseases, and now I fight savage beasts in the desert. Why can't I get my one-year-old to eat green mush?" I complained loudly in hopes my wife would take pity on me.

He reached for the bowl and knocked it out of my hand with a proud giggle. I glared at Dr. Roberts, who had just come into the room to see what the noise was all about. He often came to visit us since Cole was born. I honestly thought he liked to watch me suffer as I tried to feed my son.

"Can't you reason with him?" I huffed as I stood up to snatch a cloth from the counter. The doc laughed as he sat down and turned a page in his book. "I know you're enjoying this."

"Perhaps." He smirked. "But reasoning with a one-year-old won't do much. I think I'll enjoy my book more in there." He made a show of taking his book to the safety of the den to continue to read.

"I get it." I lowered onto the stool with a huff. "Peas are disgusting."

Cole made a string of noises and nodded.

"I know, but Mom insists, and we don't have a dog here that we can feed them to. Maybe we need a dog." I clapped my hands together. "Sue, Cole and I think we need a dog."

"Come, now." Sue clucked her tongue at us while she threaded an earring on. "Cole can play with the dogs at Shadows where they can't eat his peas." She laughed.

"Yeah, but they're never at the house." I scoffed, wondering how I could convince her. It certainly would help me when her grandmother visited, and I had to eat her meat pie. I quivered at the thought of trying to feed that rubbery steak and kidney concoction to Cole when he was old enough. Lord, I could barely choke it down.

"Abigail will be home soon. She's back from visiting her sister at any moment, and we don't need to look like we can't live without her. You look like you've had a bath in baby food."

"I have been, because your son doesn't want to eat green mush. He wants normal food like a steak or a rack of ribs."

"Yes, that's just what a baby wants." She laughed as Doc Roberts suddenly reappeared now that it was safe. "Doc Roberts, you haven't met Abigail yet. She's coming to spend a few months with us while she deals with her parents' estate. You should stay for dinner."

"Oh, yes, the famous Abigail." He grinned, and I knew we often spoke about her.

We'd met Abby through mutual friends, and when her mom passed, she was here for a while, and then her dad passed, and she knew she'd need more time to deal with everything. We offered for her to come stay with us for as long as she needed so she wouldn't have to drive so far in and out of town.

"I'd love to stay." Doc's eyebrows rose. "Just let me make a quick call to my sister to let her know I won't be joining her for dinner. If you don't mind excusing me for a bit."

"Not at all." Sue loved it when he stayed. He was like family, after all.

I was beyond thankful Abigail was coming back today. She had a real bond with Cole. She was quickly becoming family. I only hoped one of these days she'd decide to stay in Redstone for good.

Cole blew a spit bubble, and I popped it, earning me a belly laugh.

"Are you two done making a mess?" Sue asked with her hands on her hips. I could see the corners of her mouth were in a fight not to go up. When Cole belly laughed, the whole world wanted to join him.

"Yes, for the time being, I think we are." I smiled down at the little stinker. "I can't wait until you have to do this with your own little guy someday."

Sue laughed. "Remind me to give a medal to his wife. She's going to need it with his stubbornness."

"Oh, yes, she'll have to be one in a million to put up with you." I poked his belly and got another giggle.

The doorbell rang, and Sue grabbed a wet tea towel and scrubbed Cole's face then calmly went to answer the door. She glanced back at us before she opened it with a *be good* face on.

"Welcome, Abigail." Sue reached for her bags and motioned her inside. "Wow, that's a lot of bags. How was your trip?"

"Great. June insisted we do some shopping. She loves fashion, so we got lost in those little boutiques in the village. I brought you something." Abigail started to dig in her bag.

"You didn't need to bring me anything."

"Nonsense. There's only so much you can buy for yourself before you grow bored. I wanted to shop for you. Ah, here it is." She pulled out a deep red scarf. "It's cashmere."

"It's so soft," Sue cooed over the present, and I glanced at Cole and wondered how long before he'd get his grubby little hands on it.

"Five minutes before you do damage?" I asked him. "Ten?" He giggled, and I had no doubt he understood me.

"Thank you so much." Sue shot us a look, and I stood a little straighter.

"I'm so glad you like it. Hi, Daniel. How've you been?"

"Great, thanks." I poured her a glass of lemonade and handed it to her with a happy smile. I was really glad she was back. It was perfect because I hated to leave Sue and Cole alone here when I left on a mission, and I knew it could be any day now. Having Abby here for the next few months just felt right.

"Now, where is my little soldier?" Abigail made a beeline toward Cole, who kicked his legs and squealed with delight. "There's my handsome boy." She kissed his head, and I smiled at how much love they had for one another. "Well, I need to get freshened up. There was a man who thought eating spaghetti on an airplane was a wise idea." She made a face and pointed at a stain on her dress. "Please excuse me." She ran up the stairs to get cleaned up.

I smiled at Sue, who had visibly relaxed now that her beloved friend had accepted our invitation to stay. I thought there was a small part of her that believed June would convince her to stay in New York and they'd deal with everything from there. June's job didn't allow her to travel as much as Abby could.

"Glad to have her back, aren't you?" I gave her a hug.

"I sure am. I hope she'll stay awhile." She sighed. "Would you mind taking her bags to her room, Dan?" Sue handed Cole a toy while she started to set the table for dinner.

"That, I can do." I scooped her bags and headed up the stairs and down the hall when I suddenly heard a yelp. I raced into the bedroom but stopped short when I saw the reflection of Doc Roberts' face in the mirror. His eyes were open wide as he stood in front of Abigail, whose towel had fallen to the floor. Thankfully, I couldn't see anything, but the doc sure could.

"I'm so…" he shook his head as he sputtered, "I'm so sorry, I…" He leaned down and grabbed the towel and held it up to shield her. "I had no idea anyone was occupying this room." He turned his head away.

"It's all right." I could hear the humor in her voice. Abigail didn't embarrass easily. It was something I found quite appealing about her. "No harm done." She grinned at the doc's obvious dismay.

I dropped Abigail's bags on the floor and rushed to get out of there. *Nothing better when life hands you pure gold on a silver platter.*

We sat at the dinner table and waited for the doctor to join us. The look on Abigail's face when he took his seat told me she was interested in him. His neck and face were flushed, and he downed about half his water. She licked her lips and gave him a grin as she sipped hers slowly.

Oh, this will be fun.

"Everything looks lovely, Sue," he complimented my wife as he looked down at his plate.

"I hear you two have already met," Sue tried hard not to smile, "but let me make a proper introduction. Doc Roberts, this is my good friend Abigail, who I hope to convince to move here someday. Abigail, this is our friend Dr. Roberts. He's a psychologist and works in the same place as Daniel."

Though Abby was a dear friend, she did not know about Shadows or what happened there. Although Dad had mentioned more than once over the years he'd known Abby that she would prove to be a real asset someday. She was such a whiz when it came to administrative work. That was the one area Sue really needed help with. Whenever Abigail was in Montana and had time, she worked with us on the side doing some strictly non-confidential tasks. It allowed her an opportunity to earn extra cash. Her neat, concise notes and carefully done expense forms complete with numbered receipts had come to Dad's attention after Sue handed in the paperwork. Sue would always mention how invaluable Abigail's help had been, and Dad was confident in Sue's discretion when it came to Shadows. I had it in my mind that Dad wouldn't hesitate to have her vetted for Shadows if we asked.

"Lovely to officially meet you, Abigail," Doc Roberts gave her a quick smile and raised his eyes to hers for a split second.

And here we go...

"Breast?" I asked and watched as his eyes widened. I held up the dish to show what I was referring to. "Or are you more of a thigh guy?"

"Breast is fine." He cleared his throat as I smiled and waited a beat as I saw Abigail press her napkin to her face to hide her smirk.

"Shoot," I huffed, "I dropped my dressing." It took everything in me not to break into laughter. "Doc, would you mind handing me a towel?"

Abigail stared hard at me as I graciously took the tea towel from Doc and refused eye contact, knowing I'd lose it right then and there.

I waited until after dinner for a chance to get in one last jab at the doc. Sue had put the tea tray on the table and placed her homemade brownies next to it.

"Would you like some dessert, Doctor?" she asked, and I went in for the kill.

"I think the doctor's already had his dessert." I beamed at his glare.

"Dan." Sue shot me a look to behave.

"No, thank you, Sue I really should get going." Doc was all flushed, and I gloried in his discomfort. "It was lovely meeting you, Abigail. Daniel, why don't you walk me out?" he said through gritted teeth.

"Certainly." I hopped to my feet then lost it in a fit of laughter as I closed the door behind us.

"You're an ass." He laughed as he rubbed the back of his head. "I can't believe that happened."

"Where I'm just so happy to have witnessed it." I dried a

tear. I could not have asked for a better evening. "At least it was Abby. She's great."

"She's something." He sighed.

"You like her. You know, from what you've seen so far, I mean?" I held up a hand as I convulsed with laughter again. "Sorry, they just keep coming to me." He rolled his eyes and leaned against the porch railing. "I'm sorry, I'm sorry. Okay, look, you and Abby have a lot in common, you know. You're both independent people with no present attachments. She's helped us out with some work now and then, and we're going to ask Dad to consider her being vetted for Shadows. Sue just loves having her here. She's amazing with Cole. Anyway, she'll be around a lot the next few months. Just think about it, see if it's something you might want to pursue. You could just let it happen naturally."

"I'm not good at relationships." He shrugged. "I live through my sister. They're trying to have kids and all that. It's fun for me, but I don't see that kind of life for myself."

"So, just get to know her and go from there."

"Yeah, perhaps."

"It's not like you guys got to second base or anything. Oh, wait, you did." I was having way too much fun.

"It wasn't second base. There wasn't any touching," he corrected me.

"But you did get a good look."

"Goodnight, Dan."

"Night, Doc. Sweet dreams." I chuckled as I walked inside.

"I see Cole is refusing to eat again." Abigail strolled into the kitchen and admired the amazing mess of peas, mashed potatoes, and carrots that was all over the highchair and down the side of the counter.

"Nope, still refuses." I wet the sponge. "I think I'm losing my negotiation skills."

"He just knows if he holds out, you'll give in and give him the good stuff." She smiled then started to fill the dishwasher.

"Leave that, Abby. You've had a long trip. I'm sure you're tired."

"It feels good to help, I need to move, anyway, after all that sitting." She kept cleaning while I scrubbed up the little monster's mess in spite of the fact that I knew tomorrow he'd happily do it all over again.

"Come on, you little bugger. Let's get you off to bed." I unstuck his hands and jimmied him out of the highchair. I saw he had stashed more food in the top edge of his diaper. "On second thought, a good old-fashioned hosing might be in need." I tossed him over my shoulder and headed down the hall. "Night, Abby."

"Night, boys."

The next morning, we woke to Abigail's special brew. The heavenly scent of that coffee wafted down the hall and throughout the house. Once I was showered and dressed, I met Sue in the hall. She plopped Cole in my arms, said he was already fed, then gave me a kiss as she whisked off to have her own shower.

I put him down in the living room and watched him pull himself up against the table. His gummy ring hung from his mouth as he went from the table to a chair without a spill. He smiled around the ring as he looked at me, very pleased that he was able to move about independently. Cole was a baby who could do it all himself, and I could only imagine what he'd be like later on in life.

"Havin' a good morning, aren't ya, my little private?" I scooped him up and kissed his soft cheeks, making him laugh. "We have a big day today, don't we?" I noticed his orange sweatpants and cringed. I listened for the sound of Sue in the shower, then I raced us off to his room and dug around his dresser until I found his dark green cargo pants.

I'd just picked them up the other day, but Sue had yet to put them on him.

"These," I held them up to show him, "are much better than the yucky sweatpants Mom insists you wear for comfort. Cargo is fine until we get you fatigues." I shimmied on the new pants and tossed the sweats in the laundry.

I heard the water turn off and hurried down the hall toward the stairs.

Not long later, after a couple cups of Abby's great coffee and a full breakfast of bacon and eggs, I was set for the day.

"Are you ready?" Sue called as she came into the kitchen wearing a pair of navy bell-bottomed pants paired with a crisp navy woven striped top and platform sandals. I loved how she dressed even if I didn't like the way she dressed our son.

"Yes, we are now." I smiled as I held up Cole. She shook her head at his new outfit. "What? He's an Army baby. He needs to dress the part," I reasoned.

"Fine," she sighed, and we prepared to leave. "Are you good here, Abby? We should be back by dinner."

"I'll be just fine. I'll just be here reliving yesterday's events with your doctor pal." She grinned.

"It was rather entertaining. So, Abby," I could hear Sue's wheels turning, "the doctor isn't hard on the eyes."

"No, he's not, and now he's seen my V, I think we can safely say when he visits it should be that much more interesting."

I laughed, loving that she never took life too seriously. Abby was always professional, held herself with grace and integrity, but once she was comfortable with you, and in the right setting, she was a riot to be around.

"Well, at least it was the doc and not someone else like Zack or Frank," I noted, because we both knew she'd never live it down if it was one of them.

"Agreed." She laughed and helped Sue get Cole's boots on. "You three have a great day, and I'll be here when you get home." Cole gurgled at her to get some more attention.

We said our goodbyes, headed outside, and into the car where we cranked the heat.

We continued up the mountain toward Shadows, and I watched out the window. I'd never tire of this drive.

"I really missed her these past few months." Sue settled into her seat. "Could you imagine if she decided to stay here? Now that her dad has passed, she won't have any reason to come back."

"I know."

"I know she loves it here, more than at her sister's place in New York. She's never been one for the city."

"Yes, the country life is better than the city any day of the week."

"Imagine if she and the doctor got together." I could tell Sue was already plotting her next move. "It's just another reason to get her to stay here."

"Now, Sue," I gave her a pointed look, but it quickly faded because I was just as on board with keeping Abby here as she was, "we need to play this carefully. You know both of them are very independent people, so we must tread carefully. He's seen her naked, so he knows what's under the drapes. The hard part is done." I smirked and jiggled my head at her to make her laugh. "Now we just need him to get to know her personality, and that shouldn't be hard because she's very easy to be around."

"She is," Sue agreed. "We just need to plan a few dinners and outings when she's in town. Oh! He loves chess. Maybe she does, too."

"Dinner is good, but we can't be obvious about it."

"We won't," she smirked, "but sometimes Cupid needs a

kick in the ass." She made me laugh, and we continued to plot the rest of the way up the mountain.

Zack met us at the door after coming back from meeting his brother for lunch in town.

"Hey, how was Abby's trip?" He hung his coat up and gave Cole some attention.

"It was good. How's Brad?"

"Pretty good. He's nursing a hangover, so I had my fun at Patty's today."

"Could you two be any more alike?" Sue teased, giving him a hug. "Have you seen Tracy lately?"

"Not since she started dating Bruce, the guy from the bank. She seems happy."

I was happy that Zack and Tracy had dated, if only for a few months. When they separated, we all remained good friends. They knew they just weren't compatible, and that was fair enough.

"Hey, Daniel, it's all ready when you guys are," Frank called from another room.

"Ready to make history, Cole?" I whisked him in the air, dismissing Sue's warning that he just ate, and joined my family and friends in the living room.

"There's the man of the hour." Dad reached out and rubbed Cole's head, which resulted in a little brown tuft of hair standing straight up on end.

I kissed my wife on the lips and bent down to check out the floorboard that had been pulled up for the occasion. Fresh cement had been poured in a small area and was all ready to go. "Someday, Cole, you'll be the leader of Shadows. You'll be a part of a third generation of soldiers in this family." He wiggled in my arms, and I knew he'd love the idea of getting those hands dirty again. As Dad helped to steady his solid little body, I held out my son and pressed his hand into the wet concrete next to my name.

"Perfect," Mom said as she wiped a tear then snapped a few photos.

I handed Cole off to his momma, and she made a face as she whisked him off to wash his hands, and probably to change his diaper, while I lowered the board back into place, Dad hammered the nails back in, and we shook hands. The pride on his face gave me a lump in my throat.

"We're so proud of you, Daniel, and all of this." My mom wrapped an arm around my waist as we stood and soaked up the heat from the fireplace. "We always knew you'd do great things, but running this place with your father is just amazing to see."

"It is, isn't it?" I looked around and wondered if the place would always feel this warm and safe, what Cole would be like when he led his own team, and if he would love it as much as Dad and I did.

"So, Cole is getting big. Have you and Sue thought about having any more kids?" Mom pursed her lips and looked at me.

"We talked about it," I admitted, "but I don't think we're ready just yet. Maybe in a few years."

"Good for you. You do what you want and don't let anyone tell you different." She pulled my head down and kissed my cheek.

"The next time you think feeding him beans is wise," Sue handed me Cole, "you're changing him. It was like that mud pool you have out back for training."

"Good job on making Mama do it." I held up my hand and he hit it perfectly. "Come on. Let's play!"

I took him to sit on the floor next to the massive window that looked over the lake. I loved being here with him. It was the safest place on Earth and the one place I could really let my guard down. Everyone settled into comfy chairs to enjoy a quiet moment. I lifted the cushioned top from the footstool and watched as his eyes widened and he smiled. He knew what was in there. It was our favorite game to play, and he loved it.

"This is tactical gear. Can you say tactical?" I held my homemade flipbook up so he could see it better, then flipped the page. "These are fatigues. Fa-tigues. You'll wear these a lot." I looked down and rolled my eyes at the light blue sweatpants Sue had put him in since his diaper explosion. *Light blue, seriously?* I made a face as I fingered the fabric. "Daddy's gonna get you some fatigues even if I have to sew them myself." I heard Sue snicker at that, but she said nothing. Cole kicked his legs and gurgled happily as he tried to grab the book. "This is a Barrett M90," I continued.

"Some children get color and shape flipbooks, but your son gets a military grade weapons handbook." Sue chuckled as she sat down on the stool next to us.

"Never too young to learn this stuff." I held up another picture, and Cole reached out for it. "See, he's interested." I glared as he jammed the corner of the book in his mouth.

"He's teething." She chuckled.

I rolled onto my back, and two seconds later Cole climbed on top of me. "Come on," I coached him, "climb over the daddy mountain."

"Hey, Daniel?" Frank popped his head around the corner, then made a funny face at Cole, who laughed as I lifted him to fly like an airplane. "Our new weapons are here. We're about to go over the inventory."

"Oh." I looked at my watch and was shocked at how I'd lost track of time. "All right, buddy," I pushed Cole's butt over toward Sue, "go do shapes and colors with Mama." I winked at her. "Tomorrow, we learn about bush camping!"

CHAPTER EIGHTEEN

GENERAL EDISON LOGAN

I'd never forget that night. Cole was becoming quite the little man at seven and was damn fine with a toolbox already. Daniel and I were doing some repairs on his henhouse. Cole helped us out by hammering down the replacement planks. He attacked every nail like the chickens' lives depended on it. The rain poured down, but that wouldn't stop us. A job was a job.

A fox had managed to get in early that morning, and Daniel knew if it wasn't fixed right away, that damn critter would have gone right back through the same hole he'd made before. Thankfully, the neighbor's hound had set up a ruckus, and Daniel was able to chase him off before any chickens were harmed. There were plenty of feathers strewn around and some eggs eaten, but all in all, only a few very upset chickens came out of the whole episode.

Even though it was freezing and near dark, Cole kept at it. He was a fierce protector of all things, and he'd taken it personally that his chickens had been messed with.

As Daniel unloaded some supplies from my truck, I sat

back on my heels to enjoy the camaraderie of us all working together. Winter set in early in Montana, and the shadows cast long across the yard. The lights we'd set up to work by provided some hilarious shapes as the hens moved about. I allowed myself a moment to wonder what life would be like if we'd never had Daniel. Life was good. I counted my blessings and knew I was a lucky man.

Cole rubbed his fingers together as he tried to massage some warmth back into his hands. The tarp I'd used to protect us from the rain held up well, but the rain made for cold, wet hands.

"There's a pair of dry gloves on your dad's workbench. You want me to grab them for you?"

"No, thanks, Grandpa." Cole grimaced as he picked the hammer back up. "I'll be fine." He went back to work. I admired the fact that he was wired just like his father. In Montana we were often forced to work in extreme elements. It wasn't unlike service in the military; you did what you had to. There was rarely a dry set of gloves, or a new pair of boots. No, you had to work with what you had. For a soldier, it was mind over matter and live or die. Cole was shaping up to be a fine candidate for the military someday. Even at such a young age you could see it.

"Grab that end, Cole," Daniel called through the rain as he balanced a large piece of lumber. Cole scrambled to help.

Daniel never wanted the full-on stress of a proper farm. I understood that and didn't blame him a bit. Although I loved it and believed that living off your own land was the best thing for your mind and body, it was hardly something Sue could handle on her own. When Daniel was away and Cole was at school, she couldn't be expected to manage all the chores that needed to be done on a farm, even with Abby there full time. All that being said, the chickens certainly made the cut.

Shadows

I laughed when Daniel told me he wanted some for his own property. He used to say they drove him crazy at our place. I knew he secretly loved them just as much as he did the goats. He claimed he loved the fresh eggs, but I'd caught him in the coop giving them pats and love more than once.

"Would you move it, Todd?" Cole nudged the rooster out of his way as he tried to fix the floorboard. I chuckled when it didn't work. Todd wanted relief from the rain and was cold. Apparently, Cole's jacket was what he wanted, and he was determined to win the battle. "Do you want this fixed, or do you want a big ol' fox to come up through here?" He eyed him, but Todd just nuzzled against his boots and clucked something under his breath.

As I watched my son and grandson, I thought about Abby and how she had impacted all of us in some way. It was the best decision they'd ever made when they asked her to move in permanently. Abby had been traveling back and forth from her sister's place in New York to here. After she sold her parent's place, she'd become a bit of a drifter. Her heart was definitely in Montana, but she hated to live alone. She'd spent more time staying in Daniel and Sue's guest room than anywhere else. Finally, they convinced her to move in, the argument being that Sue could really use the help with Cole. She finally agreed, but only if she took on the role of nanny. Cole couldn't get enough of her, and neither could the rest of us. She was family. Now, we just needed to convince her sister June to move here, then things would be perfect all around.

"Did you hear that?" Cole asked as he stopped hammering. He had the hearing of an elephant. He looked over at the house and cocked his head to the side as he listened. "Dad, are we expecting company?" he called over to Daniel in a concerned voice.

"Not that I'm aware of." Daniel strained to listen, but the

drops on the tin roof made it difficult to hear, and the neighbor's dog barking by the fence didn't help. "Why don't you go check on Abigail and see what's up?"

Daniel knew better than to dismiss Cole's concern if he thought something was off. He'd already proved to us at a very early age that he had great instincts.

His father nodded at Cole to get moving. Cole dropped his hammer back in the toolbox and began to make his way through the slushy path toward the house.

"Cole!" I called, wanting him to grab something for me, but he didn't hear me and slipped inside the house. I tossed my gloves and trotted after him.

I caught up to him in the mudroom. He stood as still as a deer as he peered inside the kitchen. He put a finger to his lips as he felt me behind him. He was listening to something inside. We both moved forward a little to get a look. The light was on in the kitchen and made it easy to see. We spotted him then, a frail boy about Cole's age. He was talking to Abigail. The kid looked frozen to the bone, and it was obvious to me he could use some clean clothes and a meal. His dark eyes seemed too big for his pale face.

"Who's that?" I whispered as I stepped up onto the rubber mat so my boots didn't make a noise.

"He's a boy from my school," Cole whispered back. "He lives in the trailer park. A lot of the kids pick on him 'cause he lives there."

"That's not right." I felt a punch in my gut. Kids were horrible at times, and to make fun of where he lived was crap. It was hardly his fault. "Do you know him well?"

"No. His name's Mark Lopez. He's not in my class, and he's pretty quiet. I don't know much about him, really. I think he's a year younger than me."

We heard Abby mumble something about dry clothes. Cole quickly headed for the dryer and pulled out a hoodie, a t-shirt, and a pair of jeans without even a second thought. He handed them to her when she came into the mud room. Cole put a finger to his mouth and shook his head to let her know he didn't want us to be seen by Mark. She kissed his forehead and smiled down at the clothes then went back into the kitchen. I patted his shoulder, proud of his decision.

"Here." Abigail kept her voice matter of fact. I saw the boy's eyes widen at the things she held out to him, and he hesitated as though afraid she wasn't serious. Then he smiled at her and reached for them. He was obviously happy but uneasy at the same time. He thanked her as he held the clothes tight under his arm. She directed him to the restroom to try them on. As soon as he closed the door, Abigail went straight to work preparing him a bowl of soup and a few dinner rolls.

"Maybe we should go say hi?" I suggested.

"No," Cole didn't budge, "he'll get embarrassed, and he's had enough of that already. I'll talk to him at school, neutral ground."

I tried to hide my amusement at his answer. For seven, he was awfully wise.

"All right, let's give them some privacy and get back to the work." I grabbed a dry hat from a peg on the wall as I held the door open for him. He looked up me with sadness in his eyes. It wasn't pity; I knew him better than that. He wanted to help.

"You know Abby, she'll look after him, make sure he gets home all right."

"I know." He avoided the puddle and Todd as we approached his father.

Daniel glanced at us as we reached the henhouse, and I gave him a thumbs up that everything was fine. He shrugged and didn't ask questions. We all concentrated on our tasks, and soon the henhouse was better than it had been in a while, and we had everything put away.

I could tell the boy's visit was weighing on Cole. I knew he wouldn't let it go. He wasn't one to ignore someone when they obviously needed help. Once again, I felt pride in my grandson. He was going to be someone to be reckoned with one day. I could feel it in my bones.

"You boys must be frozen!" Sue stood ankle deep in a mudpuddle as she struggled with a large umbrella.

"It could be worse," Cole commented, and she smiled at me.

"As soon as Abigail gets back, dinner's ready."

"She went out in this weather, Mom?" We all knew Abby didn't venture out much. She was a homebody. "Should she?"

"She didn't go far," Sue assured him. "Ed, Meg's on her way over."

"Just a couple more nails and we're done." Daniel kissed her cheek. "We'll be right in."

"All right." She patted a chicken that came to say hello. "Gosh, it's freezing out here." She shivered and headed back inside.

I met Cole's eyes and nodded. We both figured where Abby had gone. I knew she'd question Cole about the boy when we got to the table later.

We cleaned up and gathered around the dinner table. The smell of fresh rolls and chicken soup filled the kitchen as we thanked Abby profusely then dove in.

"How was your day?" I asked Sue as I buttered my roll and looked around at everyone. I loved how we were a family that prided ourselves on family dinners.

"Well, we had a visitor tonight." Abby glanced at Cole, who looked to be deep in thought. "A young boy around Cole's age who looked entirely too thin and not dressed for this weather."

Shadows

"Really?" Daniel's face was full of concern. "Where did he come from?"

Cole spoke up. "The trailer park. He goes to my school."

"So, you know him?" Daniel glanced at me, no doubt wondering why I hadn't shared this story earlier.

"No, not really, but I think I should."

"I gave him some clothes and fed him." Abby glanced at Cole and paused, overcome with emotion. "That poor boy was sure hungry. I don't believe he gets much food. It was why he knocked on our door in the first place. I drove him home with some leftovers."

"That poor child." Meg looked at Abby. "We need to find out more about him."

"Maybe," Cole looked around the table, "you could pack me an extra lunch tomorrow, Abby? You know, just in case I run into him."

She looked at him with a smile then at Sue and Daniel as if to see if they agreed with Cole's idea.

"I think that's a wonderful idea." She patted his hand, and then we all weighed in and gave our opinions on how we could find out more about him and his situation.

It was obvious that the young boy had left a lasting impression on our Abigail, and I respected her for it. Her friendship with Sue may have brought her here, but it was her love for Cole that kept her here. None of us could imagine life without Abigail, especially my grandson.

"Drop by after school tomorrow, Cole. I'll make up a big batch of cookies," Meg piped in.

"I'm glad I went to the market this morning." Sue finished off the last of her shortcake and dabbed her mouth. "I bought some stew beef. Cole, would you like me to make a nice thick stew? I could fix container for you and Mark for lunch tomorrow. It'll stick to your bones better than your usual peanut butter and jam sandwich. Maybe even add a slice of apple pie."

His face lit up, and I smiled at Sue. She was smart, using this new kid as a way to get Cole to eat his vegetables.

"Yeah, let's do that, Mom."

———— ✫✫✫✫✫ ————

Mark would show up off and on after that day, sometimes on his own, but usually with Cole. We had all done our bit to try to find out more about the boy. We kept our distance from his life with his mother and brother out of respect for Mark, but I knew Abby and Cole kept an eye on him. Soon he became a regular at Daniel and Sue's, as he and Cole became firm friends, and one was rarely seen without the other. We began to get to know him, and his amazing appetite and humor soon earned him a spot in all our hearts. I wasn't sure who baked the most treats for the boys, Abigail, Sue, or Meg. Nothing made me happier then when I'd hear the boys chatting it up in our kitchen with Meg while they filled their pockets with her cookies, then the slap of the screen door as they bounded outside to the barn or across the field.

Sometime later, we got a troubling call, but one that would change our family for the better.

"Are you sure?" Meg covered her mouth as Daniel shared the news that the police had just shared with him. I moved closer to the phone, and Meg held it between us.

"Sadly, yes, it's true. His mother's body was found today, and it seems his brother has skipped town."

"Any sign of Mark?" I beat Meg to the question.

"No, he's not there. The neighbors haven't seen him either, not that most of them care in the slightest. If they did, I'm sure they'd have helped him well before this."

"Oh, Daniel, Cole just got here. Let me speak to him and see what he knows. Hang on." Meg handed me the phone. I could hear the police in the background and wondered what the scene was like where Daniel was.

"Grandma, I left my *I Survived* book here the other day. Have you seen it?" Cole dropped his bag on the counter and looked at the two of us as he took in the vibe.

"Sweetheart, was Mark at school today?"

"No, he wasn't. I looked for him but…" Cole looked worried. "Why, Grandma?" His chair scraped as he lowered onto it.

"Sadly, Mark's mother was found dead today, dear."

"What?" His voice was instantly upset, and his gaze flashed to me. "What happened? Where is he?"

"We don't know yet. Just a second, son, I have your father on the phone."

"Dad, Mom, are you still there?"

"We're here," Meg and I answered together.

"He didn't know anything about it, and Mark wasn't at school today." Meg tried to stay calm.

"Okay, I'll hop in the truck and check around town." I looked at Meg, and she nodded.

"All right. And I'll take Cole, and we'll check all the places the boys hang out."

"Mom, will you wait at home in case he goes there?"

"Of course!" She sounded so worried, I drew her to me as I hung up. The poor kid must be beside himself. Cole bolted for the door ahead of me.

A few days later, I was in Daniel and Sue's kitchen discussing where else we could possibly look for the boy when Cole showed up with an exhausted Mark trailing behind him. We were all instantly relieved to see he was okay. No one jumped up to rush to him right away, as we didn't want to overwhelm him.

"Can Mark spend the night?" Cole looked at his dad, and it was easy to see he needed his best friend as much as Mark needed him.

"Of course, son." He looked as relieved as I did, and I knew he'd answer all our questions later. Sue then surged forward and wrapped Mark in a big hug. She had to scurry out of the way as Abby rushed in to check him over herself.

"Mark, go upstairs with Cole and get some clean clothes, and I'll reheat some dinner for you boys." Her voice was brisk, but I saw her dash away a tear as she turned to the stove. Once they were out of earshot, Sue comforted Abby. "I wonder where he was."

"It doesn't matter now. He's back." Sue hugged her hard.

The following night, we got a call from Daniel to come for supper, as a family meeting was needed. A big decision had to be made, and we gathered in the living room to talk.

"Life shouldn't be this hard at such a young age. It's just horrible what happened to his mother. In spite of her lack of care, she was still his mom. He told me they took him into care and explained they had some people who might be willing to foster him." Abby expressed her concern while we all sat around the fireplace. "He refuses to talk about what happened, and I don't want to press him. He's still traumatized."

"It must have been awful for him, poor kid," I agreed, and Daniel murmured his agreement.

"That little boy is incredibly smart, loving, funny, and he adores Cole," Abby continued. "I mean, they've been attached at the hip since the day he showed up here." She looked at Sue. "I understand how big it is to bring another child into the family, but he needs us." She wiped a tear from her cheek, and Sue handed her a tissue.

Meg and I knew Daniel and Sue had been trying for the past five years to have another child, but it just didn't seem to be in the stars for them. I knew the idea of adopting someone like Mark would be just what they needed.

"Abby," Sue reached over and took her hand, "you don't need to sell us on Mark. We love him, too, but the question is, does he want to live here?"

"Only one way to find out." Meg shrugged and motioned toward the other room where the boys were playing. I grinned at her. I knew she was as excited as Daniel and Sue that we just might be about to get another child to love. Abby's face was a story in itself as she stood and beamed at all of us.

"Another child under our roof," she breathed and put a hand on her chest as she called the boys. It sounded like a stampede as they burst into the room.

"Mark." Abby patted the seat next to her while Cole shot me a worried look. I caught his eye and smiled to assure him everything was fine. Nothing got past Cole. He read a room like there was writing on the wall. He took in the vibe and relaxed.

"Am I in trouble for eating the last chocolate chip cookie?" Mark's big brown eyes looked around the room with worry.

"Of course not, dear." Abby wrapped a loving arm around him. "We just want to ask you something."

"Oh." Relief washed over his face.

"Mark, we know we could never replace your family," Sue said with glossy eyes. We could all see how vulnerable the boy was. "We wonder, given the circumstances, if you'd like to come live here with us instead of going with the foster parents you mentioned. We could talk to the social worker about it."

"You mean you want me to stay here? And not leave?" His face lit up when we all smiled. "Like, live here and be a part of the family?"

"You're already a part of the family, Mark." Daniel smiled and took Sue's hand. "You can have the room next to Cole's."

"What do you say?" Sue was next to tears.

"I say thank you." He sprang from the chair and leapt into Daniel's and Sue's arms. He then ran into Meg's, then mine. Abigail was now blubbering, and he ran back to her and flung himself at her. She stroked his hair and kissed him on the head. "Will you adopt me, Abigail?" Tears rimmed his eyes, and we knew he was trying to hold it together. His hand flexed on her shoulder while her chin quivered, and she cleared her throat. We all knew what those words meant to her. Sue and Daniel had their son, and now it was time for Abby to raise one, too.

"I would love to adopt you, Mark."

Tears streamed down Sue's cheeks as she smiled at Daniel.

"Can we go back to playing now?" Cole made us all laugh, and Daniel nodded at them to leave. The boys raced off, leaving the rest of us amazed at how quickly children could adapt to whatever came at them. We all took a moment to think about how much we had just impacted that child's life.

"Do I want to know what I just walked into?" Doc Roberts stood in the entrance of the room, and Abigail jumped to her feet.

"Well," she reached out for Sue's hand, "we've decided I'm going to adopt Mark, and we'll all raise him here together."

I caught Doc's face when it slipped for a half a second then morphed into a wide smile. "My goodness, that's amazing, Abigail. Congratulations," he looked around the room, "to all of you."

"It just happened. Is that..." Abigail stopped herself, and I saw a look go between them. Doc Roberts just smiled, and she cleared her throat. "Thank you."

I glanced at Daniel, and he signaled that they were dating.

Yikes. I sure hoped Abby's decision wouldn't change anything for the two of them.

"Come on, Ed, Daniel, we've got work to do." Sue pushed Abby toward the doctor and motioned for us to leave them be.

Chapter Nineteen

Daniel

"Jeez Cole, why can't you see it?" Mark complained as he balanced milk, cereal, and granola in his arms, nearly knocking over his calculus textbook on the floor. The boys were in the kitchen doing homework, and as usual, Mark was hungry. "She's basically begging you to take her to the dance." He toed the book aside as he dumped a large amount of granola over the frosted flakes.

"Michael Green's into her, and I'm not. So let him ask her."

"But she likes you."

"She's not my type." Cole shook his head, and I smiled. It was always the same argument between my boys. Girls would chase after Cole, but he was too busy with his training and JROTC to see anything else. Mark, who was also in JROTC, was the charmer and always had a young lady on his arm, even though he would say he wasn't officially dating.

"Do you even have a type?" Milk dribbled from Mark's mouth, and I tossed him a napkin as I eased into a chair at the table next to him. I had some paperwork to finish before

I drove up to Shadows, so I tried to ignore the boys' discussion as best as I could.

"I do," Cole downed half a glass of water while his eggs cooked, "and I'll know what that is when I find it."

"It better not be that new girl." Mark gave an exaggerated quiver.

"What new girl?" That got my attention, so I had to ask. Redstone wasn't huge, so new kids stuck out.

"Remember Ezra who owned the old shipping store just outside of town? It's now the UPS Store." I nodded, and Cole shook his head at me. "Yeah, anyway, they handed it off to Ezra's nephew when his wife got pregnant. Guess she had issues or something." Mark filled me in. "Now Ezra and his wife have split."

"Not surprising," I muttered.

"Right." He shook his head. "Well, now he's back to take over the store again, and his daughter Christina's with him. She spent the last few days checking out our school."

"Really? What's she like?" *Please, nothing like her mother.*

Mark considered a moment.

"Have you ever been to a movie store and popped your head through the red curtains at the back just to see if ya could get a glimpse of a side boob picture?" He tried to look innocent, but it didn't work, and I had to grin at him. "Anywaaay," he grinned back, "instead you see where all the B-rated pornos are kept, the ones with the girls who have strange titties... Like that."

"That's incredibly specific." I raised an eyebrow at him.

"Yeah, it's a gift."

I made a face at him while my son choked on a bit of toast.

"She's not sticking around." Cole flipped his eggs as he gulped some water to help his toast go down. "From what Billy told me, she only wanted to please her father by looking at the school. She'll go back to where she came from by the end of the week, and we'll never see her face again."

I made a show of going back to my paperwork to let them go on with their normal banter. I relished moments like that, just being together with the boys. I thought about how close Cole and Mark had become since he showed up hungry on our doorstep. Though they had very different personalities, they rarely clashed and were closer than most brothers. When one would get into trouble, the other was always there to back him up.

Mark's stomach was a bottomless pit, he wore his heart on his sleeve, and he had a wonderful sense of humor. He loved every moment of his life now and soaked up everything he could and never passed on an opportunity to have fun. Cole was more of the quiet, sensible type. He focused all his energy on becoming the best soldier he could be, even at such a young age. As a cadet in the JROTC program he already had an outstanding reputation. Sometimes I wondered if he missed out on a lot in life, but I also knew Cole did what made him happy, and a life as a soldier was what he wanted, and he was totally focused on that. It was what he'd wanted since birth.

"Mark," Dad came in holding a bag full of donuts, "I stopped by Zack's place, and he said he'd made your favorite this morning."

"My God, Grandpa you're too good to me. Are they chocolate, with chocolate glaze, and chocolate filling?" Mark nearly fell out of his seat as he dove for them.

"Yup, that's it." Dad smiled and handed one to Cole, who looked at him like he was crazy.

"No, thank you, Grandpa. I don't need it."

"No one needs it," Dad teased, "but it doesn't mean it isn't good."

"Yes, sooo good," Mark shoved an entire donut into his

mouth, and we all chuckled. "I'll go call Zack and thank him," he said through a stuffed mouth, then he gave Dad a hug and rushed off to his bedroom to make the call.

I thought about how I missed Zack at Shadows. Being part of Blackstone had been so good for him. He got to explore his love for cooking in the kitchen there. It was like a dream come true. He was more often found in that kitchen than outside training with the guys. It didn't surprise anyone when a couple years later he and his brother, Alex, decided to take over Patty's. He even found a new girlfriend. She recently moved close to the restaurant, and it was obvious they were well matched. I remembered our agreement, that when life changed and you wanted to embrace something else, you should go for it, even if meant you had to leave Shadows and live elsewhere. I'm just happy he didn't leave our town as well. I couldn't imagine life without my best friend.

Then there was Frank. Shortly after Cole was born, he was offered his dream position in Washington. A year later, he finally gave in to his feelings for Heather. They married and had a daughter. Zack and I gave him royal shit for actually calling his daughter Mia. We promised we'd take that secret to the grave. It was fun to hold it over him whenever his wife was around, though.

Frank was now the liaison for Shadows in Washington, but before he left, he founded a secondary team called Eagle Eye. We all teased him about that too because he'd always said he was going to have a team called that, and now he'd done it. Needless to say, Frank kept his word on a lot of things. I'd hated when he left, but now I was thankful he'd accepted the job. That move proved to be a good one for all concerned. We couldn't have asked for a better person to act on Shadows' behalf. He knew how we ran things, always listened to what we needed, and fought for even more than we asked for.

"I know that face." Dad pulled me from my thoughts as he greeted the boys then sat down across the table from me. He brushed away a few cereal crumbs as he made space for himself. The boys scurried to make room and moved their books to the den. "Worrying about things you can't control won't help, son. All you can do is be prepared for the unexpected. What's got you fretting today?"

"It's just a constant worry that our families and even some of our friends in town could become a target. The damage we bring to the Cartel on each of our missions, the loss of money with every rescue, and our constant presence in their territory has got to infuriate them."

"True." He tapped the side of his mug.

"We're much more careful than we used to be, though, and I always knew as time went on, we'd have to tighten up on the way we did things. I'm not sure about the boys' future, what it's going to be like at Shadows. I'd do everything in my power to protect them. All of them."

"I know, we'll all do everything in our power. When you're finished with this, why don't we have a meeting with the others, reevaluate everything? Maybe that'll give you more peace of mind."

"I think I need that."

"Remember, Daniel, if something doesn't feel right here," he pointed to his chest, "say something. We can't help if we don't know."

"Copy that."

"By the way, Frank called me." He caught my attention before my head spun again. Cole caught his words as he came back into the kitchen and quickly sat down next to me.

"Oh?"

"He said Ray was sending a new guy he recruited over to

the boys' high school and wanted to know if you'd sit in and evaluate him."

"Yes, I can do that." Frank had gotten Ray a position training and overseeing the new recruits at Camp Green Water. The camp wasn't that far away, and he was really enjoying his role there.

Though we now had four new men who had replaced my original friends on Blackstone, we were still a strong, unified team, and we'd rescued countless lives. "Cole, I'll give you guys a ride to school, then?" I asked as I gathered up my papers.

"Sounds good. Give me ten. Oh, Grandpa, we'll need some ammo before we head out to camp this weekend. Mark and I were practicing."

"I'll grab some from up at the house. Have a good day at school."

"Will do." Cole tucked his dishes away in the dishwasher and disappeared down the hall with a call to Mark to hurry.

"You did good, son." Dad beamed at me as he often did whenever the boys were around. "They're going to be excellent soldiers one day."

"Well, I learned from the best." I squeezed his shoulder on the way out. "See you for dinner and that meeting."

"Copy that."

The gymnasium was full of hopeful teenagers. They eagerly buzzed from table to table to see what kinds of jobs were out there. I inspected a table with three recruiters and listened as one described how joining had changed his life and helped him stay out of trouble. Another described how he enjoyed a challenge. He did a good job of sidetracking the kids who asked too many questions about how many kills he had and other uncomfortable subjects. The kids didn't realize that these recruiters were not much older than they were, so the decision on kill or be killed wasn't something they'd had to tackle, and one I hoped they'd never have to. I took note of two of their names. The third fellow, who appeared to be the oldest, and who was no doubt the leader of their group, seemed a bit uninterested when I picked up a pamphlet. He should have stood and acknowledged me even if he was unaware that I served our country. Soldiers were taught respect, and there wasn't any of that from this man.

"Staff Sergeant Peters." I addressed him by name, and he didn't seem to catch that I used his rank. That in itself should have been a big clue that I knew his world. "Where is the talk being held?"

"Huh?" He leaned back and again didn't stand like the others.

"Your career-night talk, where is it being held?"

"Um..." He leaned forward and pointed to a paper that read Room 105.

"Thanks," I muttered and signaled to Cole I was unimpressed. His face hardened, and I knew he would check him out himself.

Room 105 was just inside the main doors. I went in and settled myself at the back. When Mark and Cole came in, we chatted for a moment, and I let them know I wouldn't join them in the front, as I didn't want to be spotted. They sat across the aisle a few rows up. When Frank suggested I attend, he'd chuckled and asked me to lay low. He had realized that some of the young recruiters were already on to us. We wanted to see how they were promoting the military to the young people, and we were interested in how they engaged with those who were truly interested, and—I thought of Staff Sergeant Peters—with those who weren't.

To my surprise, Staff Sergeant Peters was the one who came in to speak. Cole looked over his shoulder at me, and I gave him a nod.

"Hi, I'm Staff Sergeant Peters, with the US Army." His

tone sounded totally disinterested, but he did manage to force a smile to some of the kids who stared up at him like he was some kind of movie star. "You'll be spending the next forty-five minutes with me." Two kids immediately stuck their hands in the air. Like typical high school students, they just wanted to ask questions. I wondered how he'd handle it. He put down his script, sat on the corner of the desk, and let the kids fire away.

"Is there a signing bonus for 92 Yankee?" a kid in the front asked.

"Oh, you want to do logistics?"

"Yeah, that's what I want to do."

"Yeah," Peters nodded with a shrug, "I can get you a signing bonus."

Cole glanced back again with a silent laugh. We both knew that was a flat-out lie. Only certain MOSs have a sign on bonus, and they were typically the least favorable.

Mark leaned over and said something that made Cole laugh out loud, and I knew this guy was about to get the full deal from my sons. Mark raised his hand, and Peters pointed at him to speak.

"I want to be special ops!"

"Okay, no problem. I can get you in." My jaw nearly dropped open at his lie.

"How can he become special ops," Cole cut in, "when that's something you must be hand-selected for?"

"Well, I mean," Peters was clearly thrown by Cole's question, "he can put in for it."

"Yeah, but that doesn't mean he's guaranteed the job, right?" Cole challenged.

"No, I guess not, but that doesn't mean he shouldn't try out for it."

"I agree with you there, but you just mislead that other guy."

"All right," he cleared his throat, "I can see how that sounded."

Cole's shoulders eased, and I could see he was happy he'd made his point. I was tempted to call Frank right then and there, but I knew I'd have to wait. I wanted to hear what else this guy was going to say.

"Oh!" A girl I recognized from Cole's engineering class spoke up. "I want to do cyber operations!"

"That's a good one." Peters smiled. "Sure, you can do that." Cole leaned forward to see the girl better.

"How did you do on your ASVAB?" Cole called to her, referring to the Armed Services Vocational Aptitude Battery test you took to help them place you in the correct field of service.

"I don't know what my score is yet." She shrugged as she looked back at Cole.

"Staff Sergeant Peters, maybe before you promise this girl a specific MOS," he paused, "military occupational specialties position," he explained to the confused faces of the students around him, "you should check her ASVAB scores first?" Cole turned back to the girl. "To be in cyber operations, you need a high ASVAB score."

Peters licked his lips and glared at Cole then turned to another kid who was already asking his question.

"How easy is it to be stationed in Hawaii?"

"That's a breeze. I can absolutely request that you be stationed in Hawaii." The kids buzzed with excitement as I tried to contain myself. I was totally flabbergasted at the lies that were being spread without regard to the importance of the decision these kids might make. Peters, on the other hand, seemed to love the role of being a yes man.

Cole chuckled. "Yeah, he can request it, but the likelihood of you getting it are slim to none," Cole tossed out, and Peters looked about ready to deck him.

Shadows

"All right, kid, what's your beef with me? You're combating everything I say."

"My problem is you recruiters blow smoke up our asses. You promise things you can't give."

"How did I blow smoke up your ass?" His cheeks grew pink, he stood, and Cole did the same. They looked ready to go to blows.

"Excuse me?" I called out in a commanding voice. The room went silent, and heads turned toward me. I knew I had their attention.

"Yes," Peters' jaw ticked as he tried to keep his cool, "old guy in the back, go ahead."

"This 'old guy' will be addressed as 'sir.'" I stood straight and gave him a glare. "I think I've earned it as a general in the United States Army." Peters' face drained of color as he stood to attention. "The reason that young man knows the information he does is because he's my son."

"Oh, sir, I didn't—" Peters looked sick as he tried desperately to find words.

"You should be ashamed of yourself. You're a disgrace to your position and to the service. You didn't speak a word of truth or give these kids one thing to help them make a decision that could potentially affect the rest of their lives." I was incredibly disappointed that this recruiter was an example of those who were trusted to represent our military, a part of my family. It was no wonder we lost so many. It was a disgrace. "And fucking remove your cover while you're inside. Mark, Cole, let's go."

"Yes, sir," both young men answered at the same time and immediately followed me out of the room.

By the time we reached the truck, our frustrations had lifted, and we found ourselves laughing.

"Oh, my gosh, Peters' face when he heard you were a general." Cole bent over and held his stomach.

"I thought for sure we'd see his pants turn a deeper shade from the piss he was holdin' on to." Mark tried to speak through his laughter. "I wish so much that was filmed."

"Please let us be there when you tell Frank," Cole hooted. "He's gonna lose it."

"I want to know how that guy even got this far in the military," I chimed in. "Who in their right mind would put that man in charge of anything, let alone be let loose in a high school with impressionable teens?"

Our sides hurt from all the laughter by the time we pulled in the driveway. I spotted Sue on the porch wrapped in a blanket. I couldn't wait to tell her the story.

"Dibs on tellin' Mom." Cole was out the door before I even turned off the engine.

"You sure you want Mark to be in charge of bringing in dinner?" I called, laughing while Mark and I grabbed the takeout from Zack's.

"Mom?" The tone in Cole's voice had my senses on high alert, and I knew something was very wrong. I approached the porch slowly, my hands squeezed tight around the takeout bag.

"Dan," Sue's face was swollen, and her eyes were red and glossy.

"What is it?"

"It's your father." She sniffed loudly, removing the food bags from my hands and setting them aside. "He's had a heart attack." Her voice broke as cold water washed over me. She lowered her head for a moment and then looked up at me. "I'm so sorry, my love. He didn't make it. He's gone."

As her words sank in, I reached for Cole and Mark and pulled them to me, needing an anchor. They wrapped their arms around me and squeezed hard. Our rock had been ripped away from us without warning. Cole pulled Sue in as she stood and came to us, and we huddled on the porch and mourned the best man who had ever lived.

———— ★★★★★ ————

"Daniel?" Sue stood in the doorway of the bathroom, face freshly washed and ready for bed. "I thought maybe we could take a hike to your dad's old camping spot. Maybe the boys could spend a few days up there. Just liven things up a little."

"That might be nice," I reached out, and she came to me and pressed against my side then pulled my hand to her cheek.

"I miss him," she sniffed.

"Me too." I held her close as I let my memories have their way as the rain pelted the window.

It took a long time for me to find peace with my father's passing. I tried to be there for my mother. She was inconsolable, but I did my best. I was so happy Sue was there for her when I was at a loss as to how to help. They spent hours talking about him, and I knew Mom was glad to have her. Cole and Mark hung their rifles on my office wall. My father had given the guns to them when the boys told us they wanted nothing more than to be in the Army. The M16s hung crisscrossed in memory of their last trip with Dad.

Sadly, it was only five months later that Mom took ill and left us too. Sue said she died from a broken heart, and I had to agree. With both parents gone, I had a new role to play in the house and even bigger shoes to fill for the boys. Lucky for me, I had the best sons anyone could ask for, the most supportive wife, and the best nanny ever. Not to mention an incredible doctor who checked in on me often. Who could ask for more? Times were changing fast around us, and all I could do was hold on and hope for the best.

After some time had passed and the weight on my heart became a little lighter, I tried to focus on things my father would have. He wouldn't've wanted us to hurt. He would want us to carry on his legacy.

I walked into the living room of Shadows where Cole and Mark whispered together about something.

"Dad," Mark's face told me they were up to no good, "any chance we could get our hands on some of those smoke bombs Frank brought in for training?"

"Do I want to know why?"

"No," Cole answered, deadpan. "You really don't."

"Should I be worried?"

"Meh." Mark pressed his lips together and wiggled his eyebrows.

"Is it for the new guy, Paul?"

"Of course not," they both lied at the same time.

"They're in the shed, but I know nothing." I smirked as they ran off to cause trouble.

Now that the boys had a good number of years in the Army under their belts and we'd selected the new members for Blackstone, we were well on our way for the new generation of Shadows operations. My father would have been so proud of what we'd done here. Shadows was so much more now than he could ever have imagined.

The new team members had arrived last month, and everyone seemed to have settled in and found their own rhythm with one another. They trained hard, under Cole's direction, and I had no doubt he would have them ready for their first mission. Frank had mentioned something about another snatch and grab. Apparently, it was the California governor. Nothing had made headlines yet, and we planned on keeping it that way. We were officially on standby, and the boys had used nearly every moment of it to prepare. Nearly…

"Cole?"

"Yes, sir?" He immediately gave me his attention.

"Can I see you in my office?"

"Of course." Mark smiled up at him then turned away, and I knew something big was up. I didn't say anything as we headed toward my office.

"Where's all your stuff?" Cole asked and looked back at me with a perplexed expression.

"Son, I took this office over when my father passed away. Everything that happens in this house runs through here first. Now that you're the new team leader and are ready to take over the house duties, it's only right that you have this office."

"Dad, you don't need to do this. I'm fine next to Doc Roberts."

"I know you are, but a leader needs room to think, plan, and needs a space that's just his." I smiled and knew Cole was excited in spite of his resistance to my giving it up. "You can paint, change the furniture, whatever. It's yours. I just need to pull those off the wall," I pointed to his and Mark's guns that were a gift from my father, "then—"

"Can they stay there?" he cut in. "Please? They mean so much to me."

"Of course, they can." I beamed with pride. "It's your office now. You do what you wish."

"I can't tell you how much I appreciate this, Dad." He smiled over at me and began to walk around the room.

I watched as my son began to plan the office he wanted. I looked down at my team's picture in the box next to my feet and remembered how excited we'd been to start the next chapter of our lives, too. We held up a sign that read Team Blackstone First Generation. The first night that Cole's team gathered at the house, we took the same picture only with the words Second Generation.

"You should know," I pulled back the curtain by the radiator, "he spends a lot of time in here." Scoot yawned and gave me a glare at the sudden invasion. "He's a jerk for being such a baby."

"He is," Cole rubbed his furry head, and in answer Scoot swatted him, "but I think we can be roommates."

"You say that now…" I dripped with sarcasm and left the little crap to sleep. He should be living in Doc's office, but that didn't happen.

"He's a Blackstone cat. We'll adapt."

I remembered when it was Cole's turn to come up with a team name, and he'd asked if he could keep Blackstone. He explained that he didn't have anyone like his mother and her bracelet who could influence a name quite like she'd done for me. I was incredibly happy that he wanted to keep it. He said it would always remind him of his mother and me.

"Maybe you can keep this wall clear for, you know, baby pictures someday." I winked, but a part of me was curious if Cole would ever want to get married. His mother and I would support him in any decision he made, but a father needed to know where his son's head was at times.

"Babies?" He looked at me and shook his head. "I think I'd need a wife first."

"You see the new girl workin' at Zacks?"

"I'm not opposed to marriage, Dad, but I love what I do. If it's meant for me to fall in love, then it'll happen, I guess, but to be honest, I have no idea what I'd even want in a woman."

"Fair enough." I nodded and thought how smart that answer was. "Just don't shut the world out too much. Time can pass quickly when you're not paying attention."

"I think if there's someone out there for me, she'll let me know."

I chuckled. "I don't doubt that. I just want to make sure

you get what I have." I dropped the subject, not wanting to push too hard.

"I can only hope I'd be so lucky." He looked at the photo of our wedding day and pulled it out of the box. He set it on the table. "This needs to stay here."

God, I loved my son.

"Cole?" Mark popped his head in the doorway and gave me a polite but devious smile. "T-minus thirty seconds."

Cole's face lit up, and I motioned with my head that we were finished. He rushed out, and I smiled. Yes, it was just what my father wanted.

Family.

Bang!

"Hahaha! He fell right on his ass!" Mark shrieked, and all I could hear was my boys' laughter throughout the entire house.

And so, it began…

CHAPTER TWENTY

Location: Montana Shadows Safe House
Coordinates: Classified

Present Day
DANIEL

I smiled at June then took a moment to enjoy the memory of it all. It was like I was back there and could feel it all over again, as if it had just happened. My love for Sue had grown every day, and the retelling of our story made me fall in love with her all over again. I had always planned on sitting down with the grandchildren someday to tell them how this all came to be. I still thought they needed to hear it but maybe they needed to be a little older to appreciate the main points, like how if you really believe in something, you can make it happen, and of course, true love was worth any risk out there.

"I had no idea that was how this place was started." June sniffed. "I sure wish I'd had the pleasure of meeting your parents. They sound like a very special couple." She wiped her flushed face with a hanky and blew her nose.

"I wish you had, too. Being here every day doing what we're doing makes me feel like they're still here in the walls we built. There's a lot of history here, not only in this house, but on this land."

"It's pretty special that Edison wrote a lot of it down." Sue ran her hand over Dad's journal. "You know, dear, you should keep a journal, too, and hand it down to Olivia someday."

"You should," June added. "The history of this place should never be forgotten."

"That's not a bad idea." I handed the book to Sue, who would put it back where we kept it, safely stored away from little hands and four legged wet noses. I couldn't help but shoot a look at Scoot, who would no doubt use it as a scratching post if given half a chance.

"Now, I'd like to address something." June moved her gaze to the kitchen. "How did I not know what happened with Doc and my sister? I feel shortchanged here."

"You've known Doc for how long?" I smiled. "He asked us to keep what happened a secret, so we did. Now they're dating publicly, I felt it was all right to share it." The truth was Doc and Abby had something happen between them years back, which included a hot kiss, though I'd never tell him I'd seen it. I'd given Doc enough crap over the years. When Mark came into the picture, they both decided to back off. He'd known how much Abigail longed for a child of her own, so when he became part of her life and then his own sister had a child, they decided to put their focus there. I knew they still had their moments; they just shared them quietly. "Love is a tricky thing, and how you choose to live it is solely up to the ones involved."

"That's very true." June made a face, and I wondered if she, too, had someone on the side. I rather hoped so.

"Come to think of it, June, you've been out a lot lately.

Anything you'd care to share?" I wiggled my eyebrows, and a tiny shade of pink dusted her cheeks.

"Why didn't Shadows stick with the K-9 unit?" I couldn't help but grin at her sudden change in subject.

"It was something we really wanted, and we tried for a few years, but there were too many issues, and we decided to just stick with them as pets."

"I see."

"Would you care to share—"

"Auntie June!" Reagan, Keith and Lexi's daughter, came running in. "You here to help make cupcakes?"

"Of course, I am!" June scooped up the bug and gave her a kiss as she visibly relaxed at the interruption. "Where's your brother? Maybe he'll want to help us, too?"

"He's still in his room." She made a sad face, and June looked over at me with the same sadness we all felt.

"Maybe we should walk over to the house and see if he wants to join us?" Sue suggested as she came in.

"Yes, please!" The little girl was instantly cheered. June reached over and patted my shoulder as a thank you for the story, and Sue started to gather up the dishes.

"It's not right," Sue whispered so only I could I hear.

"It's not, but…" I trailed off. I knew that some things were not ours to fix.

"I know." She smiled at me. "It's just when it's family, I want us all to be okay."

"We will be," I promised, but deep down inside, I wasn't sure I believed my own words. I sat on the couch; I didn't want to move yet. How I wished my father was here to cast some of his wisdom over the situation in the house. Plus, I could use the extra eye on June to find out just who made her blush like that.

"Daniel?" Savannah was suddenly next to me, and I pushed off the uneasy feeling. "Sorry to bother you, but

Frank was adamant about having me deliver these to you as soon as I finished printing and binding."

"You never bother me." I smiled and took the stack of files from her. "Thank you."

"I took the liberty of giving you a female perspective on each of the men." She pointed to some colored tabs that stuck out. "I thought it was important to point out if I saw anything in any one of their files to indicate any issues with relationships or anger. It's not just Blackstone men who live here."

"That was very insightful of you. I appreciate it." I was blown away that she'd thought to do that. "Did any of them stand out to you as team leader material?" I figured I'd ask; I wasn't sure Frank would have asked her.

"As a matter of fact, yes." She smiled and pulled out a file then set it on top of the others and flipped the cover open. "Ty Beckett is kind of amazing."

"I heard that," Mark called from somewhere, making us chuckle.

"Interesting." I tilted my head at her. "That's who Frank suggested, too." I skimmed his profile and gave a whistle when I noted where he was currently located.

"Yes, he's on one of the few teams they left in Afghanistan. Did they ask to stay? Because I thought the president pulled all US soldiers out."

"I've heard things. I think some were asked to stay. They needed eyes on what would happen once the Taliban moved back in." I ran my finger down the page. "He's special ops, so chances are they weren't able to get everyone out safely, so…" I let her fill in the rest on that one. "I also know some of the men weren't sure if they even wanted to come back to civilian life, so some probably stayed willingly."

"I wonder what Beckett's choice was."

"No clue. I just hope it was what he wanted."

"Mmm." She thought, then jumped when Mark screamed loudly. "You okay, Mark?" she called innocently and batted her eyes at me.

"Savannah!" he hollered in a tone that caused me to roll my eyes, and I knew that stupid Furby was back.

"I hid it in the cookie jar." She giggled as she explained to me. "I needed something to convince Cole to let me see the tapes."

Loud footsteps from the direction of the kitchen had Savannah on her feet and out the door with Mark on her heels.

I looked down at Scoot, who gave me an unamused glare at the interruption then went back to his nap.

"Did you hear the hyena shriek that came out of your brother just now?" I laughed at Cole, who had just come in through the back sliding glass doors.

"I was outside the window." He smirked. "I love my wife." I held up the files. "What's that?"

"Frank's files on the possible new team leader."

"Give me five, and I'll join you."

Two days later, the guys from Dusk arrived, eager to get down to business. Cole and I agreed all should be here for any big decisions that needed to be made between the two houses. We took pride in the fact that we always listened to any and all concerns a member of either team or even a family member might have. After all, we were one big unit, and we all needed to work together to make this successful.

Dell came in first, and he looked very pleased to be back. He'd always had a soft spot for the kids and the chaos they brought to our lives.

"Dell!" Olivia called. "Riddle me this. What can you break, even if you never touch it?"

"No idea."

"Seriously?" She shook her head, unimpressed. "You didn't even try."

"Fine." He pretended to think, and she rolled her eyes. "I got nothing."

"I try to sharpen your skills and I *get nothing*." She turned on her heel.

"Wait, what's the answer?"

"Google it," she huffed and walked away.

He looked at me, and I shrugged with a chuckle. Olivia was always trying in her own way to connect with the guys. She liked to try to keep them sharp, even if it was with cute little riddles.

"Do I smell cookies?" Quinn tried to shove past Dell, but Mark beat him to the entrance and blocked his way into the kitchen.

"There can only be one brother in a love affair with food, and I'm that brother. So, kindly take your dirty little thoughts elsewhere because you're not eating what's clearly marked as Mark's."

Quinn shrugged in a pretense of giving up then suddenly dropped his bags and raced for the other entrance to the kitchen. I knew it was only a matter of moments before the bickering would erupt. Mark lunged for the pan of cookies and yelped as he burned his fingers.

"And then there was me." Davie smiled as he tossed his bags down next to Quinn's. "Nice to see you, sir."

"You as well." I shook his hand and smiled at the young man who had come so far. Davie had a fear of water but wanted to work for Cole and me badly enough that he'd worked through it and had become one of the most dependable brothers we had. Though Quinn's skills had him moved to team leader, Davie wasn't far behind, and I knew I would see him in that position one day.

"Daniel?" Savannah appeared at the top of the stairs. "Ready when you are."

"Thank you, dear."

"What the hell!" Quinn yelped, and a crash made all our heads turn. Mark raced by and high fived Savannah. *God, I hated that friggin thing.*

"In fairness," Savannah seemed to read my thoughts, "your boys did start that war."

"Oh, I know." I playfully sighed then chuckled when Quinn came out with three cookies and jammed them all into his mouth. Mark's face dropped and he looked about to attack, but I held up a hand and they immediately stopped to listen. "We don't have much time before dinner, so let's start the meeting in five."

"Copy that." Mark turned his attitude immediately to work mode while the rest rushed off to drop their stuff off in their rooms.

"You really need to teach me that." Savannah watched in amazement as they scattered away.

"They're just big kids who need discipline. Oh, and at the end of the day, they all just want to be fed." I waved for her to lead the way downstairs.

We gathered around the long conference table, each person with a folder in front of them. We were all to vote for which of the three men would best fit the bill to become the new team leader.

Cole gave a rundown of each one. He used the overhead projector and pointed out all details we needed to know. After that, he opened the floor for discussion.

"I hate to say it, but Cumberland doesn't seem to have any family at all." Dell lifted the paper. "Sometimes that can work in our favor."

"I disagree," Savannah chimed in next to Cole.

"Me too." Sue nodded at her. "We're a lot to take, and not

Shadows

being used to siblings could be stressful on him. Having family teaches you a lot about give and take and about loyalty and empathy."

Cole nodded at me, and I put a mark next to his name. These were all things we needed to consider. I knew we had to look at both sides of the equation, however. Being away from family, especially if you were close, could also put a man at a disadvantage. There was a lot to consider.

"Understood," Dell agreed, "but he does have a lot of flight experience. That's a plus."

"It is." Cole watched as I added a mark on the other side of Cumberland's name.

"Beckett can fly," Savannah shot back, "and if you look at page two, he's had more time in the air than Cumberland. He's incredibly strong, too, look at his rappel scores." I couldn't help but smile at my daughter-in-law. She put a lot of time and effort into everything she did. I knew she'd have spent hours vetting these guys. I also could see she wanted Beckett. Cole, Mark, and I leaned heavily toward him as well, but it was only fair to present all the candidates in order to give everyone a chance to have their say. We had done things this way since the beginning.

"Well spotted, Savi," Dell praised her.

"What about Johnson?" Mark scratched his chin. "I find it interesting that he's only stayed a short time in his last three placements. He's a captain who's bounced around a lot."

"Maybe he's just trying to find where he fits. Different styles of a leadership aren't for everyone," I challenged.

"Agreed, but at some point, don't you have to look for the common denominator? I'm all for someone coming in and teaching us something in a new way, but if he's not able to stay long enough to gain an understanding of others and how they work, I can't see him here."

"Also, Cole is our leader, and we're here around this table

as equals, weighing in a new brother. Will he be the same when it comes to his own team, I wonder? Will we get a say in who comes in?"

"I have to agree," Doc chimed in from the back corner of the room. "I do think he can handle this job, but I'm concerned about what Mark brought up. A man needs to take a stand when he comes into a position. You can't dip your toe in then leave without giving it a good try. He does seem to skip around a lot."

"All right, Doc," Cole leaned back in his chair, "out of Cumberland and Beckett, who would you like to see come in?"

"I'd need to meet them both," he pushed his glasses up his nose, "to evaluate them, but my gut leans toward Beckett. He's impressive. It's obvious he sticks things out to the end. He was a beast over in Afghanistan, and any soldier you have to pry out of there against their will shows he doesn't give up easily."

"Agreed." Cole nodded. "I think we can all agree that someone can look great on paper and be completely off when you met them in person." He alluded to Roth. "If that's how we operated, Davie wouldn't be here today."

"Yeah," Davie laughed, "that's for sure."

"Mike?" Cole leaned forward. "John?"

They both flipped to Beckett's profile and tossed their folders to the center of the table.

"I'm not sure why we're even having this meeting, boys." Keith had been quiet most of the meeting and tossed his vote in the center of the table as well. "Two minutes into reading Beckett's profile, it was clear to me he's one of us. I think Frank needs to pull him from wherever he is before he commits to anything else."

Savannah glanced at me, and I gave her a small nod. "This isn't a job where you go home at the end of the day. This is a family with a lot of moving parts," she added. "Obviously, there's a lot to consider." She opened her folder to Beckett and slid it out to join the others. "But I'm for Beckett."

"And what about you Dusk boys? Any thoughts?" Cole addressed the others.

"Anyone who's spent eight years over there and come out alive has my vote." Quinn tossed in his folder.

"I just came for the visit." Davie grinned. "Beckett was my choice from the start."

"Mine, too." Dell looked up. "So, when's dinner?"

Cole shook his head with a smile, and I wiped the whiteboard clean.

"Well, it's settled." Cole addressed the room. "Now we just need to see if Beckett's interested in the position."

After everyone left, Cole and I hung back and took a place across the table from one another. The stack of folders was pushed aside, and Beckett's photo and file filled the screen.

"Thoughts?" I asked my son. I knew he had a lot more on his mind than just Beckett.

"I was thinking, Dad. It went me, Mark, Keith, Mike, John." He counted on his fingers. "That was the order we got married. We fell in love, tied the knot, had kids all in our early thirties. We made it work, and we used some of the property to build a mini community. But what about this new team?"

"Yeah." I agreed it was something we needed to consider.

"They will stay in the main house. There's plenty of room now that you boys have your own places." I could see he knew that but had more on his mind, so I let the silence hang for a bit.

"I never saw it before I met Savi." He rubbed his chin. "I thought this job was for guys who didn't want more. A grunt life to the end. But I was wrong. Having someone to come home to makes you want to do better all around. I fight better, I train better, I live harder, because of those three people upstairs."

"What are you thinking?" I tried not to smile. I had a feeling I knew where his mind was, and I felt incredibly proud of the son I'd raised. He had found what I had, love in its purest form, and now saw the power of it.

"Our men should have the right to find love and have a life like we did. I think we should have a plan in place to build more homes. Let them know we're thinking of their future. We can pitch it like living on a base, only here. It would be great for our kids to have a new generation coming up behind them. I see how family mentally lifts you, what it does for all of us. And when Dusk gets to this point, too, we can think about doing the same there." He paused for a moment, and his expression changed as if he'd had a dark thought then seemed to shake it off. "I want to pitch it to Frank. We might have to purchase the old Purcell land to give us more room."

"I agree, and I think he'll see the benefits of it, too." I glanced up at Beckett's face on the screen then back at Cole. "I remember sitting across the table from my dad one night, and he told me there were going to be times in my life where you were going to blow me away. He was right, and you have, countless times." I shifted to look at him. "Then there are times like this where I just think to myself you really are an amazing human being, Cole Logan. I'm beyond honored to be your father."

He smiled and reached across the table and squeezed my arm. "I learned from the best, Dad."

We tidied up the conference room and clicked off the light then walked toward the stairs.

"Daddy, look what I got!" Cole's youngest held up a book on dinosaurs. "Auntie Mia got it for me."

"A book on cats?" he teased Easton.

"Daddy," he giggled, "it's dinosaurs." He ran his little finger along the word. "See the word right there."

"Oh, I thought it said cats."

"Mommy's going to read it to me, Brandon, and Reagan."

"Lucky boy." He ruffled his mop of hair. "I'll be over soon to tuck you in."

"'Kay." He raced off with Butters on his heels. Easton reminded me so much of Cole when he was small.

"Look at those little legs go." I laughed.

CHAPTER TWENTY-ONE

Location: Cartel House, Rosarito, Mexico
Coordinates: Unknown

ERIC

"Where do you want this?" One of the workers struggled to carry a roll of barbed wire through the door.

"That way." I pointed across the room. "Any damage to my walls or floors and I cut your hands off."

"Yes, sir." His face dropped, and he yelled at his guys ahead of him to move carefully. One by one, they brought in the new materials I needed to update the holding cages. Castillo wanted a bonus room set up for something that was coming. I didn't care; I just wanted these people out of my house as quickly as possible. Every minute that door was open, the suffocating heat crept in and stole the air from my lungs. My shirt was already soaked with sweat, and my skin begged me for an ice-cold shower.

"You dyin', boss?" Alejandro eyed me from across the room. He was in jeans, a t-shirt, and boots. I shook my head at him in wonder. It was insanity that he could wear that, let alone not even show he had to be as hot as I was.

"I hate your fucking country," I hissed and grabbed a handful of ice cubes from the cooler and rubbed the back of my neck with them until they were almost melted then chucked them into the trash. "Come on." I motioned for him to follow me down the second set of stairs to the back room.

I pressed my thumb to the screen and watched it flash green as it read my fingerprint and popped open the basement door. A blast of cool air whooshed over my sticky face, and I took a moment to suck in a deep breath. The fresh air revived me as my tired lungs were brought back to full capacity. I made sure my house had the best ventilation. I couldn't imagine being able to sleep in the heat.

I ran my fingers along the stones that lined the wall. They were there to hide the soundproof padding. I smiled, pleased at my little operation. I'd spent years building it, and I never cut corners. I was meticulous in every aspect because my life depended on attention to detail.

"And you wonder why I dress the way I do," Alejandro whispered behind me as he rubbed his arms. I ignored him as he stepped through the door. I spent a lot of time down here, and I needed to be sharp. Heat made people tired and comfortable. I couldn't risk my guard being tampered with.

"Dexter said Talya showed up to work and she looked like she'd been cryin'. Everything okay with you two?"

Just the mere mention of her name made my stomach roll. The way her eyes fell when I let her leave nearly ripped my insides apart. Twice this morning, I'd picked up my phone to call her, and twice I punched holes in the wall. I never meant to fall in love. I told her that could never happen; she needed to be an afterthought. I had to hate her to get over her.

"All Talya was good for was between my sheets and under

me." The lie burned my tongue as the words slipped over it. "Hand me that hammer." He did, and I drove a temporary peg into the floor to show the workers where I wanted the entrance of the cage to be.

"I'll pass that along." He knew well enough to back off. "What is it with you and getting the sexy Latino *chicas*?"

"I have a type," I shot back. "I can't help it if they love me, too." I smirked, but it took all my effort to push like hell to get Talya's naked image out of my head. I stood and waved impatiently at the men who approached. They peered at the cages in the outer room as they walked by. I studied their faces as they entered the room we were in.

"What are they keeping in there?" one of the men muttered to his buddy, who shook his head to shut up. They never thought I could speak Spanish, and I often let them believe that. It usually worked in my favor.

"I want a thirteen-by-thirteen door there." I used English and pointed to the blue painter tape on the concrete floor. "And I want a half wall by the toilet built there."

"What about for the shower?" The foreman spoke up. "Do you want a half wall there too? A curtain?"

"Nothing." I held his gaze and watched as he swallowed hard. He knew who'd hired him, and he knew I was connected to the Cartel. In spite of not being a Cartel member myself, he knew better than to ask any more questions.

"Understood."

"Good. And over there, in that box, is a table and chair. Set that up outside the cage." I walked over and stood inside the taped off area and extended my arms. "At least this far away." The men's faces dropped. "People seem to get angry when they're held against their will," I tossed out there for good measure. They didn't miss a beat getting back to work.

"Wait." Alejandro stopped two workers who piled boxes next to the wall. "What are these?"

"No clue. I just drop off."

"Are these cameras?" Alejandro started to rip open the box on top. "If they are, they can be returned right now."

"I was told to order those." The foreman of the job looked at me, confused.

"No," I eyed the boxes, "no cameras."

"Castillo sent these over." The foreman snatched the clipboard from a worker's hand and pointed to where Martin Castillo had signed off on the invoice. "See here, six of these." He ran his finger along the list. "I believe these are heat ones, and four regular ones."

"Return them," I ordered.

"Sir," he looked nervous, "I'm not sure I can do that. I…" he stumbled, "I have a family."

We were all working for the Devil, so I felt nothing for this man or his family. It was just the way it had to be.

"Don't care." I waved him off, and Alejandro picked up a box and shoved it back in the worker's hand. He yelled at them to take the boxes back upstairs.

"I need to make a call." I pulled my phone from my pocket and headed up the stairs to leave the others to work.

"Eric, how is the new room coming together?" Castillo asked with what I assumed was a cigar clenched between his teeth. I rolled my eyes at what he'd called it. The cage wasn't some guestroom. It was to hold and prepare the girls to be sold. Nothing more.

"The *cage* is coming along, but I'll be sending back some of the supplies."

"Oh?" I knew he knew.

"You broke my number one rule."

"I didn't break it, Eric. They're for your own protection."

I pressed my fingers into my head and squeezed my eyes shut to keep from running my mouth.

"When have you ever been concerned for my protection, Castillo?" I didn't try to curb my tone. "I'm the best at what I do. That's why you use me." I went cocky, knowing he could relate. Martin Castillo was as cocky as they came. "We do this my way, or no way at all," I grated.

There was a long stretch of silence, then he gave a light chuckle, and I knew I'd made my point.

"Just hold on to them for now. You might," he paused, "change your mind later."

"I won't."

"Enough of this." His breath huffed over the mic of the phone. "I need you to meet me at the airport."

I rubbed my head at the timing. I sure as hell didn't want to leave any of these men inside my house while I wasn't there.

"What time?"

"Two hours. I want you to park across the street and watch for any guests who might come along."

"Should I be watching for any guest in particular?"

"Anyone who looks important." He drew out the last word rather dramatically. I shrugged off his cryptic answer, tired of his voice. "Text me when you've arrived."

"Yeah." I hung up and went to oversee what was happening downstairs. I needed to hurry things along.

An hour later, I showered, changed, and loaded my guns while Alejandro prepared the Escalade.

I looked over my shoulder and nodded to one of my men to watch over everything. He knew if anything seemed off, he was to report to me immediately. I shook off an uneasy feeling and braced myself to go the short distance in the stifling heat to the cool leather seats in the vehicle.

The drive down the mountain had my mind spinning in

all directions. I knew that over the last little while Castillo had changed. We'd always had an understanding on how I ran things, and I liked things to stay the same. It had worked for both of us up to now, so why the changes? The fact that this new cage was such a big deal certainly had my wheels churning. What was up with that?

"Boss?"

"Mm?"

"When does the new guy start?" He paused while I gathered my thoughts. "That youngin' Filippo?"

"Soon."

"You trust him?"

"Would he be working for me if I didn't?" I frowned at him.

"You trust me, right?"

"Yeah, because I know where your family lives, where your girl lives. I know your bank info and where your family hid your cousin after killing that kingpin in the Philippines. One fuck-up on your end, and you're wiped off the map with one phone call."

He turned onto the street and shook his head with a dark laugh. "That's fucked up. You know that, right?"

"I do." I tugged at the collar of my dress shirt. "What's leverage if there is no fear behind it?"

"I hate that I can't disagree with you."

"And that's why you're my number two, because you know I could end you at any moment."

"You want to go to church first?" He raised a brow in the rearview mirror. "Because you seem like you need a little Jesus right now."

"I'll save my confession for when I need saving." I waved him to keep going.

"There's a reason white folks get a rep," he muttered, and I smirked as I scrolled through my emails.

A short time later, the sun had set, and we were tucked in the shadows across the street from the airport. The private jet touched down slowly and came to a compete stop on the tarmac. The doors lowered, and an armed flight attendant stepped out first and looked around.

"Who are we watching, anyway?" Alejandro strained to see.

"No clue." I sighed, annoyed once again that my time was being spent here and not at home. "Just watch the street for anyone coming and going, and I'll watch the gates."

"Yeah."

We sat around for an hour, then an entourage of vehicles arrived with Castillo. A group of men stepped out of the cars. They created a lined barrier and blocked my view of who was being removed from the plane. Moments later, they crawled back behind the tinted windows and drove off, leaving me curious as to what the hell I'd just witnessed.

"That was anticlimactic." Alejandro puzzled over it.

"Indeed." I felt my phone buzz and saw it was a text from Castillo.

Castillo: Go home.

I tossed my phone aside and hit the seat in front of me.

"Let's get the hell out of here."

CHAPTER TWENTY-TWO

DANIEL

"It's a tactical bra." Olivia held up her sketchbook. "See, it holds two small handguns, a claw ring," she made a punching movement, "Mace, and right here, this small pad can read your heartbeat. When it gets to a certain level, it sends out a distress signal with your location." I couldn't help but smile. She tried so hard to help and was always coming up with something. "Now, I know there are versions of this out there already, but mine will be specific to the ladies of the house." She lowered her favorite non-prescription glasses. "But I'm not just doing this for Shadows. I'm paving the way for all women to feel safe out there."

I caught Mike's face as he looked over her shoulder, and he shook his head at me with a smile as he pretended to make an uncomfortable stretch in the area of his chest. We were all so proud of our smart little lady. In spite of the fact that her idea was totally unfeasible, which she'd only know once she had to wear one herself, it was pretty cool.

"Okay." I nodded, admiring the impressive sketch she made. "What will you call it?"

"Boobtrapment?" Mark stopped to glance at her sketch. He held a box in his arms and laughed as he continued through the room.

"Uncle Mark," Olivia scolded him, "they're called breasts."

"I'm out." Mike tossed his hands in the air. "I can't—nope, I'll not hear such words from my little niece's mouth."

Keith came in from outside and took a quick glance at Olivia's sketch. He made a noncommittal sound and hurriedly left the room without comment.

Smart man.

"I call it Backup. For the times when Blackstone isn't there."

"I'm impressed, Livi. You should present this to Frank and see what he thinks."

"Oh, Grandpa," she reached into her bookbag and pulled out her laptop, "I've got an entire presentation ready to go for Great Uncle Frank. Including and not limited to PowerPoint because apparently those are still used," she sighed, "and a small video of how everything fits nice under camouflage." I eyed her. "Auntie Cat wasn't overly pleased I used her bra, but I can't help that. She has the biggest—"

I cut her off. "I got it. You know how to set up a meeting with Frank. I'm sure he'd love to hear from you."

"Excellent." She grabbed her bag and began to pack up. Abby walked in and got a view of the sketch and a quick run-through, then Livi gave her a hug and ran out, saying she had to contact her Uncle Frank.

"Don't even go there." I chuckled at her look.

"I don't think I even know what to say." Abby chuckled, but I noticed she was a bit paler than she usually was. "Daniel? Would it be a problem if I went for a weekend to North Dakota in a couple weeks?"

"Of course not." I was surprised she even asked. "I can get Davie or Dell to escort you."

"Thank you."

"I don't want to overstep, but is everything all right?" She glanced around quickly and shot a smile at Mia as she hurried in to retrieve her cell off the coffee table.

"Sorry, running late for my class." She whisked away, but I did notice she threw me a puzzled look.

"It's nothing to be alarmed about. I've just been feeling a bit lightheaded lately. My doctor just wants to run some tests."

"You should take Sue with you." I knew Sue would be upset if she wasn't brought into this.

"She and Savi have been so busy with Brandon and Reagan." She folded her arms. "I don't want to add any more stress."

"Abby," I moved close to her and lowered my voice, "what about Doc?"

"No," she shook her head, "he has a lot going on as well. He needs to focus on his work right now."

"Fine." I stood straighter. "Then I'm going with you."

"No—"

"Abby," I put my hand on her shoulder, "I'll put it to you this way. It's me or Mark."

"Dear God, he'd have me flown out on the chopper." She laughed. "Okay, okay, but this stays between us."

"And me." Mia hadn't left after all and stood with her arms folded and a look that dared Abby to fight her. Abby reached out her hand and Mia took it as she joined us.

"I don't want a big deal made out of this. The doctor assured me he's sure it's nothing life threatening. I just need to get some tests. You know, given my age." She made air quotes and tried to laugh it off. "I'm just tired of the vertigo."

"Understood." Mia nodded at her like the professional she was. "Let's find a quiet room, and you can bring me up to speed on what's going on."

"Cole's office is free, and so is the one next to Doc's. I'll be in shortly." I kissed Mia on the head, and the two of them left.

"Grandpa!" Liam came running in. "Ethan licked a frog and told me it tastes like chicken."

"Mark!" I shouted, and he appeared out of thin air, which told me he was up to no good again.

"Deal with," I pointed to his twins, "your hyenas."

He scooped them up and whispered something in their ear that made them both giggle. I didn't want to know.

"Hey, Mike," Keith came running up the stairs, "your niece has your wife's bra on."

"Some things I don't need to know!" Mike called.

This place was a madhouse.

"I made cookies." Savannah barely had the words out as Mark and Keith came racing toward her. Liam and Ethan came up behind them, but Mark turned and grabbed the boys and twisted bungee cords around them to hook them tightly together.

"Mark!" Savannah took pity on the boys, but they just laughed and screamed for help as they toppled to the floor. Butters moved in and took his time to lick their grubby faces and made them laugh and shriek even harder.

"All mine," Mark growled in a Cookie Monster voice as he shoved two in his mouth and started to chew, bragging to his boys. His gaze shot over to me as he spat the cookie out. "What the hell! Oh, my God, my tongue's on fire."

Keith quickly dropped his on the counter and backed away.

"What kind of monster puts jalapeños in a chocolate cookie?" Mark used his sleeve to dry his eyes and took a step toward her. "You know I have a sensitive tongue."

"That's what she—" He quickly cut her off with growl, and I couldn't help but chuckle.

"And now you steal my go-to line." He tossed the crumbled cookie dramatically on the table. "I'll give you a three-second head start, because I'm coming for you, Mrs. Logan, and no one," Savi jumped over the kids and bolted toward the stairs, "no one's gonna save you!" he yelled after her.

"Dad! Untie us!" Liam shouted.

"There's no time, boys!" Mark was gone in a flash, so Keith grabbed a box of *safe* cookies and took a seat near them and propped up his feet on the tangled twins.

"Uncle Keith!"

"Shhh, you're fine." He grinned and ate another cookie. "This is fun for all of us."

Cole came in from the deck, and I waved to warn him.

"You might want to run far away, son." I chuckled.

"Oh, no, why?"

"To sum it up, your daughter is wearing Cat's bra, toads taste like chicken, Savi is being hunted by Mark, and my final advice to you is don't eat the cookies."

"Uncle Cole, help!" Ethan shrieked.

"Oh, and Uncle Keith is babysitting." I added with a grin.

"Gotcha." He laughed, but it soon faded as Cole's expression changed. I followed his gaze and looked around at the door.

"Excuse me?" Dr. Roberts stood rigidly by the end of the couch. Everything about his body language shouted something was wrong. "Might I have a word with you two?"

"Of course. Have a seat, Doc." Cole removed his gloves and coat and tossed them on the back of a chair, and I immediately moved my chair closer.

"I won't lick the toad!" Liam screamed, and I closed my eyes for a moment.

"I'd," he looked around, "prefer if we could talk in my office."

Cole immediately stood.

"Of course." I pushed to my feet. "It'll certainly be much quieter there. Is everything all right?"

"I could use a little advice."

"Isn't it supposed to be the other way around?" I joked and tried to recall if there was ever a time Doc asked us for our advice.

"Normally, yes," Doc gave a weak smile, "but I think I might need your help on this one." He looked at Cole. "This is a little out of my comfort zone."

"Well, let's not waste any more time." Cole motioned for us to follow him down the hall to Doc's office.

Just as I closed the door, I saw Mark run by, holding a paintball gun.

"Shit's gettin' real, Dad!" He grinned and held up the gun like he was about to go into battle.

I laughed and shook my head. Savi was about to regret ever pranking Mark.

The End

Acknowledgments

To my mother, my inspiration in life, my cheerleader, my best friend.

My husband, who helped "see" my vision when I couldn't.

To Elizabeth Clark and Jamie Johnson, thank you for the push in *that* direction, for spinning with me, and for always being in my corner.

To my betas and proofers, Kim Kelchner, Kasey Griffin, Veronica Nelson, Maggie Savarese, Rachel Womack, Jamie Johnson, and Elizabeth Clark.

My editor Lori, thanks for always being there.

My street team, ARC team, my reader group, and my fact-finding group, thanks for providing me a safe place to go to hang out, ask questions, and laugh!

And of course, to my readers. I wouldn't be here if it wasn't for all of you.

Thank you.

A look at what's to come...

WHISKEY

Location: Afghanistan
Coordinates: Classified

TY

"Move, move, move," I screamed at Moore as I knocked Brown in the head to wake him from a dead sleep. Fire licked the side wall and traveled up to the roof like a lit matchstick. "Grab your shit, Hill!" I dove outside and drew my gun into position to scan the perimeter. I rested my cheek on the butt of the gun and tuned out the crackle of flames as they

A look at what's to come...

consumed the hut. I closed my eyes for a second and took a deep breath to focus.

My sixth sense had never let me down before, and it had surfaced just in time. I rolled quickly to one side and *zip! zip!* I sent two bullets to my eleven and heard a groan. I sent another three to my twelve and caught sight of a man as he twisted and fell, blood spraying high in the air. I felt the heat of the flames on my back and knew it was time to move.

Moore's hand landed on my shoulder as he belly-squirmed up next to me. We moved as one, away from the burning structure and out into the night. There had been a time when this terrain made it difficult to move about, but now it was second nature to us. The loose, rocky mountainside still made us work hard as we picked our way up.

Zip! Zip! Zip! Bullets nipped at our heels as we scaled the side. We kept low to use whatever cover we could find.

"I thought we lost these fuckers thirteen miles ago," Brown hissed. "They're like friggin' bloodhounds!" The last word was cut off as bullet hit right above him. "I seriously hate this place. I need a desk job."

"You wouldn't last five minutes in a cubicle," Moore barked as I covered him, and he made his move. More bullets rained all around us.

"They look at us the same way we look at them." I motioned for Brown to move it up behind Moore. "Kill or be killed."

Hill took Brown's place and glared at me. We'd had tension between us ever since we made the decision to stay behind and accept this volunteer mission. The rest of the troops had all been called back to the US. I knew he wanted to go back but probably felt like an ass when the rest of us voted to stay. He'd kept his mouth shut then, but now it was apparently my fault he was still here. I didn't care; he was the one who made the decision. I was glad he'd been put under

A look at what's to come...

Captain Flex's command. Trouble was now, ten days in, our teams were tangled up after we'd been ambushed, and some of our men were switched up. Flex had two of mine, and I had three of his, and one, regretfully, was Hill. Our mission was compromised, and now both our teams were scrambling to make it back to the rendezvous point where a chopper would meet us to get us the hell out of there.

"Go," I ordered Hill, and he waited a beat and glared at me before he moved. Rivera then wiggled up into his spot and waited for his turn to head to the top. He was a good soldier, but he was tight with Hill and had a real attitude problem with my guys, so I kept an eye on him as well. I nodded at him, and he left. I was last.

I rolled on my back and arched my neck to watch Rivera's boots disappear. Then I started to shimmy upward. I kept as flat as possible. Bullets peppered around, but thankfully none hit me.

Once I reached the top, Moore slapped my shoulder, then we all froze when we heard the unmistakable whistle of a rocket launcher.

"Duck!" I shouted, and we dove for cover wherever we could as it hit the side of the cliff. It shook us like a carnival ride, dust filled our lungs, and rocks flew about without mercy.

I blinked back the grit that now layered my pupils I made out an opening now exposed where a rock had been. I called to the others. We took turns and shimmied inside the cave to seek relief. As we caught our breath, we all did a quick body check to see if we were injured. The shock of an unexpected attack sometimes left you momentarily numb to pain. Thankfully, we all seemed to be in one piece.

I cracked a glow stick, and so did Brown, and we did a quick scan of our surroundings. It seemed safe enough to spend a little time there. I knew we all were in desperate

A look at what's to come...

need of sleep, and with the lack of camaraderie among the team, tempers were at a fever pitch.

"Hill, watch the entrance," I ordered, and he shook his head at me as he fought to catch his breath. I held up a hand. I wasn't in a mood to tolerate his pushback. "You don't want to be here, no one's stopping you." I inclined my head at the opening to the cave. He glanced at Rivera, who looked away. *Good.* Brown got down on his belly and crawled to the opening.

"That was close." Moore puffed his cheeks at me and blew out hard. The adrenaline still rushed through our veins. "I can still taste gunpowder." He flapped his arms to relieve the stress.

Rivera butted in. "Maybe if we hadn't sat like ducks on low ground, we would've been better prepared."

I tuned them out while I tried my radio. It crackled with static, and I strained to hear around it. The reception was terrible here. Two different tones could be heard, so my guess was that Captain Flex was radioing in at the same time.

"You were the one on watch," Moore shouted, and Rivera rose to match his stance. "Maybe we should be pointing fingers at you. You were probably asleep!"

"Enough." I was tired of their shit. "We'll spend a few minutes here to rest, but they aren't far behind, and we need to keep moving. So shut up and take a break." I moved to the opening and relieved Brown. I needed to get away from all the friggin' bickering. I knew we should stay on the move, but we also needed clear heads, and the proof was in their tempers. We needed rest. We'd only had about three hours of solid sleep in the past ten days, and now that we'd been outed, they were gunnin' for us hard.

My team had been a well-oiled machine, but when we collided with the other team a few days back and got split up, tension built. I found a space to tuck myself into that still

A look at what's to come...

allowed a panoramic view of the hillside below. I needed to watch for any possible unwanted company.

Shots could still be heard, but it seemed like they were on the other side of the mountain. Where we were seemed relatively safe for the moment. I took a minute to admire the stars that shone brightly above me while I rested my body. My mind remained alert for any sound.

I'd spent just over eight years in this country, in a continuous battle with faceless men. I'd seen women and children treated like animals by their own kind. The idea of freedom was merely fiction to those who lived in this place. Hope for some kind of life might still be there, but it was buried deep with fear.

When I was ordered to return with my team to base camp, I wasn't sure what it was all about. When we were told we were going home, part of me was confused. The fight wasn't over. These people still needed our help. Then, while I attempted to get my head around it, my commanding officer pulled me aside and explained that one of our officers had been taken and we needed to get him back. He had some crucial information that we couldn't let the Taliban have knowledge of. I knew they were experts at interrogation. Though it was proposed as a voluntary mission, we really didn't have a choice. I stepped up quickly. I wasn't ready to go back to the kind of normal I knew I'd face back home, anyway. Of course, my team followed my lead. Since Flex had been in the room with the rest of us at the time, he not so willingly spoke up for his team, too.

It was important for us to remember that some of the locals were willing to put themselves out there and offer us supplies and help if need be. The citizens of Afghanistan had asked for our help, and I'd done everything in my power to do what I could. That was why I struggled hard when I

A look at what's to come...

watched our troops being loaded onto a plane. They were about to leave a war that wasn't even close to being over.

"You good, Beckett?" Moore slumped down next to me with a sigh.

"Yeah," was all I offered. He listened to the bullets hit randomly on the back side of the hill, higher up, and allowed himself to relax for a second.

"I'm nervous if Hill and Rivera meet up with Flex, I don't trust they won't mess with some Taliban and get us in trouble before the chopper arrives. They're reckless. We shouldn't separate again."

"Yeah, agreed." I closed my eyes with a nod and hated that I couldn't trust their motives.

"Listen," he cleared his throat, "I'm really worried about Brown."

"I'm watching him," I assured him, and he let it go, but I shared his concern. Brown showed some serious signs of mental wear. On a few occasions, he'd wasted ammo when he thought he saw things or reported to me on events that had happened years ago. As a Captain, I was taught to watch for these signs, and I definitely saw them in Brown. But, I reasoned internally, we were only a few days away from our return to the United States. I hoped he could hold it together just a little longer.

"Remember when Brown soaked Jamie's boots in cat pee, and for the rest of the summer we called him catpiss?" Moore chuckled.

"You can't mess with Brown." I smirked as I remembered how he was always the fun one. Practical jokes were taken to a whole new level if anyone dared to mess with him, or us too, for that matter.

"I had so much fun watching him fuck with people." He rubbed his face. "I miss that Brown."

"Yeah, me too." I nodded. I knew we were close to losing

A look at what's to come...

our lifelong brother mentally if we didn't get him some help soon. "We should get moving." I pulled back and struggled to my feet then called to the rest of the men.

It didn't take long to understand why the Taliban had pushed us in the direction they had. We soon found we could no longer go any higher. We were now forced to head back down; it was the only way we could go. After a long struggle through thick, low scrub brush that tripped you up and only provided about an inch of ledge for your boot to hold onto, we found ourselves at the top of a twenty-foot slope that went straight down into dark water. Dark water that held God only knew what.

"Shit." Moore struggled to keep his footing as he peered down. "Beckett, please don't tell me we're going for another dip."

"Shh," I held up a hand and slipped my night-vision goggles on to scan around us, "we have five coming over the east ridge."

"Have we been spotted?"

"I don't think." I ducked low, careful to balance my weight on my toes, and the others followed suit. The men threaded their guns over their shoulders and started to make their way toward us. I searched for options, but the only one that would save our asses was below us. The water.

"Rope," I whispered to Brown through the radio. He made quick work of removing it from his rucksack. I did the same and tied a knot in the ends to make it longer then made a loop. "Moore, you're up first," I ordered, mainly because he was right beside me. He wrapped it around his waist. "We don't have much time, so this'll be fast," I warned him.

"Brown, tell me when to stop." He flipped down his night goggles and gave me a thumbs up. With our heels planted, we lowered him quickly, and at a signal from Brown, we stopped him right above the water. Moore slipped the loop up over

A look at what's to come...

his head and let it go as he slipped into the water without a sound.

We repeated the action until only I was left. Using a root that was sticking out of the ground, I made a pulley and hoped to hell it would hold my weight. I tested it, and it felt solid. At a sound above me, I froze, and I heard them walk right over my head. Dirt hit my shoulder as I flattened to the side of the rock. I prayed the guys were out of sight in the water below. I inched my blade out of its sheath and steadied my breathing. If I was going to have to kill, it was going to need to be silent. Tonight, we were the prey, and one hell of a bounty was sure to be on our heads. One wrong move and it would be over.

I heard voices, and they seemed to be arguing. I knew they were close and only needed to go a few more yards before they would get to the spot where we'd been earlier, and then they'd soon be right on me. I had a very short window to get out of there. I moved carefully and eased my weight out and over the side then rappelled quietly down the mountain, staying as close as I could to the rock face.

Just as I slid into the water, I reached up, and with Moore's nod, I gave the rope a sharp tug at the same time as he threw a rock as hard as he could in the opposite direction. It hit farther up on the side of the mountain. The diversion worked, and the men fired their weapons in the direction of the sound. I prayed they didn't hear the rope as it smacked hard in the water. The last thing I needed was to have them discover the rope that would lead them right to us. It sank under the water, and I quickly gathered it to me. I held my breath and kicked toward the direction where the men hid in the wet plants that grew up from the muddy bottom. I slowly coiled up the rope as I went so none of us would get tangled in it and looped it on my belt.

I led them in a slow, measured swim away from the cliffs.

A look at what's to come...

I was sure the others struggled as I did as we moved through the dark, awful water, concerned that something would either grab us and pull us down or we'd hit a booby trap hidden underneath somewhere. It played on your head, and I could feel the sweat burn my eyes as I tried to push back the thoughts. Finally, I found a ledge where I could get my feet under me. There was a spot where the brush grew out over the rocks, and we could get ourselves under it. That was where we spent the night. If it wasn't for the cover of the brush, and the dark water to conceal our whereabouts, we'd surely be dead.

Hours later, the sun lined the mountaintops, and we drank in what was waiting for us if we dared move. There must have been at a least seventy Taliban members crawling over the mountainside we'd rappelled down. They scoured the hills looking for any sign of us.

I glanced at Brown, who'd barely moved all night. His eyes were cast straight ahead, and he seemed to be in a trance.

I slipped back into my head, too. It was all we could do. That, and pray they'd move on soon.

I remembered my parents' faces when I Skyped them on the night I got word that our special "volunteer" mission was about to ship out. They'd thought I was about to return home with the rest of the US troops. They had music on and held sparklers when the call connected. I felt horrible when I shared my news with them, but I knew their life just wasn't for me anymore. Not now, anyway. Maybe never. They'd respected my decision to stay and tried hard to hide their disappointment and fear. My sister, Shelly, was the only one who allowed herself to show she was pissed. She held up her daughter who was now nearly a year old and shook her head at me with tears in her eyes. She told me I'd missed so much of her life already. I promised her this would be the last

A look at what's to come...

mission, but I knew the truth. If I was offered another, I wouldn't hesitate to take it, and I thought she knew it too. I was a soldier. I was meant to make a difference here, there was no end date on freedom for these people. I stayed because that was all I knew how to do. I just had to survive.

Shouts pulled me from my thoughts, and we watched as the Taliban started to cheer and hoot. They held their weapons in the air and jumped around. A few ran back up the slope.

"You think they found Flex?" Hill hissed to Rivera, who shook his head. I hoped to God they hadn't found the other team, but they'd found something, and it was time for us to move.

We were used to all types of elements as soldiers, but it didn't help that wet boots and slippery rocks made your ankles and knees ache. Mind over matter was what kept me going, but two hours in and Brown was dragging, so I drew back and checked in with him.

"How's the hip doing?" Brown had taken a pretty bad hit to the hip a few nights back when we were outed, and I noticed he now had a bad limp.

"Fine." He squeezed his eyes shut for a moment like his head was in a battle.

"Four days from now, I'll buy the first round at some dive bar with greasy burgers and fries." He nodded, and we walked a little farther in silence. His eyes twitched when I looked over at him, and I decided I should give him a little reminder. "Whiskey."

"Alpha," Moore huffed over his shoulder.

"Tango," Brown answered in a low voice, and I felt a little relief come over me.

"Good." I squeezed his shoulder. "Not much farther."

Hill glanced back at me with a scowl. He and Brown often seemed to butt heads. I knew they'd gotten into it back in the

A look at what's to come...

States over some girl. Hill was used to getting the women. I never asked about it because, frankly, I didn't give a flying shit as long as they did their jobs.

A while later, something in my gut warned me we weren't alone. I held up my hand to warn the others to get low.

My heart pounded in my chest and my fingers flexed on my weapon when I heard the pounding of horse hooves.

"Dammit," Moore groaned, "there's got to be at least seven of them."

"Possibly eight." I squinted at something slung over the back of one of the horses. In a last-ditch effort for help, I cupped my mouth and sent our signature signal through the mountains in hopes my echo would find the ears of our fellow soldiers. It was a deep wolf howl that went high at the end to ensure my team knew it wasn't an actual wolf. The idea was to stand out against nature without drawing too much attention from the enemy.

"Should we drop?" Hill hesitated, and I glared at him. He looked at me then turned away and did his annoying habit of combing his hair with his fingers. Moore called it his Kenickie move. Moore's thing was to always reference movies. I guessed everyone had something. I shrugged it off and concentrated on Hill.

"If you drop your weapon, I'll shoot you myself," I snapped. We would never surrender, especially to such animals.

The men pointed their guns at us as they approached and circled us with whistles and shouts. We moved into a circle, backs to each other, and kept our weapons held high. If this was it, we'd go out swinging.

"I will soon live like a king," the leader of the pack said in Pashtu. "Round them up and bring them back to camp," he ordered.

"We won't be going anywhere with you." I let him know

A look at what's to come...

I spoke Pashtu as well. They warned us not to let the enemy know if we could speak their language. That way, we could eavesdrop if captured, but today I didn't care. They wouldn't get their bounty because we'd fight to our death.

"Ah," he smiled and tilted his head at me, "you speak my tongue?" He spoke in English. "Good. You should know I always get what I want. So, do yourself a favor and get moving."

One of his men pointed a gun in my face, and I shoved it upward so hard I could hear the crack as his nose broke. He fell backward and flew over the horse's ass, tumbling to the ground. The leader shook his head and nodded at another man who went to stab me, but I stepped out of his way and grabbed his arm, twisting it at the elbow. It snapped, and he cried out as his knife fell to the ground.

"Enough!" the leader ordered, and they all pointed their guns at me. "Fire!" They hesitated for a split second, I'm sure because of the bounty on our heads that was about to be lost, and then fate suddenly was on our side.

Bullets whipped through the air, and the men jolted in their saddles then fell to the ground near our feet. I popped two in the leader's head as he tried to ride away. I raced after the horse and grabbed the reins. We could use the horses to give our feet a break. As I circled back, I grinned at the familiar face.

"Heard your call." Captain Flex stepped out of the shrubs. He signaled for the others to join him.

"Appreciate the timing." I shook his hand.

"Finally," Hill grunted as he approached and motioned for Rivera to follow. "I couldn't do another day here." I wanted to punch his face in for his lack of respect.

Moore rolled his eyes at me, and I looked away, happy they were leaving so I didn't have the urge to give him a

A look at what's to come...

black eye. I hated being down two men, but we'd be better off without those two.

"Who's that?" Dustin, one of Flex's men, pointed to the body draped over the horse I held by the bridle.

"Don't know." Hill moved forward and went to investigate. He poked the bulge with his rifle, and the body jerked. "He's alive, whoever it is."

"Untie him," Flex ordered.

"Copy that." Hill loosened the ropes around his arms and legs and let him fall to the ground with a thud. Hill pulled off the blanket he was wrapped in and roughly ripped the sack off his head. "Oh, shit, it's a kid."

The young boy, maybe nine years old, blinked at the sunlight while tears streamed down his cheeks. He sat up when he saw us and wrapped his arms around his knees for protection.

I bent down and removed his gag and inspected his cuts. He studied my clothes then looked up at me with confusion.

I handed him my water and urged him to drink some. He hesitated at first but took it and swallowed a good amount. His wrists were bloody, and his neck was rubbed raw, which told me he likely had been on the back of that horse for quite a while.

"Hungry?" I spoke in Pashtu, and when he didn't answer, I switched to Dari. He nodded, and I handed him a protein pack.

"He's one of them, Beckett." Flex came up next to me and stuck the barrel of his gun in the kids face. "We need to keep moving."

"He's a child." I pushed the tip of his gun away. "Just because he looks like them doesn't mean he's one of them." We learned that lesson day one of being there.

"Just shoot him and be done," Hill huffed.

"You shoot him, and you'll have me to deal with." I

A look at what's to come...

grunted, and he waited a beat before he stepped back with a curse.

I looked the kid over and noticed his clothes were expensive looking and his satchel had beadwork on the side. It was unusual to see such items on a typical Afghan child.

"Wait here," I told him and pulled Moore and Brown aside. "I think this kid is someone important."

"Because of his clothes and the bag?" Moore looked at the kid. "Maybe, but shit, Beckett, that's extra baggage."

"He's a kid." My gut screamed at me to take him with us.

"He could also make us an even bigger target." Moore shrugged.

Brown rubbed the back of his head nervously. "He could be carrying drugs or maybe even be a mole. Fuck, this entire thing could have been planted for us to take him. They're most likely watching us right now." He looked wildly around.

I shook my head. This wasn't Brown's typical thought process, and even Moore gave him an odd look. He was slipping. The three of us had been ridiculously close growing up. I knew Brown better than he knew himself, and right now my brother needed to get the hell out of this place. The signs were all there in his eyes and in the constant movements he made. Yes, those tics were a dead giveaway that he needed help. I knew we had to get him home fast.

I stepped back and turned to face the others.

"Let's vote. Take the kid, or leave the kid?"

"I think I speak for my team when I say leave 'im. We aren't going to get sucked into another of your volunteer fuck-ups." Flex looked at the guys, and they all nodded in agreement. "We aren't far from where the truck's waiting, but I'm not taking a kid."

I turned to Brown, who shrugged but hit my shoulder to indicate he'd side with me. Moore nodded to imply the same.

A look at what's to come...

"We need to leave before they come." Brown looked about, worried. "We need to go," he repeated.

I turned to Moore so only he could hear. "Go with them. I need your ears. Meet me at the last check. We'll take the horses, and you go in the truck with the others. Get settled at the house, but don't let your guard down. Safe place or not, keep your eyes open."

"You sure?" His face twisted as his eyes went to Brown. I knew he wasn't sure it was a wise idea to leave me with only Brown, but Brown needed one on one, and so did the kid.

"Yeah, keep Anderson and Gail close, but yeah, go." I didn't trust that the others wouldn't sell me out and trap me somewhere. I trusted Moore with my life. I knew he'd have my back, especially with the other two guys.

"Be safe." He fist-bumped me and raced to join the others. I knew they'd get to the rendezvous well before we would, but I wasn't going to leave the kid here. The horses would help as long as we could keep out of sight of the Taliban.

I crouched back down in front of the kid and rubbed my chin. I knew we didn't have a lot of time to get out of there. We were too exposed, but I needed a minute.

"Where are your parents?" He shrugged, and I could see his cheeks pink up. "Are you hurt?" He shrugged again, and I looked at his bare feet. I leaned back, untied and wiggled a boot off one of the dead men. I held it to the kid's foot, but it was way too big. I looked around and spotted a smaller size and tugged them off the guy with a hole in his chest. I handed them to the kid, and he slipped them on without hesitation.

"We need to move, okay?" I patted his head, and he nodded but looked unsure. I peeled back a small Velcro flap on my jacket and pointed to the flag on my arm. "I'm not here to hurt you." He hopped to his feet then stumbled to find his footing. He'd hung over that horse too long. I

A look at what's to come...

scooped him up and sat him on the back of the horse then jumped up behind him on the saddle. Brown mounted up but looked a bit awkward on the horse. I knew we'd make better time on horseback. We just needed to be extra careful. I kicked hard, and we took off toward higher ground. I checked back, and Brown seemed able to follow. I hoped he wouldn't fall off the damn thing. His face was a picture of concentration, and it almost made me laugh. I was glad I'd ridden a bit as a kid.

About the Author

J.L. Drake was born and raised in Nova Scotia, Canada, later moving to southern California. Though she loves the weather in Cali, she would sell her left kidney for a good rainstorm. Jodi's love of the seasons back home in Canada definitely appear in her books.

When she's not writing, you can often find her sitting somewhere along the coast of Huntington Beach, reading, or at home curled up on a couch with her two children and husband, binge watching Marvel movies.

Authorjldrake.com
Facebook Reader Group

Suggested Reading Order

Broken

Shattered

Mended

Honor

Escape

Trigger

Demons

Unleashed

Freedom

Omertà

Courage

Darkness Lurks

Darkness Follows

Darkness Falls

Behind My Words

Christmas at the Cabin

All In

Quiet Wealth

Quiet Secrets

Quiet Power

Quiet Empire

Shadows

Whiskey

Alpha

Tango

Milton Keynes UK
Ingram Content Group UK Ltd.
UKHW011957190124
436321UK00004B/210